MICHAEL VAUGHN

RESURRECTION

HAYDEN KELLER RETURNS

MICHAEL VAUGHN

BOOKS BY
MICHAEL VAUGHN

2013 Powerhouse Press Trade Paperback Edition

Published in the United States by Powerhouse Press
Resurrection / Michael Vaughn

First Edition: October 2013

ISBN-13: 978-0615914619
ISBN-10: 0615914616

1. Paranormal psychic powers-fiction 2. Soul transference-fiction
3. Serial killer satanic ritual-fiction 4. Horror dark magic-fiction
5. Demonic possession -fiction 6. Police good v/s evil-fiction

Manufactured in the United States of America

Table Of Contents

Chapter 1

Taking Human Form

It was four o'clock in the morning. No one in their right mind woke up at that hour. Still, the alarm clock sounded as he laid there staring up at the ceiling. Every morning started out that way, but this particular morning something was different. A demonic look covered the face of Vincent Russell, and he was no longer in control of his body for the most part. Oddly enough, actions he wished to take faded from his mind in a matter of seconds. The thoughts which replaced them were not his own.

Vincent's mind was struggling to process what was happening, but he was given no answers. In an instant, his brain attempted to fight a formidable force he had never encountered before as he laid there asking questions like - where the hell am I. He couldn't begin to explain the chilling feeling he had come over him while lying there in his bed, and offering resistance to the evil spirit now battling for his physical existence was futile. Eventually, his thoughts vanished altogether - that's why he laid there without moving a muscle.

The demonic force which was taking control of him now occupied his body. The spiritual transference itself came at a price for both the host, and the new inhabitant. That was a trade the demon would gladly make to avoid burning in hell. Growing accustomed to its new surroundings, soon it gained physical strength along with the basic senses most of us take for granted. The feeling of confinement that came with being housed in a human body took some getting used to, but the evil entity was alive once more. The feel of the beating heart, and air repeatedly filling the lungs of what was once Vincent Russell served as a reminder. He blinked his eyes once or twice. Vincent was still trying to fight what was slowly taking hold of him, but it was no use. Within a matter of minutes the total transformation, and spiritual takeover was complete.

Lost somewhere in the abyss - Vincent Russell was gone, traded places with the evil entity perhaps, but the spirit inside his former body was no longer his own. Looking over at the clock, and then at the woman lying beside him, he could hear her complain even through the pillow as she said, "what's wrong with you? Turn that damn thing off." Had Mrs. Russell known it wasn't her husband she was speaking to she would have never tried to fall back asleep. In fact, she would've hastily departed from the room. She would have certainly screamed, and probably called the police. The demonic spirit which now possessed the body of her husband displayed his violent nature as he reached over snatching the cord out of the wall which immediately put an end to the loud buzzer blaring into his ear. He could hear her say, "it's about time you got your ass up."

Half asleep, she rolled over looking at him, and she could tell something was wrong. Even in the dark, it was obvious Vincent wasn't himself at all. He stared at her with great distain. That's when he reached over grabbing the pillow she had placed over her head to block out the noise coming from the alarm clock, and he forcefully shoved it into her face. She tried to scream, but he had cut off any airflow she had, and he held the pillow firmly in place. She struggled for a minute or so trying to pull away, but he aggressively applied more pressure while suffocating her with her own pillow. Mrs. Russell squirmed, and wiggled to no avail. Her arms flailed in the air. She tried to breathe, but it was hopeless. He kept the pillow over her mouth, and nose cramming her head further into the mattress with brutal force. Finally, she stopped moving altogether, and then he took the pillow away to reveal his first kill.

Completely satisfied with his actions, the only thing he said as he got out of bed making his way to the bathroom was, "this is going to be a hell of a day." Upon entering the bathroom he flipped on the light, and twisted the handle on the faucet. Allowing it to fill with water, he leaned over to rinse his face. He looked over at the straight razor which sat close by, and he picked up the shaving cream. Applying the lather, he flipped opened the razor, and he drew it near his cheek. He then turned his head touching the cold steel blade of the straight razor to his skin. Moving it downward in short deliberate strokes, he trimmed away the stubble which covered his face.

Looking up into the mirror, he stared at his reflection with a chilling glare in his eyes. He was simply trying to become familiar with the way he looked this time. Not that it mattered, every "body" was expendable including the one he now inhabited. That's when he did what most dare not. Taking the straight razor placing it high up on his left cheek, he sliced it open leaving a horrid gash stretching the length of his face. Blood steadily dripped into the white washbasin as he rinsed what was left of the shaving cream from his chin. Without making a sound, he grabbed the towel hanging on the wall next to him. Blotting the blood from his left cheek, he held the towel in place for a minute. Pulling it away he admired his appearance in the mirror once more. This time he looked completely demented as he tossed the towel on the bathroom floor. Fiercely determined, he boldly growled, "Hayden, you never looked better."

Chapter 2

Sense Of Fear

Suddenly, Sister Lee's eyes popped open wide. She was no longer in deep meditation. She now had a foreboding look on her face. Blood drizzled from her nose, and she wiped it away. She knew there was much more bloodshed yet to come. The moon was full, and the wheel of the years was positioned at a very dangerous place. The watchtowers were out of sync, and Sister Lee knew what it meant. The portholes in time were in alignment with one another forming an open door allowing Hayden Keller to escape. She knew evil had once again taken on a human shape. The dark days were at hand, and they would have no end, not until she put an end to him. Nearly breathless, she gasped, "he's back!" She stood removing her hands from the tapestry which covered her table.

This time, Hayden was a thousand miles away in a little town way down in South Georgia. Though she had never heard of the place before, she knew he wouldn't stay there long. She knew where he would go, and who he would try to hunt first. Eventually, he would be coming for her. It was only a matter of time. Sister Lee blew out the candle, and she backed away from the wooden table which sat in the center of the room. Turning toward her vast collection of books on the shelves behind her, she placed her hand on them. It was pitch dark in the conservatory where the books resided, but that didn't hinder her in the least. Steadily, she ran her fingers across them. She didn't need light to find that which she sought. She would know it when she touched upon the binding of the one she was searching for.

Her eyes were even closed as she used her extra sensory perception to gain the answers she wished to have. All of a sudden her hand stopped moving, and a jolt of energy shot through her fingers. It coursed through her hand into her arm before surging through her body. She had found the book containing the secrets of the dark arts, and death. This would not be the first time she had used it. She carefully removed the book from the shelf. It was old, large, and leather-bound. She held it using both hands, and she carried it into the next room. She placed the book on an altar which had symbols representing the five magical elements. They included fire, air, water, earth, and spirit. It was there that she opened the book, and carefully turned the pages as she began to read it through aloud. Her face showed signs of grave concern. Following each line of ancient text with her finger, she read whispering each word unto herself. She knew she had to cast a circle for protection, and she stopped reading long enough to do just that.

Turning her palms upward, she slowly lifted her hands in the air as she looked up from the book. With her hands raised slightly above her head, she began chanting words not spoken since the days of old, casting a circle around both herself, and the book. It was the only way she could ensure she was shielded from the evil which lurked in the shadows. Uncertainty now existed in Sister Lee's mind. It was an uncommon occurrence she found unsettling at best, but she knew, without question, death would follow wherever Satan led Hayden. Soon enough, he would make his way back to Jefferson County. The town of Chanceville would not be prepared for his arrival, but Sister Lee would, no doubt. Men with two lives didn't grow on trees though. She had serious hunting of her own to do prior to Hayden Keller's inevitable visit.

Sister Lee held secrets she revealed to no one. Why she sought to end Hayden's reign of death, and destruction was one of them. The good of humanity was worthy of her efforts alone, but she had her own reasons for ceasing his earthly existence. It stemmed from the vision of an ancient prophetess. Grave words which her mother's seer spoke to her as a child stayed with her all the days of her life, and she heeded them. She was merely five at the time, and already communicating with spirits. *"Gifted beyond all others,"* was a compliment bestowed on her by the old woman holding the cats-eye crystal. The words which the prophetess shared were complex, and dated as old as the ancients in a time now forgotten, but they were as follows: "Vos sunt iuncta in vita et etiam morti cum uno quae non potest tenuit in igne inferiori." The translation was simple. Even as a child Sister Lee understood their basic meaning. It was her adult life she spent questioning who they referred to. Plainly put, those words spoken by the ancient mystic stated, "you are joined in life, and even in death with the one which cannot not be bound by the fires of hell."

Throughout her youth, her mother questioned if the mystic referred to Satan himself, but that answer didn't make itself clear at the time. It was nearly forty years later when Sister Lee discovered her link to the scarred lion. Another two hundred years had passed between that day, and this one. The hunt had spanned centuries for them both. Hayden sought blood, and served as the harbinger of souls, while Sister Lee fought to preserve her own. She continually harnessed the minds and lives of others to return Hayden Keller to his proper place. It came with great cost of course, but Hayden could never be given the soul of one so, powerful as she. Armed with only fragments of information, and spotted visions, her work was made difficult, yet it had to be done. His face would change from time to time, but

12

the scar forever marked him. That was the one thing she could count on when it came to identifying him and she referred to him as the scared lion for centuries. They were connected eternally it seemed. Sister Lee wanted no part of him, but she was given no choice. It was inevitable he would find her someday. She sought to prolong the arrival of that moment for as long as possible. Only one question remained unanswered regarding her fate. She couldn't see that part of the future no matter how hard she tried. It was her weakness, not knowing her own demise, where or when it would come. Many might claim that's a gift in a way, even though it left unknown what was to come of the scarred lion, and the one gifted beyond all others. Some things are just not meant to be seen. Sister Lee accepted that in exchange for the power she possessed, but there would come a time. A gifted exchange would have to be made if she were unsuccessful in her attempts to rid the world of Hayden Keller, but she delayed it hoping for some other way to gain the sacred knowledge.

Living with diminished capabilities in the physical world was something she didn't relish, but more than that there was one obstacle which prevented her from making that exchange, one worthy of accepting her gift. Until that person surfaced, she had to remain among the living. All that she knew must be preserved, and passed down, for there would always be a need in the future. The world turns not on its own as they say, but for now, the details of Sister Lee's death yet to come remained a mystery even unto her. Clinching the tiger's eye crystal in her left hand, and the bloodstone in her right, in time she would come to know her reason for existing, and her eternal purpose. For now, it seemed she was tasked with sending him back from where he came. To do that, she had to take every precaution, arming herself against the darkest of forces.

Chapter 3

The Devil Went Down To Georgia

While Sister Lee went through this ancient ritual searching for answers to Hayden's exact location, Hayden searched for something to wear in Vincent's closet. He pulled his jacket off the hanger, and slid it on over his black tee-shirt. Taking a seat on the edge of the bed, he put on his boots while looking over at the dead body of Mrs. Russell lying there crossways on the bed.

A sinister grin started to form when his first thought surfaced. Clearly, for once she was completely silent. Hayden imagined the life he spared Vincent from having to endure. If he hadn't killed her, poor Vincent might have spent the rest of his life putting up with her. How tragic would that have been? Hayden pictured that as hell on earth. With that in mind, he considered it a shame he had to come between the two of them.

All of that was just Hayden's morbid sense of humor at play. He took no pity on anyone. Sympathy was something he was incapable of possessing entirely. Possession of emotion, and someone's body, was a totally different story. Hayden certainly appreciated the loan of Vincent's body. It spared him from spending more time in hell, even though that's where he belonged, but he had his deal with the devil that he had to make good on in order to keep walking this earth.

The prince of darkness still held him accountable for six souls every seven days, and Hayden knew he kept strict count. As it turned out, he had been in town less than an hour, and he already had one down. Reaching over on the dresser he picked up Vincent's wallet along with his keys. Dauntlessly placing them both in his pocket, he left the bedroom whistling a tune as he walked toward the front door.

Exiting the home of Mr. and Mrs. Russell, Hayden found something waiting for him outside which took him by surprise. Stepping foot on the door mat covering the front stoop which read, "*Welcome*," he couldn't help but notice the large truck parked in the tiny driveway. He pulled the keys out of his pocket looking down at them, and then he looked up at the bread truck.

Walking toward it, Hayden twisted his head in mild disbelief. He looked in the cab before he climbed up in it. He almost found it amusing when he muttered, "hell, I guess I'm the bread man." That was a new one on him. He then admired the storage capacity in the back of the delivery truck. He looked at it saying, "man, the bodies I could stuff in there."

Hayden was still as twisted as ever. He could hardly wait to hit the road in that thing. Shifting it into neutral, he cranked up the box truck, and rolled out of the driveway. Taking the front tire over the curb, he ran over the mailbox with the back tire. He looked in the side view mirror at what was left of it, and said, "damn, I love this job."

He had no idea where he was until he hit a sign that directed him south toward Valdosta. That was the wrong direction of course. Hayden slammed on brakes, and made a u-turn out in the middle of nowhere on a two lane stretch of road with no shoulder on either side. He ground the gears as he jockeyed the Sunbeam wagon back, and forth until he turned the coach completely around. All the while he growled, "tell me I can't drive this thing." He was definitely getting the hang of it, a true feel for the vehicle. What it offered in body storage capacity it lacked in easy maneuverability, but that didn't stop him from getting pointed in the right direction. He had a number of important stops to make, and the day itself wasn't getting any younger. There was only one thing Hayden delivered though, and it wasn't bread that's for sure.

Sister Lee now knew more about him, but Hayden was still unaware of her existence. Nevertheless, he was on a mission to find the man with two lives that had sent him straight to hell. His only link to him was Ashley Pennington, and that town up north called Chanceville.

Ben had put Hayden in his proper place when he saved Ashley's life, and Hayden could never allow that to happen again. He had to discover how Ben knew his name, and where to find him. He was certain he could find the answers to his questions if he could locate Ashley. Chalk it up to the quality time they spent together. Hayden had a feeling she missed him.

Once again he hunted her, but this time it was in an effort to find out more about Ben. Still, he had many miles to cover before he could lay his gruesome hands on her, but Sister Lee sensed he was coming. She could feel it deep in her heart. No third eye was needed to reveal that.

Chapter 4

Keep On Trucking

Hayden pulled onto the highway heading north toward some place called Tifton. He drove for miles before he exited on some little country-ass road that led to a small town just off the interstate. It was damn cold flying down the highway in a sunbeam truck with open doors.

Storage capacity or not, Hayden thought to himself, *this job sucks* as he ventured off Highway 75. The demands made by the human form he inhabited were irritating at times, but at that point all he wanted was a cup of coffee to help warm his bones. That didn't seem like too much to ask for at five o'clock in the morning, cause after all he was the bread man for God sakes. He'd quickly lost his fascination with the bread truck, but even he had to grin as he thought *who would ever suspect the merchant of death to pull up in the sunbeam-mobile.* Seeing a diner up ahead in the distance, Hayden knew two things - he needed a cup of coffee, and a new set of wheels.

There was a chill in the air, and the wind was brisk as it swept across the small town square directly across from the diner. It was still dark outside when Hayden stepped out of his vehicle. There were hardly any cars on the road at that hour of the morning. It was never too early for Hayden to kill, but right at that moment, all he wanted was a hot cup of java. He tended to be hasty in his pursuit of new victims after spending time in the most uncomfortable place ever created. He was aware of that, but it made his job difficult. Everything came with its share of headaches one could say, but to stay within the confines of his deal with the devil, Hayden was going to have to pace himself.

Sister Lee was tasked with a mission of her own. She had to protect Ashley Pennington at all costs. She had to do that in order to shield Ben from Hayden Keller. That would be difficult to achieve given the distance between she, and them, but the outcome wasn't predictable given so many variables. What was certain was someone good would die in the process if she failed to stop Hayden. It wasn't all selfless sacrifice on her part. If Hayden found Ben, he would surely discover her role in his demise, and the game would be over.

She had no choice. Sister Lee had to enlist the help of others, something she didn't like doing, but the alternative was unthinkable. To her credit, she had divine spiritual guidance, a complete understanding of the stars, and knowledge of the inner workings of the mind. Mental transference, mind control, call it what you will. She possessed the power to do just that. Who she would place in harm's way remained in question. It had to be someone bold, and capable of rendering lethal force. Only that type of individual could stop him without having his own life snatched in the process. Even then, there were no guarantees though. It would take time, but she would find such a man. Sheriff Baker was certainly capable, but he was needed in Chanceville.

Sister Lee turned her efforts to discovering Ashley's whereabouts since that was the most prudent course of action. Upon knowing that, based on proximity, she could decide who to select to defend against supernatural forces, and the man he would assist in facing down evil. He would need knowledge he did not possess, and such a man as she sought was hard to advise. Two things were certain. He would have to be forced to accept help from those he would normally not turn to, and his eyes would have to be opened to something he did not believe in at the moment. The best way to do that was through facts, clues, and history. Nevertheless, the confrontation was destined to take place, but much was within the gifted fortune teller's control.

Sister Lee's elaborate plan to find another hero to save the girl from Hayden would ensure Ben Goodman's life would never be placed in danger, and his identity would remain unknown to the evil one. Nothing was more important than that, even if it meant the lives of others.

As Ben tossed and turned in his bed during the early morning hours, he could definitely sense something was wrong. The mental connection he shared with the palm reader told a story all its own. What many would dismiss as simple insomnia, he knew was something altogether different. Blurred images of the scarred lion, and the town he never wished to visit again faded in, and out of his brain preventing him from falling asleep. It was instinct, seeing to it he gained no rest. It had grown sharper after he suffer his first death and the chill he felt when in Hayden's presence would never again be mistaken. He was growing aware of the mental connection that had been established. Sister Lee knew it too, and she immediately severed all contact.

She could still see clearly through his eyes. The gifted palm reader now knew he was on the west coast based on the time showing on his alarm clock. Which city he lived in she couldn't be certain, not without more time, but she didn't have any to spare. For now, just knowing Ben was nowhere close to the scarred lion gave her a feeling of reassurance she could keep him hidden from Hayden Keller.

Chapter 5

Marked For Death

Hayden stepped inside the empty diner, and took a seat at a corner table. The waitress hollered, "I'll be with you in a minute sweetie." She had no idea who just walked in her door. Hayden snarled at her warm greeting. He heard the intermittent noise of cookware clanging in the kitchen, and he was thoroughly familiar with the sound of a knife blade hitting a cutting board. Suddenly, Hayden developed a real appetite for something other than coffee. About that time, headlights appeared through the window of the diner.

Just outside, Hayden could hear the voices of two men as they exited their pickup. Over the sound of them slamming the doors shut, the word that caught his attention was kill, and Hayden knew how to do it best. As the door swung open, the cold air entered the room. Hayden still had no cup of joe in his hand, and he was growing ever impatient.

One of the men yelled out to the waitress calling her by name, and she jokingly said, "don't get your pants in a wad. I'm coming." She then told Clint to behave himself as she looked at him through the window of the kitchen.

He and his chubby hunting partner just laughed as Roscoe mumbled, "she knows you too well." Hayden didn't appreciate them sitting next to him. He liked his space, and they were in it even if they were regulars there.

The waitress brought out two cups of coffee, and she placed them on the table in front of Clint and Roscoe. She proudly stated, "I made them just how you boys like 'em."

Clint reached over gently slapping her on the tush adding, "you know how I like it, alright."

Sherry stopped as she looked over her shoulder at both of them before walking over to the table where Hayden was seated. Preparing to take Hayden's order, she gave Clint a look that indicated she was annoyed. A smirk appeared on her face when she looked away saying, "I swear, one of these days."

Roscoe remarked, "I told him you were going to turn him over your knee if he keeps it up."

Sherry's retort was, "I would, but he'd enjoy it too much." Clint's head began to bob up, and down as he took another sip of coffee. Hayden hadn't tasted the first drop yet, and these two yahoos were being treated like they owned the place. Sherry asked if they would both be having the usual before she turned around to take Hayden's order. When she asked, "what will you be having darling," Hayden growled hot coffee without so much as looking up at her. She clarified that's all he wanted, and she quickly informed him, "you're in luck sugar cause that's the only way we make it around here."

As she walked away, Hayden said, "I'd just settle for some on the table." There was a tone of vengeance embedded in his voice, and he didn't care who he offended with that remark, but Sherry never heard him over the banter of the hunters sitting next to him. Both of them were decked out in their hunting attire. In fact, they were covered in it from head to toe, and hunting was all they seemed to talk about.

Clint described the events that unfolded just as he remembered them from a previous hunt. He started off with, "I wasn't up in that stand hardly no time when I saw that deer step out from behind the tree. I eased over raising the barrel of my gun just a little, and I put my sites right on him as he moved closer to that little old creek to get him a drink of water. About that time, he raised that head of his up, and bam I shot him right there. Hell, he never even saw it coming." Clint was pretty proud of that story. He must have told it countless times, never tiring of it. It caused Hayden to think back on some of his previous kills, and for him that made for a fairly enjoyable morning.

As Sherry approached the table, she overheard part of their conversation, and she warned them saying, "you two know the rules. You better not be talking about killing Bambi inside the diner," but that didn't hush them up for long. As soon as she returned to the kitchen, Roscoe said, "I'm going to get me a big one this year. I can feel it."

Clint grinned big as he said, "you're going to have to do a damn sight better than you did the other weekend." That spawned a conversation about their previous hunting season. Roscoe bragged about the twelve point buck he bagged that year saying, "that's how it started out for me last year, and I ended up killing one bigger than the one Eugene shot the other day."

Clint argued with him just to get him riled up a little as he pointed out, "hell, it wasn't that big."

Roscoe protested, "hell yeah it was, and I got pictures to prove it." That's when Roscoe reached in his back pocket to grab his wallet as he leaned to one side lifting part of his fat ass out of the chair. Sure enough, he pulled out a photo of him, and his deer which he shot the year before.

Clint couldn't believe he had the picture on him as he said, "let me see that thing. What else you got stuffed in there?" Hayden found that part mildly amusing. Roscoe was a die-hard deer hunter, and Hayden thought to himself, *that's exactly how he will die.* When Roscoe pointed over at the photo telling Clint to count the points on the deer's antlers, Hayden questioned in his mind if the two of them collectively could count that high. Clint boldly stated, "it looks like ten to me."

Roscoe pointed out two more nubs as he said, "see that little one over there, and here. That's a twelve point buck."

Clint said, "I can't believe you call that thing a point. Hell, that's hardly a little tit."

Sherry sat the hot cup of coffee down on Hayden's table as Roscoe pulled the picture away looking at it himself before placing it back inside his wallet. As he put it away, he said, "that's a trophy if I ever saw one." That's when Hayden chuckled out loud where they both could hear just before taking a swig of black coffee. Roscoe looked over at him, and he posed one question to Hayden. "Do you do any hunting partner?"

Hayden sat there holding the cup of coffee in front of his face with his elbow resting on the table as he claimed, "I've done my fair share."

Roscoe carried a smug look on his face as he turned looking over at Clint. All he said was, "he don't look like much of a hunter, does he?"

Clint had to agree with his hunting buddy on that one as he grinned shaking his head saying, "no, he don't." About that time, Sherry sat a plate of eggs, and bacon in front of Clint. Roscoe was already wolfing down his biscuits which were covered in sausage gravy. In between bites, he and Clint had their fun as they glanced over at Hayden laughing at the thought of him claiming to be a hunter.

Hayden wasn't sporting a pair of camouflage coveralls or even a hunting jacket like Clint and Roscoe. On the surface, it was easy for them to dismiss him as being a hunter, but they had no real understanding of what game he was after. Hayden was definitely a hunter through, and through, he simply preferred to kill people instead of deer. Roscoe asked him, "you ever kill a buck?"

Hayden looked up saying, "yeah, I killed a Buck once," and he left it at that.

Roscoe felt the need to press him for details as he asked, "well, how big was he?"

Hayden looked over sizing him up. The fat hunter was only given a partial view of his face. The right side of it was all Clint and Roscoe could see. Sitting his coffee cup down on the table in front of him, Hayden said, "he was every bit of two hundred and seventy pounds, but I don't have a picture of him to show you."

Roscoe couldn't believe what he was hearing, but he had to ask one more question as he and Clint finished up their breakfast. "What did you get him with?"

Hayden was done talking. Lifting his hands up in the air he held them in front of him. Clint chimed in with, "he's asking what you used to kill him. Was it a bow or a rifle?"

Hayden boldly stated, "I killed him with by bare hands."

His tone was serious, and Roscoe paused for a second wondering if Hayden was crazy or just pulling his leg. He looked over at Clint asking, "are you believing this?"

Clint immediately said the first thing that came to mind which was, "bullshit."

He dug into his last bite of scrambled eggs and Roscoe just laughed as he laid a tip on the table for Sherry saying, "I've heard enough of this shit. Come on, let's get out of here."

Hayden sat there expressionless as he said, "happy hunting gentlemen." They paid him little attention as they walked out the door. Clint informed Roscoe he was going to have to get some gas, and that was the last thing Hayden heard them say as they left diner. Not only did they not know they were now being hunted, they also told Hayden right where to find them. Hayden thought to himself, *this is going to be like shooting fish in a barrel, even deer aren't that dumb*. He got up from the table, and he stepped outside looking in the direction of the truck as it pulled out onto the road.

Chapter 6

Vengeance Is Hayden Keller

Sherry saw the diner was empty, and she yelled at the cook informing him she was going to the restroom for a moment. Bob looked up from the grill as he cleaned it, and he just nodded his head. As she walked into the bathroom, Hayden quietly slipped back inside the diner. He looked over at the counter, and his eye caught something he wanted. He paid the cook no mind whatsoever. He was busy in the kitchen doing God knows what as Hayden moved in the direction of the counter. Once there, he lifted the clear plastic lid off of the cake box without making a sound. It wasn't the three layer chocolate cake Hayden was interested in acquiring. It was the long stainless steel knife used to cut it that was of use to him. He then followed the path Sherry had blazed to the restroom, and he stood just outside the door. Holding the knife behind his back, he waited for her.

He would have barged right in and killed her while she sat on the commode, but Sherry had locked the door, and Hayden planned on taking care of business in stealth mode. She had pissed him off by not serving him first, and he meant to set things straight. Sherry opened the door only to be startled by Hayden's presence. In fact, he downright scared the hell out of her. It was the first time she had seen the open gash on his left cheek since he had been sitting with it turned to the wall when she took his order. The sight of it left her without words. She was frozen with fear. The sinister look he had on his face didn't help put her at ease either. She hesitantly muttered, "I thought you left already." Hayden explained he had forgotten to give her a tip, and

Sherry responded, "oh, that's alright." She felt a cold chill of death run through her veins as he spoke.

Almost apologetically, he said, "I still feel as though I owe you one." Sherry could sense something wasn't right about him, and the entire situation. He stood there without any money in his hand as he said, "run." That was the best tip he could give her at that point, but she had nowhere to run.

Hayden had her cornered as he pulled out the knife. He quickly ran the back of the blade across his tongue tasting the chocolate frosting which cleaved to it. It gave him time to see her eyes fill with terror before he unleashed his wrath upon her. Whispering his name, he introduced himself to her before she could scream. As soon as she opened her mouth to call out for help, he drove the nine inch blade straight into her throat pinning her to the bathroom door behind her. The hilt of the knife crushed her esophagus, and her head slumped forward with her eyes still wide open.

Hayden grabbed her by the hair as he lifted her head, allowing him to look into her eyes one last time. He let go of it, and her chin bounced off the handle of the knife as her head leaned to one side. Hayden watched the blood stream off the handle of the knife making its way to the floor. He looked down with satisfaction at the puddle of blood pooling at Sherry's feet. She had truly gotten under Hayden's skin catering to the hunters, and not tending to him first. Hayden now thought how fitting it was that he got under her skin in the end. He would've skinned her like a deer, but he didn't have time. He had to track down his new hunting buddies before they hit the woods. For Hayden, it was the start to a beautiful morning. He still had to acquire a new set of wheels but he felt certain he could get a deal on a pickup, no money down of course. His guess was it would come with a full tank of gas, and a couple of firearms.

Chapter 7

Trophy Kill

As Clint pulled into the Stop and Go station, he looked over at Roscoe while turning up his nose. That's when he said, "damn boy, was that you?"

Roscoe started to laugh as he joked, "it must be a polecat or something."

Clint had a sick look on his face as he said, "it's something alright. I think something must have crawled up and died inside of you. Damn, that's bad!"

Roscoe shook his head pointing out, "you know I don't do well with eggs."

Clint quickly reached over to roll down his window, and that made Roscoe laugh even harder. Pulling up next to the gas pump, Clint gladly climbed out to fill the tank. Roscoe informed him, "I'm going inside to grab me one of those Thirstbusters. You want anything?"

Clint candidly said, "maybe an air freshener for the truck." Roscoe added that he was going to the bathroom so he may be a minute. Clint took that opportunity to tell him, "while you're there make sure you don't need a change of drawers." Roscoe just laughed once again. Clint filled the tank, and he took his sweet time before climbing back inside the truck. He left the window down to let in some fresh air. Roscoe's silent fart was impressive, perhaps even one for the record books if they measured potency, and the longest hang time. Clint didn't give a shit how cold it was. The stench Roscoe left inside his pickup almost made his eyes burn. He pulled around to the side of the store to wait on Roscoe. He was hoping to make him believe he had left his ass at the store. He had actually done it one time. They enjoyed playing pranks on one another, but it was all fairly harmless in the end. Cutting off the engine, he sat there looking down at his watch. Clint questioned how long he could possibly take in there. He wanted to be up in the stand before sunup, but nature had unfortunately called his hunting partner.

As Clint leaned his head back resting his eyes, Hayden pulled into the parking lot next to the gas station. He had found his prey. He observed the truck for a moment before getting out of his vehicle. Walking over to it, he didn't make a sound. As he neared the driver's side of Clint's truck he could see a logging chain lying in the bed of the pickup close to the cab. His instincts were all that was driving him at that moment. Without even thinking, Hayden reached in the bed of the truck picking up the heavy chain with his right hand.

The sound of the steel links in the chain hitting the side of the truck caused Clint to open his eyes to see what was going on. Sticking his head out the window looking toward the back of the vehicle, all he saw in his last living moment was Hayden as he wrapped the chain around his neck. Clint's face became blood red as he reached for the chain cutting off his air supply. Hayden pulled the chain hard severing all blood flow to Clint's brain. He then pulled Clint out of the truck through the window using the logging chain. Clint's neck snapped before he hit the ground.

Hayden reached inside the cab of the truck pulling out one of the rifles which was resting in the gun rack. He bent down to hook the loose end of the chain to the towing hitch on the back of the truck. That's when Roscoe rounded the corner munching on a bag of pork rinds while slurping on his big gulp. He saw the truck, but no Clint anywhere to be found. He looked around with a lost expression glued to his face as he questioned, "where the hell did he go?" As he moved closer to the vehicle, Hayden stood up looking right at him. Roscoe immediately questioned what he was doing in the bed of their truck.

Hayden hoisted Clint's head in the air using the logging chain, and Roscoe damn near choked on a pork rind as he dropped his drink. He just stood there dumbfounded in complete disbelief. Hayden placed his boot on the bumper of the truck as he said, "now that's a trophy if I ever saw one. I didn't bring my camera. You want to take the shot?"

Roscoe became furious. The sickened feeling he first felt was now replaced with rage. He wanted to kill Hayden with his bare hands as he rushed toward him. Hayden raised the hunting rifle he was holding in his right hand, and he let go of the chain which was wrapped around Clint's neck. As Clint's head bounced off the tailgate of the truck, Hayden lowered the weapon pointing it right at Roscoe. Staring at the barrel of the gun, Roscoe froze like a deer in the headlights before turning to run in the other direction. Hayden fired one shot, and Roscoe fell forward hitting the pavement hard. He was unable to move his legs.

Hayden removed the chain from Clint's neck, and he hooked the free end around Roscoe's feet as he said, "what do you say we take a little weight off of you fat boy?" He tossed Clint's body in the bed of the truck as if he were a sack of garbage, and he climbed inside the pickup placing the rife on the seat next to him. Pulling out of the parking lot, Hayden drug Roscoe to his death as his body bounced along the pavement behind him.

Hayden pulled off onto a dirt road just before sunup, and he unhooked the logging chain from what was left of Roscoe. He threw the chain in the bed of the truck, and he pulled Clint's body out tossing him on top of the mangled mess that was once his hunting buddy as he said, "this is where you get off." Hayden now had a pickup truck with a full tank of gas, and two hunting rifles. This was all the makings for a great day in Hayden's twisted world.

As he tore off down the road in search of his next victim, Bob began to wonder where Sherry had run off to. He looked outside thinking she may be on a smoke break before walking back to the restroom to check on her. Seeing her hanging on the door, he became sick to his stomach. He puked on his way to the phone before calling the police. As a car pulled up in front of the diner, he flipped the switch next to the door turning the neon "open" sign "off." A few minutes later a patrol car pulled into the parking lot. Bob unlocked the door to let the officer in and he led him to the place where Sherry drew her last breath. Even the officer couldn't believe what he was seeing. He had a borage of questions for Bob which he couldn't answer. All the while, Hayden was now headed out of town on a major highway as he listened to Willie Nelson sing "On The Road Again." Seeing a sign for a Huddle House up ahead, he decided to pull off for a piece of pecan pie.

Chapter 8

Killing Spree

Hayden had already amassed four victims, and it wasn't even lunchtime yet. Authorities had only found one so far, and that was the waitress in the diner he left pinned to the door of the bathroom. Bob, the cook, was still sick about the whole mess, but all he could tell police was he heard her talking to two of her regular customers that morning. At that point, Bob's statement, and the fingerprints they lifted off the murder weapon were their only real clues. It would be several hours later when the bodies of Clint and Roscoe were discovered, and as for Mrs. Russell, well she wouldn't be found for a day or two.

Hayden was already in another state by the time police found the two hunters he had bagged earlier that morning. He grinned as he recalled that stupid look on Roscoe's fat face right before he shot him. He didn't have a picture of it to tote around in his back pocket, but he had Clint, and Roscoe's wallets. Their picture IDs would just have to serve as his fond reminder of the kills he made on his most recent hunt. He was still behind the wheel of Clint's pickup truck. With four bodies to his credit in less than four hours, Hayden made a mental note that he was going to have to apply the brakes to his fast paced killing spree.

It was Tuesday, and Hayden couldn't afford to take another life before the passing of the next Sabbath. He detested the thought of not being free to kill, but that was his deal with the devil, and there was no going back on it. If he broke that rule, he would never escape from hell ever again, regardless of the anomalies in the space time continuum. That forced him to find a place where he could lay low for a couple of days. An abandoned trailer ten miles south of Montgomery seemed like as good a place as any. The accommodations weren't desirable, but Hayden needed a place to hide-out, and serial killers on the run can't be choosers.

To see to it he didn't overstep his bounds, he had to separate himself from people altogether in order to avoid killing them, even he knew that. His psychopathic urges were nearly impossible to control, and killing came as natural to him as breathing is to most of us. He had a difficult time restraining himself from taking life wherever he found it. He certainly didn't like adhering to the constraints which were placed on him, but that was his lot in life according to the master which he served. Hayden lived in misery, and sowed it harvesting souls for Satan.

He pulled up to the old rusted box of metal that someone once called home, and he surveyed the area. It was well hidden off the road tucked behind some trees. A long dirt drive led up to it, but it had been years since anyone ventured down it. Now, it was completely overgrown with tall grass and weeds. Time was not on his side even though Hayden hummed that classic tune made famous by the Rolling Stones as he stepped out of the truck to inspect the old vine covered wobbly box.

Taking a look inside the trailer, he noticed a stained couch, and a busted coffee table just inside the door. Most people would have preferred not to even touch it, but Hayden made himself right at home. The dried up piece of snakeskin resting in the corner next to the closet didn't faze Hayden a bit. He hoped to find the owner of it, because that meant dinner. Yeah, Hayden ate snake, and just about anything that moved for that matter. He'd be the first to tell you everything tastes like chicken, including rat. He was quite the connoisseur alright. Looking the place over thoroughly before stepping outside to relieve himself in front of the trailer, he knew the next four days were going to feel like eternity, but he had been to hell many times, and it was a far cry from that place.

When he walked back inside, he left the door standing open. Eventually, the foul air which lingered in the living room would dissipate, either that, or he'd get used to it. Feeling the need to take a load off, he treated the place as if he owned it. Plopping down on the old dirty couch, he tucked his hands behind his head. He stared up at the damaged ceiling above him, and thought *well I'm home.* As the sun began to set, and the mosquitoes began to emerge, he soon questioned if he had truly escaped hell at all. Hayden quickly lost his love for that place as they attempted to feast on his face, but Hayden was forced to endure their constant pestering in order to live to see another day. He laid there with a dismal look of disbelief on his scarred faced as he swatted them away while staring up at the stains on the ceiling.

The abandoned bread truck sat in the parking lot of the Stop and Go station all afternoon. Police finally showed up on the scene after they received a call from the convenience store owner telling them he wanted it moved. Officer Lackey pulled up next to the sunbeam-mobile. He looked it over without even stepping foot outside his patrol car. He thought to himself, *I don't have time for this shit. Hell, we're after a cold blooded murderer, and here I am on bread truck patrol.*

He really didn't care to have to deal with the store owner, but when Lackey walked inside the convenience store, Haddad started in on him as soon as he came through the door. He was babbling with that thick Arab accent of his about how that damn bread truck was costing him business. "It is blocking my store sign. See? You can take it away, right?" Officer Lackey looked around the store as he responded to Haddad. "Well, someone owns it - I'm sure they'll be back for it." Lackey's words did nothing to calm down the store owner.

Haddad exclaimed, "it's been there all morning. I have a business to run, and no customers come."

Lackey explained, "business might be off because of the murders that took place in town." Haddad listened closely to Officer Lackey's every word. Nothing Lackey shared with him was good news, and Haddad's face reflected that. He then told Haddad they just found two more bodies on a road not too far from his store. "It looks like they were dumped there several hours ago," he said.

A concerned look came over Haddad's face. He lowered his head as he slowly rubbed his neck with his hand while he looked down at the floor. He was obviously in deep thought. Lackey could tell the news really disturbed him, but then he looked up saying, "I want that bread truck out of here. It's bad luck! It's no good!" That's what Haddad kept saying as he pointed to it through the window of his store. Lackey assured him he'd take care of it. Even he found it odd that it had been there all morning left unattended. As he opened the door to walk out of the store, Haddad tried to sell him on buying something. Haddad said, "hey! You want coffee, how about a Slim-Jim? Lackey had to admire his persistence as Haddad added, "I got hot dogs in the back." Officer Lackey shook his head no as he exited the store. Haddad was still in the middle of his sales pitch as he said, "what about a donut." Disgusted, Haddad turned looking at the truck which blocked his store sign. It was parked out by the road. Poking out his lips, he stared at it as he watched Lackey walk toward it. He started talking to himself as he shook his head saying, "that truck, it's no good."

Officer Lackey stuck his head inside the vehicle. There was no sign of anything that looked suspicious other than the fact it was missing its driver. He walked around behind the vehicle, and he wrote down the tag number before turning to walk back to his patrol car. That's when he noticed something that caught his eye. It was on the ground next to the side of the store. A serious look formed on his face as he moved closer to investigate. It was a hunting cap which belonged to Roscoe, and there was a blood trail on the pavement that led out to the street. Lackey damn near dropped his notepad as he scrambled to get to his radio. Picking up the microphone he said, "this is Officer Lackey. I have a blood trail over here at the Stop and Go on State Road 41. You need to notify the Cook County sheriff, and highway patrol. I also have an abandoned vehicle I believe might be involved. It has a Georgia plate, the tag number is 2074 FME."

When the dispatcher asked what type of vehicle it was, Lackey paused for a second before volunteering that it was a bread truck. He knew if he was wrong about this one he'd never live it down. Still, the blood trail was real, and within less than twelve minutes Haddad's parking lot was filled with blue lights. Haddad's eyes got big as he watched more law enforcement officers pull up in front of his store. He walked outside to see what was going on. He still didn't see a tow truck, just droves of patrol cars. He became hysterical as he watched them stretch crime scene tape across half of his parking lot. Things just seemed to go from bad to worse,

35

and he knew this couldn't be good for business.

Within an hour, prints taken off the bread truck were matched to those found on the murder weapon back at the diner. The Cook County sheriff complimented Officer Lackey on his efforts to help them find what now appeared to be a serial killer. The sheriff slapped Lackey on the back as he looked at the truck saying, "well done. I got to hand it to you, this is a fine piece of investigative work."

Lackey looked over at him as he replied, "yeah, I just had a bad feeling about it as soon as I pulled up." He sold that line with confidence, and the sheriff bought it. Sheriff Tyndall didn't say it, but at that point he wished his deputies were half that smart as Lackey appeared to be. It didn't take them long to determine the name of the company which owned the vehicle. Getting in touch with them was another story. It had not been reported stolen at that point, but late that afternoon it was brought into question what the hell happened to the driver of that vehicle. Upon getting a hold of the routing manager, it was made clear to police that no one had seen or heard from Vincent Russell since three o'clock the day before.

Initially, the state police believed Vincent was probably a victim of the killer, and his dead body had yet to be discovered. They were right in a sense. Vincent had fallen prey to Hayden Keller, just not in the way authorities expected. A statewide manhunt was now in effect for the bread man throughout Georgia, and Hayden was holdup in a poor excuse for a mobile home which happened to be located in southern Alabama. He spent his time hatching a plan in his mind as to how he would go about finding Ashley Pennington, and he was dead set on returning to Chanceville to get the answers he needed.

Chapter 9

A Cold Case Mandate

It was 8:30 a.m. Thursday morning when Chief Cielinski of the Indianapolis Metropolitan Police Department issued his statement to the press concerning the overwhelming number of unsolved cases currently in the hands of the IMPD. Many of them were long outstanding cases with no real leads to go on. One reporter referred to them as the cold case files when he asked, "is it your administration's policy to overlook the growing number of cold cases your police department has managed to stack-up over the past five years?"

Chief Cielinski pointed out that wasn't the case at all. He stated in certain terms, "I would first like to point out I have only been in charge of this department for nine months, and we have made a great deal of progress in that short period of time addressing major issues which needed immediate attention. That said, I assure you reducing the number of unsolved cases on record is my top priority at this point."

The next question that followed was, "how do you plan to go about doing it?" Cielinski paused a moment before speaking, then he proudly announced he had issued a mandate to those under him to put whatever resources were necessary in place to see to it that the number of cold cases on record were reduced by fifteen percent by the end of this year. That got everyone's attention as they all made a note of that, and the room was buzzing with comments from reporters at that point.

One of them could be heard saying, "that's aggressive alright." Chief Cielinski closed his folder as he stepped away from the podium, and with that statement he concluded his press conference as he exited the room.

Captain Rollins witnessed the whole thing, and he knew whose shoulders that burden would rest on. It wasn't three minutes after the press conference when Chief Cielinski called him on his cell phone as he left the government center. Rollins picked up the phone knowing it was the Chief of Police. All he heard him say was, "Bob, I guess you heard what took place this morning during the interview."

Captain Rollins replied, "yes sir."

Chief Cielinski said, "well, now you have your mandate. Don't fall short on this one if you ever plan on becoming chief. Everyone will be watching you understand."

Captain Rollins sat back in his chair pushing himself away from his desk using one hand as he braced himself for the challenge the chief just placed on him. All he said was, "I'll see to it that we are successful just as you promised. I'll put my best detectives on those cases immediately."

Cielinski responded with, "that's what I want to hear Bob."

The Captain looked up from his desk with a grim look on his face, but then he smirked seeing Detective Callahan pass by his office window on his way to the head. The captain stood up from his chair quickly making his way to the door of his office. Opening it, he leaned his head out firmly saying, "Callahan, my office, right now." The detective looked over his shoulder at him attempting to explain he had some pressing business he needed to take care of, but Captain Rollins shook his head no saying, "whatever it is, it can wait."

Callahan dropped his head toward his shoulder as he turned around to walk back to his office. The seasoned detective stood in the doorway looking inside at his boss taking his seat behind his desk. He didn't mince words when he asked, "what is it now?"

The captain looked him straight in the eye saying, "I have a new assignment for you. You're going to oversee the cold case division of our department."

Callahan looked at him somewhat puzzled. His response to that was, "I was unaware we even had such a division. Who's currently a part of it?"

Rollins grinned saying, "right now just you, but I'm planning on reassigning more detectives to that area very soon. Right now you're the best I got, and I expect results. The Chief of Police has said we will reduce the number of cold cases we have on record by the end of this year, and we will make good on his promise."

Callahan immediately started shaking his head in protest. "I have real cases on my desk that need my attention. If I don't follow-up on them they could add to that growing pile of unsolved cases," he said.

Captain Rollins replied, "this is not up for debate. I expect you to handle those cases as well, that's why I'm putting Buttweiler with you."

Callahan emphatically said, "oh no, not Buttweiler." Rollins cut the detective off before he could say another word telling him, "I want you to pull thirty cases from archives, and get started immediately on assessing which ones are most likely to be solved given what's in the file. I expect a list of the ones you will be working on my desk first thing in the morning. Is that understood?"

Callahan knew the captain was serious about this by the tone in his voice. He didn't have to add that their careers were riding on this. The thought of working with Buttweiler on a bunch of old cases no one else was able to solve seemed bleak at best. Even if he could compile a list of the ones he felt were possibly solvable, he knew it would take countless hours to reopen all those cases. Trying to generate new leads with Buttweiler's assistance seemed almost like punishment. Still, Callahan reminded himself the captain was counting on him to get the job done. Maybe he could make a detective out of Buttweiler yet. God knows he had taken the test five times already, and never came close to passing.

Ten seconds later, Rollins asked Callahan if he knew how the door to his office worked, and that meant their meeting was concluded. Callahan nodded his head just once pulling the door shut. He could see the captain point at him through the glass window, and he knew what that meant as well.

Chapter 10

A Pile Of Unsolved Murders

Detective Callahan mumbled, "morning," to Lieutenant Shaw as he passed him in the hall on his way downstairs to the records room. The lieutenant couldn't help but notice Detective Callahan seemed to be in a bit of a hurry to get somewhere, and he didn't look happy about it. The Lieutenant simply thought he just woke up on the wrong side of the bed that morning, and he probably hadn't had his first cup of coffee yet, but he was wrong.

The day had started out pretty well for a middle-aged detective with no family to speak of, and Callahan had already downed his second cup of coffee by the time he entered the precinct. He liked it black with plenty of sugar. What he didn't care for was being sent down to archives to research a bunch of old cases no one had been able to solve. He was a cop though, and good cops do what they must to bring about justice even if it takes decades to do it.

Passing the holding room where the evidence locker was located, he thought back to some of the biggest busts he had made in recent years. Many of them were quite notable. A long distinguished career had now led him to one place he never imagined seeing, the basement is what most called it. Technically, it was a sub-floor. Either way, the damn thing was underground with no window anywhere to be found.

As Callahan entered the records room, he stopped dead in his tracks. He stood just inside the door looking around at the tall filing cabinets which lined the walls. Near where he was standing was a small desk equipped with a computer, and a sign-in sheet. He didn't bother using it. He was a bit overwhelmed. The place was huge, filled with countless rows of shelves which were packed with paper housed in boxes, and numerous file folders. The massive number of records he was staring at left him without words. All he could do is clear his throat.

Two seconds later, a short tubby man with thinning hair wearing a white short-sleeve shirt, and black rimmed glass stuck his head out from behind one of the shelves. His name was Henley, and he manned the desk inside the records room. Callahan could see him peeping around from behind one of the tall shelves positioned almost in the center of the room. Henley was looking straight at him, yet he didn't say a word. Henley had spent more time in the archives room than anyone could ever imagine, and he had never been visited by a legendary detective. He questioned if he was seeing things. He stammered a little as he spoke. Still, he managed to ask, "can I help you with something?"

Callahan's response was, "you must be Henley. I'm looking for the unsolved case files."

Henley stepped around the corner carrying a large stack of folders which he placed on the nearest table. He looked up at Callahan happy to assist him in that endeavor asking him, "are you looking for cases that date back before the eighties, or after?"

The look on Callahan's face was that of utter surprise. Henley pointed toward the back of the room saying, "cause anything prior to 1990 can be found on that back wall. All unsolved crimes that occurred within the last twenty-two years comprise these two isles. Oh, and that set of filing cabinets over there."

Callahan tried to take in what Henley was saying. Still, his face showed some sign of bewilderment. Could there really be that many unsolved cases? That's what he had to ask himself. Suddenly, his new assignment took on a whole new light. The job certainly hadn't become any easier, but Callahan saw a lot of shelves filled with the names of a lot of people whose families still had no closure. At this point, that's all they could be given. The disconcerted look on Callahan's face faded as he realized this was his chance to do his part to help rectify that situation.

Henley waddled over to his desk asking, "so, how did you know my name is Henley?"

Callahan replied, "it's my job. I'm a detective."

Henley smiled a little confessing that he didn't see too many detectives down there in his records room. Motioning with his hand for Callahan to follow him, he took him on a tour of the room. The first thing he pointed out was what he called the hot cold cases. That equated to anything that had ended up unsolved in the last five years. He was constantly juggling those folders as they aged. He was serious when he said, "yeah, archives really keeps you on your toes."

Callahan listened to him as Henley led him to the other side of the room. Walking at a slower pace than he was used to, they passed what seemed like continuous rows of shelves and file cabinets. Even though he was a bit out of his element, and completely lost when it came to finding what he wanted, he realized the little guy in front of him knew the records room like the back of his hand.

When the detective went to introduce himself, Henley up and surprised him by saying, "you're Detective Callahan, I know. I've been following your cases for years. Over three hundred arrests, with two hundred and eighty-three convictions, and that's just in the last eight years." Callahan looked at him in near disbelief. Henley knew his stats just as if he were some kind of famous baseball player, and if there was one thing Callahan loved it was baseball.

Henley astonished him with his ability to locate anything in that room within seconds, and the detective was forced to ask, "are you a baseball fan by any chance Henley?"

Henley paused for only a second before saying, "no, I don't believe so. I've never watched a game really. Why, do you like baseball?" Callahan did his best to suppress a smile from surfacing as he nodded his head. Before he could say a word Henley asked, "shall we continue?"

The next five minutes were filled with history concerning the migration of files throughout the room, and how to go about searching for something using Henley's complex filing system. His method was unique to say the least. Somewhere during the lengthy lesson, Callahan interrupted him asking, "how long have you been in this room Henley?"

Henley paused for a moment, then he gave Callahan the history on when he first took the job as filing clerk assistant. "That was back in 1984, but two years later they eliminated that position altogether when Mr. Portman retired. That's when I took over archives, and I've been in charge ever since," he said.

Callahan cut him short again asking, "am I to understand you have worked down here for almost thirty years?" Henley bobbed his head just once as he pointed out, "its actually been twenty-eight years as of May of this year."

Callahan found that remarkably believable, and truly priceless. Looking at Henley, he said the first thing that came to mind. "You know where everything is in this room, don't you. I tell you what - if I need something, I'm coming to you for it. How does that sound partner?" Henley instantly latched onto the word "partner." His mind raced, envisioning scenes from Miami Vice, and Hill Street Blues as Callahan added, "that's what partners do. They help each other out, right."

Henley eagerly replied, "yeah, and they watch each other's back." That comment made Callahan grin.

"Yeah they do," he agreed.

He couldn't help but like Henley. Callahan knew the world inside the archives room couldn't be that exciting. Watching your partner's back down there most likely consisted of making sure they didn't fall off a ladder or something, but the fact was he did need Henley's help. Maybe together they really could clear up some of the old outstanding cases. Having Henley as his partner sounded a hell of a lot better than being stuck with Buttweiler, but that wasn't his call.

Chapter 11

Breaking In A New Partner

While Callahan may not have found archives to be the most exciting place on earth, his portly little partner did. Henley saw all of those records within the walls of the archives room as critical pieces of history. Even though many of the victims were no longer living, Henley felt each file had a story to tell, and a life all its own. That's why he never felt like he was all by himself down there. In Henley's mind, he was surrounded by the people whose names appeared within those documents. Everyone's name could be found within that room - witnesses, victims, medical examiners, and key members of law enforcement. Even the names of those responsible for the crimes themselves could be found there. When he shared his take on things with Callahan, it gave him a new perspective. He'd never look at a manila folder again in quite the same way after that. No one could deny each file contained important information, and Henley had laid his hands on just about every one.

He guarded those files from the time he unlocked the records room to the time he secured it for the evening. To pass the time he read over eyewitness accounts, and viewed photographs of crime scenes. Henley even studied verdicts along with the sentences which were handed down by the court judges. The appeals process often turned the archives department into a happening place, in Henley's mind. That said, he had never had a detective refer to him as partner. Callahan's words sounded damn good to him. So much so that he couldn't wait to pull the first pile of records for him. He anxiously asked, "so, what are we looking for?"

Callahan replied, "murders occurring in the last ten years. That's where we'll start." Henley pointed toward one of the tall shelves as Callahan said, "I want thirty of them." The theme to Nash Bridges started playing inside Henley's head as he pushed the stepladder in that direction. This is as close as he'd ever get to being a cop, and here he was partnered up with the legendary Detective Callahan. Classic lines from numerous Dirty Harry movies ran through Henley's mind as he handed Callahan one folder after another.

Amassing a pile of unsolved murders, Callahan took the stack of files over to the table, and began reading through them. Henley returned to his clerical tasks occasionally looking over at him imagining what it must be like to work the streets, and catch a killer. He found it rather difficult not to say something, but he tried his best not to disturb the detective. Henley just appreciated having a live person sharing the same room with him for a change. The fact that it was Detective Callahan made it all the better. Whenever the detective asked for something, Henley was right on it. Callahan made notes as he read through each file, and Henley would occasionally look over his shoulder at what he was writing, then he would go about his duties. Hours later, Callahan was still hard at work never bothering to pay attention to the time. He stopped looking at his watch after he read over the third file. When lunch rolled around he was lost deep within one of the cold case files. It was a brutal slaying that occurred five years earlier. The killer had viciously beaten a thirty-six year old man with an aluminum baseball bat outside Victory Field. Callahan had visited that place many times. It was the home of the Indianapolis Indians. Callahan was a season ticket holder. It wasn't until Henley pulled out a ham and cheese sandwich, along with a bag of chips which he had in a paper bag on his desk that Callahan realized how late in the day it was. As Henley crunched on some stale potato chips, Callahan looked over at him. He slowly stopped chewing. Swallowing what he had in his mouth in one gulp he said, "I'm sorry. Am I disturbing you?"

Callahan replied, "hell no Henley. I was just thinking I know a place that serves the best bratwurst in town. You and I ought to go there sometime." Henley certainly liked the sound of that, but he knew he had to remain in the archives department until he locked the doors for good at five o'clock each day. When he pointed that out, Callahan said, "let me use your phone for a minute." Just at that moment, Buttweiler stumbled into the records room. He looked lost, of course. Callahan put down the phone saying, "I was just about to call you. What's for lunch?"

As usual, Buttweiler didn't have the answer to that question either. All he said was, "I don't know, you tell me." Buttweiler always said that regardless of the question.

At least he was consistent. Callahan pulled a ten dollar bill out of his pocket handing it to him as he said, "I have quite a few case files to go through. I'm going to need your help, I'm sure. Why don't you grab me, and my partner here two loaded bratwursts." The detective looked over at Henley confirming that he wanted his all the way. He eagerly shook his head yes taking what was left of his dry ham and cheese sandwich stuffing it back in the bag.

Buttweiler just looked at Henley as he pointed to Callahan saying, "that's my partner. I'm Henley by the way. I'm looking forward to working with you."

A befuddled look graced Buttweiler's face as Callahan said, "make it quick, cause I'm hungry."

Flexing his newly acquired spine with Callahan resting one leg on his desk Henley added, "you heard the man. He's hungry." With that, Buttweiler made his exit determined not to screw up his new assignment which the captain had given him even though he was now playing the role of errand boy.

Chapter 12

Gruesome Killings

The rest of the afternoon was spent reading over more cold cases. Callahan had started making his list for the captain. Buttweiler struggled to keep his eyes open while reading through one file after another. Not sure of which one to pursue investigating, he started a new stack. Henley was all too happy to keep them coming.

Callahan looked up from what he was doing. It was clear his newly assigned partner had no clue when it came to determining which cases were viable to reopen. Offering him some guidance, Callahan told Buttweiler, "pick three cases out of the ones I have in front of me. Those are your cases. You'll be responsible for the outcome, whatever it may be, but I'll tell you this, if they end up going unsolved, you should seriously consider another line of work."

Buttweiler looked Callahan in the eye. He certainly wasn't the first one to make that suggestion, but coming from Callahan it sounded serious. For once, Buttweiler really didn't wish to ask why he said that. Not because he didn't care to know what moved Callahan to make that statement, he just didn't want to appear clueless for a change.

Callahan glanced back down at the list he had comprised, and Buttweiler broke down asking, "why?"
The seasoned detective never looked back up at him. He was now busy studying another case file. All he said was, "you tell me." That was his challenge put to Buttweiler, and he expected him to provide the answer. There were only a

half dozen case files on the table in front of him, and they were all related to one another. Buttweiler read through them all again trying to pick between them.

Finally, he said, "I don't guess it matters, they all look the same. None of these people died without being tortured. Hell it makes me sick just to think about what was done to Melanie Karnes, all of them for that matter. Wendy Fitzgerald, Craig Bradshaw, you name them. Whoever killed them was one sick bastard."

Callahan looked up at Buttweiler with what some might describe as a slight smile emerging on his face even though he spoke of some of the tragic circumstances surrounding the murders. Pointing out some of the details concerning what the victims endured before dying wasn't pleasant, but it was enlightening.

Buttweiler was now aware he had uncovered something, a critical link missed by others. It was knowledge only he, and Callahan shared at the moment. He quickly looked back at several case files, and then he grinned himself as he looked up at Callahan. "They're related," he said.

Callahan nodded as Buttweiler added, "that's why they look the same. He used a different murder weapon in each instance, but one man is responsible for all of these murders."

Callahan's response was, "that's right. Good work, you solve one, you solve them all. Now tell me why these cases were never solved in the first place." Buttweiler thought for a moment, but no answer came to mind. Callahan said, "look where they occurred, and when, and pay attention to who worked each case."

Thumbing back through the files, Buttweiler said, "different investigators on the cases for the most part. Different murder weapons like I said. They probably figured they were searching for someone that knew the victim personally only working that one particular case. They never knew those cases were related."

Callahan responded saying, "right again, my friend. They never bothered searching for a serial killer because of the M.O."

"Yeah they didn't see the pattern."

"How could they? We wouldn't have been led to that conclusion without all of the cases placed right here in front of us."

"Yeah, the puzzling part is why the drastic change in the method of assault, and the divergence in victim selection."

Callahan had multiple reasons roll through his mind which addressed that, yet he kept his thoughts to himself. It was time someone took off Buttweiler's training wheels. Sink or swim, he had to learn to think for himself. Still, it was good to see him doing it for once.

Callahan was simply proud to see young partner making such strides, putting the pieces of the puzzle together for himself using only what he had in front of him. Before their partnership ended, he planned to have him working independently on his own cases. This was just the start of things to come.

Henley listened closely to everything they said. He couldn't believe it. They had only been at it for a little over six hours, and they had already determined six of the unsolved murders were perpetrated by a serial killer. Callahan pointed out the only way to prove that was to find the killer, or at least matching evidence to tie the cases together. Hearing that, Henley realized the original investigators were at an extreme disadvantage. Not knowing about the other cases made their job that much more difficult.

He had looked through those files himself on occasion just out of curiosity, sometimes during his lunch break. He could even recount some of the details about each one. Still, he never saw what Callahan did. The ironic part was the serial killer had been in Henley's presence the whole time, hidden within the pages of the unsolved case files, of course. This discovery was the most exciting thing Henley had experienced in the records room in almost five months.

There was only one other day that compared to this one as far as Henley was concerned. That was when Miranda Scroggins first graced the Archives Department with her presence. She was sent there from the mayor's office to conduct an informal audit of the records room. That was the most spectacular week of Henley's adult life. He remembered every little detail about her, especially the way she smiled when he paid her a compliment. Whenever she went to pick something up her left foot would leave the floor just a little, and Henley always stopped what he was doing to watch her walk across the records room in her high heels. She seemed to do it with virtually no effort at all.

Henley got a warm feeling deep down inside whenever he managed to make her laugh, even just a little. He was heavily into Miranda, no doubt. His glasses still steamed up whenever he recalled just how perfect she looked in her skirt, wearing her tight pullover sweater. With that said, this particular day was right up there with Miranda in Henley's mind. They were trying to track down a real serial killer, and here Henley was at the heart of the investigation. At that point, he couldn't resist asking if there was anything he could do to help. Callahan looked over at Henley telling him, "pull every unsolved murder you have on record dating back to the year 2000."

Henley came alive saying, "it's going to take a while, but

I'm on it partner."

Buttweiler smiled right along with Callahan as Henley trudged off down the aisle pulling more boxes off the shelf as he went along. "What do you expect to find," Buttweiler asked.

Callahan said, "you tell me. What do you think those additional files will tell us?"

"I guess they'll tell us if he committed more murders in the area, and how long he was actively killing."

Callahan pointed out how critical the timeline was saying, "when you're dealing with a possible serial killer, the timeline is everything. It can even be your best friend at times during your investigation, but without it you don't have a case." Buttweiler paid close attention to Callahan as he said, "one of those related cases may hold a set of fingerprints or some other clue we can use to identify the killer. I once solved a case with a matchbook found near a crime scene. Little things can lead to big breaks in a case."

Working a cold case usually forces investigators thinking of reopening it to look at every detail. Things that sometime get overlooked in an initial investigation are usually scrutinized much harder years later - the drawback is the time lapsed though. The hardest thing to overcome is evidence erosion, and peoples less than perfect memories. That being the case, even Buttweiler realized there was a strong possibility they would discover the killer's identity with the help of the additional files. The more information they could gather about him the better their chances were.

Given the fact that there were multiple victims, and crime scenes belonging to the same killer, odds increased dramatically that they would uncover some pertinent clue that would help them solve all the cases. He would uncover who was behind the murders, Buttweiler was confident regarding that, and he seldom ever possessed that feeling with any conviction.

What they didn't know could kill them though. They were right about the cases being connected. They were all the handiwork of one man, and that man was Hayden Keller. Buttweiler simply referred to him as a cold blooded killer for the time being which he certainly was, but neither he nor Callahan had any real understanding of what they were now hunting. Catching Hayden Keller was like trying to catch a handful of sand. It was damn near impossible, Satan saw to that.

Chapter 13

The Path Of Evil

While Callahan and Buttweiler attempted to pick up where others had left off in a bold effort to find the trail which led to Hayden Keller, Sister Lee traced the path of evil using an entirely different method. She channeled her thoughts as she chanted mystic phrases repeating the same words over and over again. What was revealed to her was Hayden's exact location, but she only gained a glimpse of it before her vision faded. That was all she needed. She kept her vision short for good reason.

Hayden was a hunter, and his senses were extremely acute to the point of knowing when he was being watched for any length of time. That was something he had perfected over centuries of stalking others, and his out of body experiences gave him the ability to sense that which most of us cannot. Hayden had an intimate understanding of the spirit world, but he was under the impression Satan ruled it. He had no knowledge that there was another that dabbled in the spiritual realm with enough power to send him back to hell. Sister Lee's plan was not to reveal that to him until it was time.

Hayden was still hold up in that trailer biding his time, waiting to make his next move. She knew she still had time to halt him from finding Ashley. She had already discovered the girl's location herself through Ben's thoughts using her telepathic powers. Sister Lee was linked to him now. She had been ever since she gave him the premonition which helped him save Ashley's life. That's how powerful Sister

Lee was. She could penetrate the dreams of a man she had never physically met, and she could alter the course of his destiny at will provided the stars would permit it to be so. She was a dangerous woman indeed, capable of invading the thoughts of others, and stealing that which she wanted. What's even more amazing is she did all this without anyone knowing.

In rare cases, she spoke through others in order to accomplish her mission. When it came to actual thought transference, Sister Lee's abilities were unparalleled, but fortunately she used them to shield the world from evil. Satan didn't make it easy for her though. Evil continually changed its appearance. The truth was evil had too many faces to count, and it covered the earth at times. Still, there was one left to oversee that evil would never take over the earth entirely, not while she was living anyway. Talk about your purpose driven life, Sister Lee had it.

She had found Hayden before. She would find him again, and one day it would end for good, or so we should hope. Her most recent efforts to track down the evil one yielded her Detective Callahan. He was now the latest tool in her arsenal, and Sister Lee knew exactly how to use him. She had carefully placed each piece on the board necessary to defeat Hayden Keller. It was no easy doing, but Callahan, Henley, and even Buttweiler were a part of that. She arranged the pieces in such a way that evil could never discover their whereabouts until it was too late, and she moved each piece using her mystic powers. In a world filled with pawns, Callahan was her knight making him one of the most dangerous pieces in play.

Callahan's role would be critical in her efforts to stop Hayden Keller, but Sister Lee would even sacrifice him if need be in order to end the deadly game. You don't think he ended up in the records room with Henley and Buttweiler simply by chance do you? Truthfully, nothing really happens by chance, not in Sister Lee's world. Sure the chain of events which unfolded to place him in the archives department were many, and they appeared to come right from the top down. With that said, who do you think forced that reporter to ask the Chief of Police for the IMPD about those growing number of unsolved cases in the first place? Now you know.

There wasn't much Sister Lee didn't know except how it would all end. There was one person's future she couldn't see, but even that would reveal itself in time. The lives she changed as a result of her intense transcendental meditation sessions were numerous, and it was all in the name of vanquishing the evil one forever. Unfortunately, some would have to be made expendable. She knew there was still time to stop Hayden Keller. The only question was - would she.

Three men now hunted him, and more would follow. The man with two lives was still breathing, and the woman who could see all was now able to observe the girl herself using her third eye. She was safely hidden within the city of monks. Sister Lee found her hard at work studying inside her dorm room. There was another girl in the room with her that in no way resembled the girl of faith. Her tongue piercing wasn't the only thing separating them, but she was leaving as Ashley continued reading one of her textbooks. She had a pile of them on the small desk next to her chair. Her thoughts were only on her studies at that moment, but Sister Lee knew that would soon change.

Ashley was trying to prepare for her mid-terms, and college life took some getting used to. Her first semester at Grand View brought its share of challenges. Life had been extremely difficult after losing her family at the hands of Hayden Keller, but she somehow coped. No one could ever explain the senseless killings or the violent nature of their deaths, no one that she knew anyway. She was doing her best to move on with her life while never forgetting the ones she loved in the process. Therapy helped, and she was fortunate to still have her grandmother's support. Her home was now Ashley's when she wasn't in school, and she was the one that encouraged her granddaughter to give college life a try. She felt it would be good for her to be around girls her own age, but little did she know Hayden Keller once again hunted her.

A confused look appeared on Ashley's face as if she were having trouble locating something. She marked her place in the book as she sat it to the side. Picking up another book she had in the sizable stack next to her, she began flipping through the pages in search of the answer she was looking for. Turning to a page somewhere near the middle of the book, she ran her finger down the page, then she began reading. She paused briefly after reading over something. Maybe it was the picture within the book that caught her attention. Whatever it was she found inside the pages of the book appeared to be disturbing. The look on her face indicated that without her uttering a word.

She was distracted by the noise coming from the hallway outside her room. Ashley looked in the direction of her door. She could hear someone approaching, a group of people it seemed. She turned her attention back to her books in an effort to pursue her studies some more while trying her best to block-out the voices of her classmates passing by her door. They were jabbering away about what Andy Holloway did in Professor Kim's class. Apparently, whatever he did made an impression of some sort. The chatter in the hallway seemed almost never-ending. She found it difficult to focus even with the door closed.

Using only her minds-eye, Sister Lee continued observing as Ashley looked back at the book she was reading. Laughter erupted just outside her room. Chatter then persisted surrounding the social plans of others for the week following their exams, and the continual interruptions made it nearly impossible for Ashley to concentrate on what she was doing. Annoyed by it all, she looked up holding the book she had in her hands. Distracted by their voices, and her own concerns, Ashley was forced to ask herself, "what's the point?"

Sister Lee opened her eyes leaving Ashley to her continued search for the information that eluded her, but the gifted palm reader had seen that which she sought. She was satisfied the girl was safe for the time being. She now had to concentrate on arming Detective Callahan with critical knowledge that was crucial to capturing Hayden Keller. In order to do that she would have to use Buttweiler, and Henley to provide him with that which he needed to know. She had a short period of time to open his eyes to the fact that this was no mere man he was after.

Making Detective Callahan believe in things beyond his understanding wouldn't be a simple task. After all, he was a cop, and cops tend to believe that which they can see, hear, and touch. Getting him to buy into the fact that Hayden Keller was a demonic spirit that possessed the bodies of numerous men would not be possible without evidence, and lots of it. Even then, it would take someone he trusted to advise him as to whether that was even possible given the evidence. That trusted person wasn't Sister Lee, not at this point anyway. She would have to place two more pieces on the board in just the right order before she could begin to advise him on what to do next. The bishop which she chose was Father Tomas, and the rook, that was Sergeant Gant of the Des Moines Police Department.

Sister Lee stared at the tapestry which covered the wooden table. She sat before it drawing her hands together, and she lifted them up off the table slightly as she said, "recolligo simul congressio induco venatio." The words she spoke were in the language of old. They were ominous in nature, and they meant "gather them together, and guide them in the hunt." Sister Lee delivered them with a serious tone as she looked up toward the map which hung on her wall. That map contained all of the major star formations that resided in the heavens, and Sister Lee was intimately familiar with them all. She focused on one in particular concentrating all of her energy in the stars forming the constellation of Orion. It was the path to finding Hayden Keller, for it was the sign of the hunter. The path which evil took was a treacherous one indeed. Callahan would have to follow it if he ever hoped to stop the beast that committed the heinous murders which were still unsolved. What he would discover would place them all in harm's way.

Chapter 14

Manhunt

Hayden only had one thing in common with police, at times they both hunted men. Law enforcement officials were obviously much more selective in their efforts than Hayden had ever been though. They were now on the hunt for one Vincent Russell, a forty-seven year old, white male with blue eyes, and black hair that was now starting to gray. After matching the prints found on the steering wheel of the bread truck to the ones on the knife used to kill the waitress in the diner, police now believed Vincent Russell was responsible for the murders which occurred in Cook County.

Mrs. Russell's body had been discovered two days earlier. Police had found her lying on her bed with the pillow Hayden had used to smother her still covering part of her face. That discovery left little doubt in their mind that Vincent was their guy. Mrs. Kemp, the neighbor from next door had to ask police what was going on. They didn't reveal much to her at first. They simply asked if she knew Mr. Russell very well, and when she had last seen him. As they snapped photos of the room, and gathered forensic evidence, a body bag containing Mrs. Russell's corpse was placed on a small gurney, and wheeled out the front door before it was placed inside the ambulance. Mrs. Kemp about had a heart attack right there on the spot. She was the one that first noticed the damaged mailbox. She had knocked on her neighbor's door to let them know someone had vandalized it, but no one came to the door. When she asked, "is that Mr. Russell," police informed her it was his wife, and they were now searching for Vincent. Unnerved, she asked, "you don't think he did this, do you?"

The officer interviewing her tried to ease her anxiety a little in order to get the answers to the questions. He said, "we don't know that for sure. We'd just like to get a hold of him, and ask him some questions. Do you know any places he tended to frequent, or anyone he had close ties to, maybe a friend or a relative that visited from time to time?"

Mrs. Kemp looked perplexed as she said, "no, not really. Vincent kind of kept to himself most of the time, but he always seemed like such a nice guy. She pointed at her fence saying, "he even fixed the latch on my gate once." The officer taking her statement had heard this kind of description more than once in his long career on the force.

No one ever came right out and said the suspect was anything other than a model citizen. In fact, they always tended to be one of the nicest guys you'd ever be blessed to meet. It didn't matter who they interviewed whether it be Vincent's boss, or those he saw daily in each of the stores on his bread route. Whatever they told police wouldn't help them get one step closer to the killer, because Vincent wasn't the one committing the murders. Hayden was in control now, and he was simply using Vincent's body to do his dirty work.

Hayden had occupied the bodies of many men over the centuries. To him, those bodies were merely nothing more than a change of clothes. That's not to say he didn't get attached to a few of them along the way, but he always knew there would come a day when he would part with them for good. That point in time was usually when they no longer served him well. What was left of the person remaining inside that body wasn't a pretty sight. Their spirit would never fully regain control of their body, and all that was left was a shell of a person that once existed. They wouldn't be able to effectively communicate with the outside world. Hayden would leave them imprisoned in their own body in a sense if he left them alive at all. The police had no understanding of this, but what they did know is Vincent had obviously snapped, and it appeared that he was now on a rampage.

The statewide search for the missing vehicle belonging to Clint had now spilled over into neighboring states as authorities believed their suspect was on the move with no plans of coming back anytime soon. Hell, they didn't even know who Hayden Keller was, but they had a picture of Vincent along with his prints. They believed he was headed north. That, combined with the tag number on the missing pickup truck, would be enough to go on for now as the Georgia State Patrol contacted law enforcement authorities in Alabama and Tennessee. Yeah, the manhunt for the bread man now covered three states. Who would have ever figured that?

When police interviewed Vincent's route manager, his only concern was getting the bread truck back, he had a route to cover. At that point, police explained it was evidence for the time being since it was believed to have been used as a getaway vehicle in connection with a string of murders. The routing manager just looked at the police officer with a stunned expression plastered on his face as he asked the rhetorical question, "now, who in their right mind kills someone, and uses a bread truck as their getaway vehicle."

The officer looked right at him as he said, "I don't think he was in his right mind when he smothered that poor woman he was married to before murdering that waitress, and those two hunters up in Cook County."

With that, Vincent's boss was left without words, wondering if they, in fact, were after the right guy. He couldn't imagine Vincent ever harming anyone. He was physically capable of doing it, but he was a nice guy for Pete's sake. Now, he was being accused of committing violent murders, none of it made any sense at all. As far as he knew, Vincent had never uttered a cross word toward anyone. Still, he was missing, and no body had been found matching his description. That automatically drew some suspicion, and the fact that Vincent never missed a day of work in nearly four years led his boss to question just how well he really knew him. Maybe he was the killer. At least for some it was starting to look that way. That trail grew colder with each day that passed. Eventually, all the leads which police followed would lead them to a dead end, but for now they hunted.

Chapter 15

Those Possessed

Hayden's time spent waiting for the seventh day to pass was much like torture. He detested every waking second that he sat there looking out the busted window of the trailer as he watched the steady drops of water fall from the edge of the rust covered roof after the let-up of the rain. It was mind numbing listening to each drop hit the ground just outside the door. For someone that longed to live again, this part of life held no enjoyment at all. Without killing, Hayden could never feel truly alive.

Enraged by the slow passage of time, he became violent hitting the walls with his fist, even kicking them at times. He tore into them with utter fury, damaging them further as he cursed and raged. His wait forced him to accept the walls he would forever be imprisoned within, and he was reminded of his servitude. Hayden was a demonic spirit encapsulated in the body of a man, and his hands were bound at the moment as he was forced to endure the long wait before the kill. He despised the Sabbath with a passion. Perhaps that's why the devil had prohibited him from collecting souls on that day. Maybe it was to deny Hayden any pleasure whatsoever causing him to abhor the Sabbath as much as Satan. Either way, the devil made the rules which Hayden had to live by, and the prince of darkness never had to explain himself to anyone. The earth was his domain for the time being, and he determined, to a large degree, who stayed in it.

Lucifer had what Hayden longed for, a chance to live, and kill again, and again. With that, he controlled Hayden making him do just about anything he pleased. Hayden would kill, and Satan would pull his strings, now he was tormenting him. No one escaped being worked by Satan including Hayden Keller. It's true Lucifer used Hayden as his henchman, but his purpose was grander than one may have imagined. Satan's real reason for having him kill centered around causing those in the world great pain, not just his actual victims, but those that cared for the ones he stole from this life in the name of Satan.

Few lives were shielded from Hayden's wrath indefinitely, but all were spared on the day of rest which the Lord had made. Knowing that, we should all take solace in that blessed moment, and look upon life with hope on that day. In the scheme of time passage, not all days are so wondrous. Nevertheless, it was a daunting challenge for Hayden to simply get through as he tried to collect his thoughts in order to plan his next move, but he was incapable of focusing on anything. All he kept asking himself was will this day ever end. With no answer coming back to him in his mind, he drove himself mad as he continued to lash out in anger until he drained the body he now possessed of all its physical strength.

Hayden fell backward onto the nasty sofa, one of his legs hung off the edge of the armrest, and the other he tossed up on what was left of the busted coffee table. He looked over at some brown crud that was ground into the filthy carpet not quite sure of what it was. It could have been shit, dirt or a mixture of both for all he knew. Another spot on the carpet looked like grease or motor oil, it really didn't matter, but it gave Hayden an idea of sorts.

He knew he had to conceal the tag number on that truck parked outside just in case he rolled up on a cop. He never liked retaining the same ride more than a few days tops. Suddenly, it became clear to him as to how to do it when he looked outside at the wet ground. The rain had stopped completely, but the ground was still soaked, and therein lied the answer to Hayden's dilemma.

A satisfied expression made its way to Hayden's face as he walked outside staring at the red clay which covered the ground in front of the trailer. It was now soft and wet, slick, and sticky to the touch. He reached down grabbing a handful of it in his fist. Picking it up, squeezing it through his fingers, he hurled it at the truck spattering the red mud all over it. He purposely aimed for the license plate making sure he made it unreadable. To avoid drawing particular attention to it, he plastered the entire lower portion of the vehicle with mud spatter. He admired his work, looking at the truck as he rinsed his hands off using the water that had accumulated in a large puddle right next to the truck. That thick red mud stained his hands, and it stuck to that pickup like glue.

Hayden knew what he was doing without question. He had learned a thing or two about avoiding capture. He had even mastered throwing police off his trail over the years. Hayden had been doing it for almost a century, ever since cars replaced the carriage. Constantly changing vehicles, and never traveling in one particular direction were critical keys to him seldom being caught. When he was apprehended, he would simply take over the body of another human being, and after he escaped, he would leave the person he possessed in a vegetative state.

The growing number of people filling the mental wards during the early 1900's, that was in part due to Hayden. The use of a new body from time to time certainly had its advantages. It made it virtually impossible for police to connect various murders. With that new body came a new set of fingerprints which Hayden was able to leave at the crime scenes. To law enforcement officials, Hayden's handiwork appeared to be a growing rash of serial killers emerging one after another, and no one could explain the reason behind it.

Only those that had been possessed by Hayden Keller's demonic spirit had answers, but they weren't talking. That being the case, few of them were still left breathing when Hayden was done with their body. On those rare occasions when he did not end their life altogether, they were forced to watch as he stepped out of their body, and into the skin of another person. The last thing that person usually saw was Hayden Keller walking away in the body of someone else. Before they died, all they were left with was an empty grievous feeling deep down inside which they could not express in words. The visions they had seen, left them permanently scarred. Some would be held accountable for crimes that couldn't be explained, and they were heavy weights to bare in their tortured minds.

Most would never speak a coherent word ever again, just wailing cries of anguish in the dark of night. The fierce overpowering hollowness, and pain they felt could only be seen in their eyes as Hayden departed from them. Unable to say a word as he exited, they seemed mentally dead to the world by the blank expression they carried on their face. Their minds fought to suppress the visions of horror which continually ran through their brains after being taken over by Hayden Keller. They were in hell, battling it every second of their existence even though they remained on earth until their dying day.

Hayden did them no favor leaving them alive. Most of them committed suicide within several months of the possession taking place. Yes, Hayden was responsible for that statistic increasing as well, but the devil didn't give him credit for those lost souls. He was only charged with the precious ones he sent straight to hell before the start of the seventh day. That's why Hayden hated leaving any of them alive to see another sunrise, although they would never again see it the same way.

It's no surprise that for the rest of their lives they would all live in fear of the evil which lurked in the shadows. Most would never speak ever again, and the ones that did would suffer from what sane people saw as grossly tormented hallucinations. They weren't really hallucinating, they were reliving the nightmare over, and over again faced with the blood which covered Hayden's hands.

Chapter 16

Killer On The Move

Police continued their search for Vincent Russell while Hayden subsisted on prepackaged meals, peanuts, beef jerky, and beer which he found inside the large toolbox behind the cab of Clint's truck. The hunters had certainly prepared to make sure they had something to eat while they were out in the woods. Hayden loathed that the physical form he now possessed required nourishment to keep living. That was something he never had to worry about outside the body. Still, it had its tradeoffs. Despite the weaknesses he encountered in a physical form, he could inflict great pain. Hayden reminded himself of that as he reached into his back pocket. He pulled out Clint and Roscoe's Ids, and smirked as he stared at their faces. He couldn't help but think back to when he killed them at the Stop and Go station. The amusing thought that ran through his mind at that point was, *they sure as hell weren't prepared for the kill though.*

There wasn't much Hayden found enjoyable about the crappy place he was in, but thinking back to when he killed Roscoe always brought a devious sneer to his disgusting face. Several days of roughing it out in the sticks was enough to drive anyone a little insane, Hayden was there when he pulled up to the place. He now felt at home in the body of Vincent Russell, even though it took him a while to get used to it.

Time passed as if the earth stood still, but Hayden knew it wouldn't be much longer before he'd be free to kill again.

When that time came, he knew he was going to have to part with Clint's truck. Hayden detested that. Clint's truck fit him well, but authorities would soon be on the lookout for it if they weren't already. He planned on making his way north to Chanceville where he could find out more about Ashley's whereabouts. Perhaps, if he was lucky, he could find out the name of the man that sent him straight to hell. This time, Hayden planned on returning the favor. He, no doubt, wanted to send him to face Satan for a change, but not until he got answers as to how his name was made known to him.

As night began to fall, Hayden prepared to head out, and a killer was on the move once more. When he approached Highway 65, he was faced with a choice. North would take him right where he wanted to go, but it would also reveal his whereabouts to police when the stolen vehicle was found abandoned somewhere along the side of the road. Hayden always liked to keep them guessing, that's why he turned south. He planned to dump the truck once he reached Mobile. It would be months before anyone found it submerged under water down in the delta. Hayden had used that dump site before.

He figured he could pick up something more stylish for the long drive up north, maybe a late model caddie of some sort. Flying down the highway making good time he thought, maybe an escalade. I've never driven one of those before. He compared it to the image of the bread truck he left sitting at Haddad's gas station, and he then told himself, you can never go wrong with a good SUV. Seconds after coming to that realization, a content look of resolve faded from his despicable face. That thought had triggered something else altogether. It brought back to mind the chance encounter he had with Ben at the Petrol Station, and

Hayden became livid as he pressed the accelerator all the way to the floor.

Barely halfway there, Hayden passed a parked car sitting in the dark in the center of the median along the highway. Within seconds it pulled out turning on its lights as it closed in behind him. Hayden knew who it was. This wasn't the first time some highway patrolman had pegged him doing eighty in the fast lane, but he really didn't have time for this. That's when he reached down placing his hand on the gun which was resting on the seat beside him.

He knew he had best pull over immediately before the cop had a chance to run his plate, and find out the truck was stolen. Hayden's finger gently rubbed against the trigger of Clint's rifle as he pulled over into the safety lane stopping the vehicle as quick as possible. The highway patrolman didn't even have time to flip on the siren. He was forced to follow Hayden right onto the shoulder to avoid passing him, and that's when he got his first real look at the vehicle. The lower half of the truck was covered in mud, and the plate on it could hardly be seen.

The patrolman had an odd feeling about this one for some reason. Perhaps it was because Hayden pulled off the road so quickly in front of him, but something didn't seem right. Not really knowing what to expect, he turned on the strobe lights with the flip of a switch as he peered through the windshield of his car at the muddy truck parked in front of him. That little voice inside him said, proceed with caution, but that was usually the case anytime he pulled someone over after dark, especially along that stretch of highway. He hadn't called it in, but that vehicle certainly looked as though it might match the description of the vehicle they received an APB on just one day earlier.

As Officer Danford shined his spotlight toward the cab of the truck, Hayden stuck his left hand out the window holding an open beer can. He dropped the empty can on the ground next to the driver's side door as he sluggishly announced, "I promise, I haven't been drinking officer. I swear. Someone else put this in here." Hayden sounded drunk as hell when he said it.

Danford opened his door in order to hear what Hayden was saying. The officer was totally taken by surprise at that action. He had pulled over more than his share of drunken drivers, but this poor son of a bitch must have been three sheets to the wind for sure if he thought he was getting out of this one. Hayden allowed his left arm to hang there outside the window. He clumsily moved it in an attempt to deceive the patrolman into thinking he was just some drunk driver out for a joyride instead of the cold blooded murderer they were on the look-out for.

Officer Danford stepped out of his vehicle. He raised his chin as he looked the truck over. Summing up the situation in his mind while holding his flashlight in his left hand, he walked toward the pickup with his right hand comfortably resting on the handle of his gun. As he neared the truck he looked in the bed. There were beer cans galore. Hell, there were so many it looked as though he had been out collecting them for the better part of the day. That's when the officer chose to walk around the rear of the vehicle, and approach the passenger side door. Leaning his head forward slightly as he peeked in at Hayden, he figured he could observe him without being noticed.

It was dark inside the cab as he raised his flashlight pointing it directly at Hayden shining it right in his face. "Well what do we have here," he bellowed. The second he said that, Hayden pulled the trigger firing at him right through the door. Danford fell back stunned by the deafening sound of the rife that nearly shot him right in his loins. Highly pissed that he missed, Hayden slung open the driver's side door chambering another round as Danford hastily tried to un-holster his weapon. By the time he raised it to fire the first shot, Hayden had a bead on him aiming the hunting rifle straight at his chest. He charged toward him without fear.

It was dark, and Hayden was on the move when Officer Danford managed to squeeze off two rounds. The first one missed entirely, and the second one nearly grazed Hayden's ear as he moved around the rear of the truck. Danford retreated toward his vehicle, but that only brought him face to face with Hayden. Before he could fire another round, Hayden placed the barrel of the rifle right between his eyes. The officer froze at the site of the muzzle looking him right dead in the face. So ended the age old question of who wins out when the man with the rifle meets the man with a pistol. This time it was Hayden Keller.

The real question was - why didn't Hayden pull the trigger one last time. He ordered Officer Danford to drop the gun while he still could. Hayden confessed, "I don't want to shoot you, but I will if you make me." The officer didn't doubt that for a second. Here he was faced with a life or death decision, and it was his own life hanging in the balance. If he tried to fire his weapon he was dead, no doubt about it. Maybe he could wound Hayden, but his life was over. He would never see the result of his effort. He would never know the outcome of his action other than there would surely be a long caravan of patrol cars escorting him to his final resting place, and twenty-one guns would be fired in a salute to honor his memory. He had been a part of it before, but this time he would be the one laid to rest in a pine box, and that downright sucked.

All facts weighed and considered under split-second pressure to act, dropping the gun, and living to fight crime another day sounded good at that point. Could he trust Hayden not to blow him away if he let go of the gun? Maybe or maybe not, but he could certainly trust him to pull that trigger if he didn't do just as he said. The last thing he wanted to do was give up his weapon, but circumstances being what they were, that now fell behind not wanting to have his head blown to pieces on the side of the highway. The truth of the matter was he didn't have a great deal of time to think about it. He dropped the gun.

Standing there next to his patrol car, Hayden ordered him to get undressed as he forced him to remove his uniform. Officer Danford felt uncomfortable stripping down to his skivvies right there on the side of the road, but Hayden was now in control of the situation. It never occurred to Danford why Hayden preferred not to shoot him, or what he planned to do to with his uniform and patrol car. Danford logically assumed Hayden didn't want him to be able to follow him. Without clothes, a weapon, and access to a vehicle, that would certainly make it rather difficult to catch him, he thought. He now worried about how he was going to explain this to whoever picked him up, but he didn't have to worry for long.

As soon as he removed his trousers, and shirt placing them right next to where he stood, Hayden said, "turn around and start walking." Hayden then warned him not to look back. Officer Danford turned taking comfort in that believing he was going to live to tell this story to his grandkids someday whenever they asked about the worst day he had on the force as an officer. Hayden denied him that tale.

Officer Danford took several steps in the direction of the trees which were thirty feet or so in front of him, and Hayden grabbed hold of the business end of the rifle. Instead of pointing it at the near naked highway patrolman, he gripped it tightly as that murderous look filled his eyes. Using it as a bat, he swung the rifle with everything he had bashing Danford upside the head with the stock of the gun. He hit him so damn hard he broke his neck with one blow. Danford fell forward hitting the ground with a thud as Hayden kept his promise not to shoot him. He picked up Danford's hat placing it on his head. Then he grabbed Danford's pistol which was lying on the ground along with the rest of the officer's clothes. He pulled Danford's body up next to the patrol car, and he began to change into his uniform. Walking around to the driver's side of the car he climbed inside unlocking the passenger door. Hayden immediately returned to the other side of the vehicle to load the dead officer's body into the car.

Hayden couldn't have planned this any better. The vehicle was headed south, and it would be morning before it was discovered. Police would probably think he was somewhere further south like Mobile, or even Tampa, Florida. Hayden cut off the emergency lights after turning the patrol car around. He was moving north, and there was no stopping him now. He knew what he had, and that was a ticket to ride all the way to the North Alabama state-line without the slightest concern of being stopped along the way. That put him closer to Chanceville, and Hayden couldn't wait to get there, but there was still time to have a little fun on the way. It wasn't every day that he got to play cop. Hayden found that quite amusing as he cruised up the interstate.

Chapter 17

I'm The Law Around Here

Hayden sat beneath an overpass just off of Highway 280. There was time enough for him to have his fun at the taxpayer's expense, and he planned on making the most of the experience. He sipped on a cup of black coffee as he waited in the dark while listening to the police scanner. Out of sure curiosity, he flipped some of the buttons on the console just to see what turned on what. Even though he had graced the back seat of a patrol car more than once, this was the first time he had ever sat in the driver's seat.

Chewing on a stale honey bun, Hayden looked over at Officer Danford slumped over in the seat next to him. He tossed the pastry down in the floorboard next to Danford's feet as he said, "I don't see how you eat this crap." He took a swig of coffee swishing it around in his mouth trying to wash the taste out as a car pulled off the interstate. Hayden watched, and waited for the car to pull off the highway before he cranked up the patrol car, and he kept his distance as he followed it for several miles.

With the dead corpse of Officer Danford riding shotgun, Hayden observed the vehicle for quite some time before making his next move. As he closed in tight on the vehicle he could see it had Virginia plates, and he knew exactly what to do. Flipping on the blue lights he wasted no time in pulling them over. The guy inside the Honda Accord lifted his hands from the steering wheel asking his wife, "what the hell did I do?"

The young woman in the passenger seat said, "I told you

to be careful. Were you speeding?"

The man behind the wheel responded, "I was going sixty-six, what the hell."

The young woman in the passenger seat told him, "just be nice, and let me do the talking, okay." Hayden continued watching them bicker from where he was sitting while the guy argued with his wife saying, "I think I can handle this myself." That opened up a whole other argument as the blue lights continued to flash behind them. She began to berate him for the last time he spoke those words out loud reminding him of how that ultimately worked out.

Sitting there on the side of the road with lights flashing, Hayden just waited. This was the part he relished most. The prey had been caught, and they didn't even realize it. He watched the two heads in the front seat of the Accord move as they turned to speak with one another. He could see their faces clearly as he enjoyed the show. It was a fairly young couple, and she was giving him hell. The funny thing was this time he hadn't actually done anything wrong except for having the misfortune of taking a turn which happened to cross paths with Hayden. That was almost always a grave mistake indeed.

Hayden looked straight ahead as he placed a wooden toothpick in his mouth that he had retrieved from the drink holder near the center console. Glancing up at the mirror, he put on his shades. Before getting out of the car he reached over slapping Officer Danford on the shoulder as he said, "don't worry, I'll handle this one." Hayden was one twisted devil for sure. He closed the door to the patrol car as he placed Officer Danford's hat on his head. He, of course, adjusted it squaring it properly as he took the tips of his fingers sharply running them across the outer rim of the brim. His mouth moved slightly adjusting the placement of the toothpick as he walked toward the driver's side door of the Accord.

Hayden placed his left hand on his nightstick as he approached the vehicle. His right hand rested on the handle of Danford's gun. Within seconds, Hayden drew his black baton tapping the butt of it against Phil's window. The guy in the driver's seat stopped talking as he turned to see Hayden standing right outside his door. When he rolled down his window, Hayden instructed him to cut the car off. Phil complied as he asked, "is there a problem Officer?" Hayden just looked at him without saying a word. He then leaned down to take a closer look at Phil's wife who was sitting in the passenger seat. She was ready to explain their way out of this, and she already had the perfect excuse in her mind for whatever her husband had done wrong.

Hayden halted her from speaking as he said without emotion, "let me see your driver's license, and registration." Phil reached for his wallet, and Hayden told his wife to keep both hands where he could see them. She knew at that point something wasn't routine about this traffic stop. Still, she tried to explain that she wasn't feeling well, and her husband was just trying to get her to a bathroom as soon as possible. That prompted Hayden to tell her, "if I want to hear from you I'll let you know." This wasn't the southern hospitality they were expecting, and Phil managed to muster up the courage to stand-up for his wife as he handed Hayden his license.

Hayden read the name as Phil said, "my wife was just trying to help Officer, that's all. Hayden looked down at him, and his face showed no sign of emotion at all. That's when Hayden said, "I don't want to hear any lip out of you either Phil." Hayden then added, "I guess that's why they named you Phillip. They must have realized you'd just never know when to shut the hell up." Phil's wife placed her hand on his arm. Hayden said, "I told you to keep your hands where I could see them lady."

She was now scared, and Phil tried to defuse the situation by saying, "you're scaring her. She's not used to someone speaking to her that way. I assure you we wouldn't harm a soul." Hearing that, Hayden toned it down a bit as he asked if he was making Phil a bit uncomfortable as well. Honestly, he admitted he had been in more pleasant situations, but he just wanted to get this matter settled so they could get back on the road. He was certain both he, and his wife could use the nearest restroom they came to, but after this encounter he simply wished to keep driving until he crossed that Georgia line.

Phil, and his wife refrained from saying anything further in an effort not to provoke Hayden in any way. At that point, they both would have gladly accepted a ticket in exchange for ending what seemed like an escalating confrontation. He had heard stories of how crooked cops in small towns preyed on passing cars breezing through on their way to somewhere worth being, but Phil figured this one would top them all. Unfortunately, he hadn't seen the worst side of Hayden yet.

In classic southern fashion, Hayden twisted his head a little removing the toothpick from his mouth, and he held it in his right hand while staring down at Phil. His left hand still carried the night stick, and Phil's ID. Hayden began to speak saying, "well you see here Phil, this is the great state of Alabama where I can do just about any damn thing I want. Seeing as you aren't from around these parts I guess I'll just have to educate your dumb ass."

Phil promptly responded by saying, "you can't talk to us like that."

Hayden dropped the toothpick on the ground where he stood as he reached grabbing the handle of the nightstick with his right hand. He forcefully swung it cracking Phil right in the jaw with it, then he growled, "what did I tell you about that lip Phil."

Blood started to drizzle from the corner of his mouth, and Hayden stared down at him placing Phil's ID in his pocket. His face remained stoic as he reached down for the door handle telling Phil to step out of the car. His wife reached over pulling the keys out of the ignition as Hayden dragged him out of the car. Phil immediately apologized for anything he had said that may have offended the officer. His only desire at that point was to get the hell away from Hayden.

With his teeth tightly clinched together, Hayden listened to him before removing his forearm from Phil's chest. He contained his temper, and told him, "wait right here while I run your license, and if it checks out I'll let you go." That part sounded damn good to Phil, but his wife wasn't buying it.

As Hayden walked back to the patrol car, Phil's wife told him to get back in the car. She held the keys up next to the ignition in an effort to encourage her husband to start the vehicle, and flee the scene. She was now terrified as she said in a panicked tone, "we have to get the hell out of here." Trying to keep his voice down, Phil slowly looked toward the front of the car saying, "what happened to just be polite, and do what the officer says."

Julie outright ordered him, "get your ass in the car now, or I'm leaving without you." She didn't have time to argue over what was said earlier. All she knew was Hayden wasn't about to just let them go on their merry way. Call it women's intuition, but she had a bad feeling about what was to come.

Phil looked back toward the patrol car hoping it would all end peacefully, but that's when he saw Hayden reach for the shotgun inside the cruiser. He knew that couldn't be good. Phil immediately hollered, "crank that fucker up!" He slung open the driver's side door jumping in as Hayden took out the rear window of the Accord with one shot. He pumped the shotgun again chambering another round, and Phil hit the gas peeling back onto the road as if Julie, and he were a modern day Bonnie and Clyde. They may have both imagined killing one another at some point in their relationship, especially when they didn't see eye to eye on things. However, now they were both committed to working on staying alive.

Hayden now had what he longed for, a high speed pursuit with him wearing the badge for once. He knew how it would end, but for Hayden half the fun was getting there. Taking people like Phil and Julie with him was a game Hayden knew how to win. He followed them staying right on their tail before repeatedly ramming their bumper several times sending them into a tailspin as they went sliding off the road. Stomping on the brakes brought the patrol car to a halt, and Officer Danford's corpse flopped forward hitting the dash just as Phil and Julie's car slammed into a tall pine tree. Hayden sat there in the driver's seat next to the dead state trooper never taking his eyes off of the wrecked Honda Accord. He waited for any sign of life to emerge from the vehicle. Julie's car door opened, but she never made it out.

Hayden was fresh out of toothpicks, but he pulled a box of matches from his pocket placing one them in his mouth as he walked over to assess the damage. He had to see the carnage for himself. Phil was still breathing thanks to the airbag, but Julie had spoken her last words. Hayden found that to be a little ironic. He figured the only way Phil would ever get the last word in with her was for him to outlive her, and here they were. He walked around the back of the vehicle as he opened the driver's side door. Hayden then said, "your wife really isn't looking well." Tears started to flow from Phil's eyes at that point. Hayden asked him if he had any final words before he took him before the judge.

Totally enraged, Phil screamed, "no!" Before he could utter anything else, Hayden removed the match from in between his lips, and struck it on the side of the Accord. Tossing the match, and Phil's license inside the car he watched with satisfaction.

The flames spread rapidly covering the seats, and the last thing Hayden said to him was, "by the way, everything checked out. So, I guess you can be on your way." Hayden then turned to walk away from the vehicle leaving Phil pinned in the front seat behind the wheel. Once the leaking fuel caught fire beneath the car, it became engulfed in flames.

Chapter 18

Free Ride

Hayden neared the Alabama state line as he pulled off Highway 65 heading toward Killen, Alabama. Don't think for a second he didn't find some irony in that. He drove through Athens savoring the final moments he had as a highway patrolman. His career wasn't long or distinguished to say the least, but for Hayden it was a hell of a lot of fun. He looked over at the dead body of Officer Danford which was seated in the passenger seat next to him. Danford looked anything but authoritative in his fruit of the looms.

They call it Alabama the beautiful, at least that's what it reads on the welcome sign when you enter the state, but Hayden scoffed at that slogan. He wasn't buying it for a second when he approached the busted sign of the Victory gas station which sat next to an old shutdown car wash off to his right. The desolate stretch of road he was on didn't offer much in the way of scenery, and Hayden hadn't spotted anything worth looking at since he swapped rides losing the bread truck. As luck would have it though, something caught his eye, and it wasn't the rusty dumpster surrounded by tall grass a hundred feet away from the gas pumps. Parked next to it was the mother of all trucks. It was big, fast and loaded with just about every option available. It was no Cadillac, but when it came to trucks, it was as close as one could get.

Hayden knew he had to part with the patrol car. After cruising the highway with a corpse as his riding companion, he figured it was time to upgrade. If he was going to leave

Alabama, he might as well do it in style by taking something worth having with him. That truck was it. The red, and gold testament to American engineering was calling his name out loud, and Hayden had to answer it. He turned the patrol car around driving straight back toward the two pump gas station where he pulled off the road to admire his new ride. Looking it over from the exterior, he pictured himself behind the wheel of it in his less then right mind. The only thing he had to do is make the current owner of it an offer he couldn't refuse.

The art, or a fair exchange, never took place when Hayden dealt with anyone. His negotiating tactics were rather limited in scope even though they had proven to be a hundred percent effective over the years. Never had he failed to acquire any vehicle he set his sights on, hell he was marauding around in a police cruiser for God's sake. Some damned old redneck from Hooterville wasn't about to stand between him, and that sweet machine. He took out his flashlight, and pointed it inside the vehicle shining it through the heavily tinted glass in an effort to check-out the interior. It was plush, leather seats, wood grain console, cruise control, you name it. He didn't care if someone was inside or not, that would simply allow him the opportunity to go ahead, and get the negotiations underway.

It was pitch dark outside with the exception of the lights shining down over the gas pumps. None of that prevented him from peering through the windshield, and into the glass of the driver's side window. Just about the time he reached to check to see if it was unlocked, the owner of the vehicle departed from the store carrying a case of beer. He saw someone near his truck shining a light inside it, but he obviously didn't know who it was. He never would have come off with such an attitude had he thought it was a cop, but seeing as he loved that truck every bit as much as Hayden, he hollered out, "hey! What the hell do you think you're doing? Get the hell away from my truck!" As Ronnie picked up the pace a little moving closer to his fairly new F-350 in an effort to see to it that no one scratched it up trying to break into it, Hayden raised his head. He waited for Ronnie to round the rear end of the crew cab pickup before he enlightened him to the fact he was wearing a badge. Even though it belonged to Officer Danford, it made no difference. The fact that he was out of jurisdiction really didn't matter either. Hayden planned on flexing the long arm of the law one last time before ditching the uniform, and he didn't give a shit what part of the country he was standing in.

When Ronnie saw what Hayden was sporting, his whole demeanor changed instantly. With his adrenaline rush quashed, in a huff, he let go of a breath of air as he faced Hayden wearing Danford's uniform. One hand held the flashlight, and the other rested firmly on the handle of Danford's gun. Hayden appeared imposing as usual, and his head didn't move as his eyes cut down toward the case of beer Ronnie was carrying. He promptly lifted it placing it in the bed of the truck as he said, "I'm sorry officer, I didn't know it was you." Making no real distinction between local or highway patrol, he continued explaining, "I thought somebody was out here messing with my truck."

There wasn't much time to get to know the guy. Hayden stared at him a second, remembering various details about him that he would surely reflect back on as he drove on up to Chanceville in his crew cab. The scar on his left cheek was hidden from Ronnie's line of sight. It was concealed by the dark for the most part. Hayden preferred for people to see it though right before drawing their last breath. Easing the tension, he finally spoke saying, "yeah, I understand. It's a nice one alright. I've been on the lookout for one just like it. I don't guess you'd mind showing me your license and registration would you." Hayden's tone didn't deliver that in the form of a question.

Ronnie was caught off guard for a second time, but he replied, "yeah, I can do that. What seems to be the problem?"

He unlocked the truck to get to the papers he had in the glove box. Hayden spouted something along the lines of, "well there's been a rash of auto thefts lately. I believe this vehicle may be part of them."

Ronnie just kind of grinned saying, "there ain't another truck like this within fifty miles of here." He bragged about how he had to special order it through the dealership, and waited for damn near a month for it to finally arrive. Hayden listened acting as though he wasn't impressed, but make no mistake about it, he certainly appreciated all the effort Ronnie had put forth to see to it that he was handed such a sweet ride.

Pretending to be a bit of a hard-ass was no stretch for Hayden at all. He even thought he would have made a hell of a law enforcement officer. He never stopped to consider his ability to gage right from wrong. He was too far gone to realize how far off the mark he really was. It never once entered Hayden's mind that he possessed a warped sense of justice along with the body of another man. Hell, everything he had was stolen right down to clothes he was wearing, and the skin he was in. He hated to part with the uniform, but he was keeping the badge because he was a pragmatist, and that thing could come in handy at some point in the future.

Hayden was definitely insane, but he was far from crazy in

a stupid way at least. Ronnie handed the registration papers to him, and he dug inside his back pocket pulling out his wallet. Hayden glanced at the name on the papers, and then at the truck itself. He looked up at Ronnie as he handed Hayden his ID. Making a show of it, he pushed his lower lip forward as if were scrutinizing something. That's when Ronnie proudly said, "see, it's all mine."

Hayden grinned a little at that point thinking to himself, *not for long you idiot*. He neglected to let Ronnie in on that little secret though. All he said was, "well it would appear that way, I guess." Using his best southern drawl Hayden asked, "whatcha got in this thing?" He walked around to the rear of the vehicle still holding Ronnie's license in his hand. He had already made that his.

Ronnie smugly revealed what was under the hood as he said, "a 6.2 liter V8, with 350 HP, and a six speed automatic transmission with overdrive, of course." Hayden finally rendered a look of extreme interest as he walked around to the driver's side door.

It was now time to close the deal in Hayden's mind. He was fairly certain he'd be the one leaving in Ronnie's truck along with plenty of beer, and full tank of gas. Standing with the left side of his horrid face pointed toward the lights mounted over the gas pumps, Ronnie noticed the fresh scar on Hayden's cheek. He couldn't refrain from asking Hayden how he got it. Ronnie was expecting to hear something worth repeating regarding his injury, but Hayden just looked at him saying, "it just comes with the job sometimes." Ronnie could tell it was obviously something he didn't wish to talk about when he abruptly changed the subject of conversation back to the vehicle in question. Hayden said, "hell, I bet you even got one of those quick start buttons for this thing don't you."

Ronnie just smiled as he held up his key chain for Hayden

to see. Without saying a word, he pressed a button, the engine cranked right up. Ronnie said, "hell, it almost drives itself, don't it."

Hayden was impressed to say the least. He managed to mutter, "well, I'll be, that's something alright."

Placing his hand on the handle of the nightstick, Hayden extended his hand as if he were going to give Ronnie his license back. When Ronnie went to reach for it, Hayden drew the black baton from his belt, and forcefully jabbed Ronnie with it right in his gut. He invariably bent forward clutching his stomach with one arm as he struggled to find a breath of air. He was out of luck. Hayden waylaid him over the back of the skull with it, and Ronnie didn't know it, but the deal was struck. He hit the concrete hard, and Hayden looked around to make sure no one else was in eyeshot. That's when he began to pummel him, clubbing him relentlessly until Ronnie's blood covered the side of the truck.

When the violent attack ended, Hayden kicked him once for good measure just to make certain he was dead even though he had stopped moving after the third blow. Spying the nearby dumpster, he thought *how convenient* as he picked Ronnie's carcass up off the ground slinging him over his shoulder. He wasted no time hurling Ronnie's corpse into the dumpster. Peering over the edge of it, he sized up how much room was left inside the trash bin. Thinking only of Officer Danford, he looked back toward the patrol car. Ronnie looked lonely lying atop the oversized garbage bags, and empty boxes. Hayden planned on giving him some company. Walking in the direction of the cruiser, Hayden spoke his thoughts aloud confessing to himself, "my work is never done."

Hastily opening up the passenger door of the car, he removed Officer Danford's body. There was no tossing Danford over his shoulder, his body was now in full rigor. The dead officer was literally stiff as a board, and Hayden had his work cut out for him just getting him out of the front seat. Two hundred and ten pounds felt more like three hundred as Hayden hooked his arms under Danford's, and drug him over to his new resting place. He looked at him as he leaned him up against the dumpster. Hayden was tempted to go inside the store just to see if they had a disposable camera he could capture the moment with, but he knew time was ticking. Still, he couldn't help but stare at the frozen look of pain on Danford's face at that moment, and he questioned if he should just leave him there propped up in front of the rusted trash bin.

The vision of Danford braced against the dumpster in a frozen seated position wearing nothing but boxers, and a crewneck tee almost made Hayden form a sick grin. The image was truly priceless in his mind. Hayden thought to himself, *this is where you and I part, partner*. With Danford leaning against the dumpster snugly wedged between it, and the ground, Hayden bent down grabbing him around the legs in order to lift him. He quickly shoved him into the trash bin making the pointless introduction. Hayden carelessly said, "Danford, meet Ronnie," as he closed the lid on both of them, and started to walk away. Just at that moment, Ronnie's cell phone rang from inside the dumpster. Hayden wasn't believing this shit. Here he was trying his damnedest to properly dispose of two dead bodies, and Ronnie's cell phone was sounding the alarm.

Hayden stopped where he stood as he turned looking back in the direction of where he stashed the bodies. All he heard was a ring tone spewing out an old country song made famous by Bocephus himself. Hayden was slightly pissed he didn't take the time to search Ronnie's pockets, but he couldn't help but find a little irony in the words of the song that played on his phone. As Hank Williams Jr. sang, "if heaven ain't a lot like Dixie, I don't want to go." Hayden responded, "well, I don't think you'll have to worry about going there." He was forced to climb in the damn dumpster to fish out the phone. Danford's hardened oversized carcass made it more challenging, but Hayden had learned to accept the fact that his job tended to get messy at times, and this was one of them. He should have been used to it with all the time he spent killing others, but even he encountered the unexpected sometimes. This one forced him to go dumpster diving in order to fix it.

Despite what he combed through in the trash bin, he knew he had Vincent's clothes in the back seat of Danford's vehicle. Dirty as they were he was ready to change back into them. There was little that fazed him really, even the overpowering sour stench filling the metal garbage bin. He gained a strong whiff of it every time he bent down. Hayden had lived, and died numerous times, too many times to count. He had seen just about every filthy thing on the planet, and he was at home there half the time. As he rummaged through the dumpster, he took that opportunity to relieve Ronnie of his wallet as well as his phone. Climbing out, he stepped on Danford's face, and the expression didn't change at all. He was like a flesh statue, just not a very pretty one. Hayden closed the lid for the second time, and promptly removed the shirt he was wearing. It was covered in blood, and he didn't want to mess up his brand new truck. Tossing the shirt in the back of Danford's car, he pulled out Vincent's old duds. He was going to have to get used to being a civilian again. For the short period of time he wore the uniform, he brought a new meaning to the term bad-cop. The transition wouldn't be difficult for him though.

Standing next to the patrol car with the door left hanging open, he quickly stripped down changing clothes before making his way over to his newly acquired vehicle. He looked at the blood spatter covering the driver's side door as he opened it to climb his ass up in the cab. It was a hell of a nice ride, too nice to have Ronnie's blood covering one side of it. So, Hayden took it upon himself to pull it around to the carwash next door. He planned to clean the thing up as best he could before hitting the road. Truth was this was the most care he had given anything in decades, but this wasn't all about keeping something in mint condition. This was about not getting caught.

Hayden placed the case of beer in the back seat of the truck, and disposed of the bloody clothes. Venturing back onto the highway he headed toward Nashville. Soaking in the feel of the leather upholstery, he could hear music playing on the radio. Turning up the volume, it was no surprise to hear it blasting out some Tim McGraw. Hayden hated that guy just like he hated everything else he encountered in life. Frustrated to no end, he kept pushing the tuner button in search of something he could tolerate. He eventually, found an oldies station playing something by the Edgar Winter Group. He came in on the tail end of it. Even though the words were much too upbeat for Hayden's taste, the message it delivered couldn't be more appropriate given the moment. An evil snarl made its way to Hayden's monstrous mug as he moved his head to rhythm of the tune as the EWG sang "come on and take a free ride." Hayden even started to sing with them. His only thought at that point was *ready or not Nashville, here I come.*

Chapter 19

Dark Forces Near

Hayden was moving closer to Chanceville with each mile he covered in Ronnie's pickup. It would only be a matter of time before he found what he was looking for unless he was stopped somehow. Sister Lee attempted to tap into Henley's mind to enable him to help Callahan discover the missing piece of the puzzle. Whether or not she could do it in time remained to be seen. Other things had to take place before that could happen, and Buttweiler's inability to recognize what was in front of him presented a daunting challenge to the all-seeing palm reader.

Strangely enough, the team she had assembled consisted of a young tech savvy cop with little confidence in his own investigative abilities. Sister Lee didn't really understand much of what went through his mind. Plainly put, she and Buttweiler didn't speak the same language. Callahan was different. There was little which cluttered his thoughts most of the time, and his skills as a detective she didn't doubt for the time being. They had always served him well, but he was a dinosaur though in an emerging world of technology. Eventually, he would become what some might see as obsolete because he had no desire to keep up with the latest gadget. In fact, he was doing good just to complete his reports using a computer, not that he was gifted at it by any means. Shortcomings or not, Sister Lee needed him more than anyone. Then there was Henley. The man was a walking encyclopedia holding more information between his ears than even he was aware of. That knowledge would have to be used in a specific way to unearth dark secrets

Callahan wasn't ready to believe. Obviously, there was much Henley didn't know about catching killers. Sister Lee would have to use his curiosity to extract the information Callahan needed to hear and see.

Few understood Sister Lee's form of communication, and less could imagine her hidden talents. She possessed the ability to read people's palms, minds, hidden signs, and even the stars themselves. She could see the future through the eyes of others. It was like something out of a science fiction movie, yet she was real along with the other powers she held secret. Her plans to connect with Buttweiler were placed on hold as he combed the internet using his cell phone looking for information related to victims. He would uncover something Callahan would've never found, but more importantly, Sister Lee knew she could count on his lack of understanding to bring everything to Callahan's attention without exception given time. Time, unfortunately, was something she had little of since the window into a man's mind is limited.

Invading a person's thoughts from a distance without being detected is a challenge even for someone as gifted as her. She had soon exhausted her energy concentrating on Henley's subconscious. The fact was he packed a lot of information in that brain of his, and sorting through it took more time than she had given to her. She had to take frequent breaks, and rest before trying to tap into the information he held in his head. Henley's subconscious was a busy place, more so than anyone she had encountered before. He may have only been a glorified file clerk, but he held the IQ of a genius.

Henley was a far contrast from Buttweiler, but that was all part of the plan. Buttweiler's talents lied elsewhere, and they would be needed if anyone was going to stop Hayden Keller. Sister Lee thought about him as she sat there at the wooden table in the center of her parlor. She recognized it was Buttweiler's determination to attempt to solve the case on his own that got in the way for the moment. It caused a complete breakdown in communication between the three men. That didn't stop her from working her magic though. She took that moment to find a solution to the problem as she looked at the vast collection of books on the shelf behind her.

Taking one of the books down off the shelf, she ran her hand over the cover. What it contained wasn't what she was looking for. Sister Lee's speed reading capabilities far exceeded those of any Harvard grad. She never had to bother cracking the cover to thumb through it to determine it held no key to solving her dilemma. Without hesitating, she scanned the entire wall of books in her parlor. Putting the one she held in her hands back in its place, she pulled another one down that was covered in dust. She ran her forefinger across one of the pages near the front of the book in search of something important. She was fairly certain it held secrets that had eluded her. Seconds later, she looked up with the answer she had been searching for. Concern was embedded in the lines of her face, and a look of question instilled itself in her black eyes. Doing her best to shield herself from the dark side, she quickly closed the book - for it contained power even she wished not to wield. She wished to return it back in its proper place on the shelf, yet she paused a second. Her hand rested on the book, and she thought of an incantation she had not used before.

The ancient seer she knew had used the spell more than once. The effects were devastating, and she had warned her of the cost associated with practicing the dark arts. Sister

Lee grew to respect the old woman's wisdom. She saw firsthand the destructive nature of its power, and what became of the ones who used it for their own purpose. Spells cast from that book drained physical strength from the one who summoned forces in the dark. In time, it sucked the life right out of the spell-caster. The book itself fed on the life-force of others. Still, it had a place in her collection for its magic was great. Letting go a deep breath she accepted evil must be fought by any means necessary.

Now determined, she walked into the room containing the altar toward the rear of her house. She believed Buttweiler's stubborn nature could be used to benefit her if it was channeled properly. For some reason, he reminded her of Deputy Singer, except his belief system was altogether different. Buttweiler was moldable, unlike the deputy. Stubborn to a fault she knew without question one day he would become a believer in many things unseen.

Sister Lee raised her hands, holding them over the large leather-bound book which still rested on the altar. Her hands started to tremble a little as she spoke these words out loud, "dume oreyis laboram shatar rei." She chanted the words thrice sealing the spell with, "no slumber, no peace." Translation simply meant, "come what may he shall work without rest, if he fails he shall ask for help until then he shall have no peace."

Chapter 20

Related Cases

Buttweiler waded through a stack of case files setting aside any that appeared to involve a dead body, and a missing vehicle. He had picked up a few tricks from Callahan in their brief period of time working together. He even used the time of deaths corresponding to each decedent to develop a timeline as he charted each murder location to construct a path in an effort to track the killer. He was compiling a detailed database of related cases.

Callahan knew what he was doing. He also knew it would take time to comb through the pertinent facts in each case. Developing the proper timeline was easier said than done. There was a lot of guesswork involved early on. Still, he was impressed for once with Buttweiler's initiative. Finally, he had stopped asking for answers, and now he was searching for them himself. He had no idea how detailed Buttweiler's spreadsheet was, and what an important piece the computer would play in tying the related cases to one another.

Even with the ability to analyze fifty cases at once with the touch of a button it wouldn't be easy. There would no doubt be several cases that were included in that pile that were unrelated, but it was a great way to start out. The ones that did belong to Hayden were so random as far as direction, and location Buttweiler began to ask himself which ones were committed by the same individual. It wasn't as smooth a process as he had hoped it would be, but he knew he could accurately cross reference the data to piece the timeline together with extreme accuracy. The results would be something he wasn't prepared for. None of them would be.

The number of cases were growing, and the timeline appeared to have no end. Soon, Buttweiler found himself repeatedly questioning if he had messed up. Surely, he was now including cases that were unrelated. At first, he said nothing, he just continued building the database. With time, his mind became weighted down with doubt, and concern. Sister Lee's spell had a hold on him. Regardless of his stubborn streak, it brought him to a point of utter confusion. Eventually, he was forced to share what he had discovered with Callahan. He had tried to make sense of it, but he needed to make sure he wasn't traveling down a road he should have never taken.

Laying out what he presumed was the path of the killer, the map became covered with sporadic points marking the dumpsites belonging to Hayden Keller. He hesitantly asked, "can you look at this for a second?" Callahan walked over to the table where Buttweiler was working. He looked down at the map in front of him, and then at the long list of murders which Buttweiler had compiled. That's when Buttweiler looked up at Callahan saying, "I know this can't be right, but this guy looks like he's all over the place. I just can't seem to find a logical path for the direction he takes. Am I missing something here?"

Callahan surveyed the data as Buttweiler explained he didn't want to ask, but he felt he had no choice. That's when Callahan informed him, "all good cops know when to ask the right questions, and that includes when to ask for a second pair of eyes on something." What Buttweiler saw as total confusion Callahan tried to piece together using some form of twisted logic because that's how the killer operated.

He knew that much when he handed Buttweiler the first stack of folders. Callahan studied everything closely as he leaned forward resting both of his hands on the table. Buttweiler watched his eyes as he stared down at the map. There was rapid movement on them, and a look of serious determination on the detective's face.

Buttweiler had numbered each murder on the map according to the order in which they were committed. He had made several corrections whenever he happened to come across new cases that seemed to fit somewhere within the murders he had already charted. He questioned himself in his mind if he had made a mistake on a few of them. That thought plagued him as he made mention of it to Callahan.

Peering back down at the list for a moment, and then over at the number covered map, he tried to pick up on what Callahan was taking in. Buttweiler even added, "I tried to number them correctly. Maybe I made a mistake."

Callahan could tell according to the TOD.s, and the dates corresponding to them, Buttweiler hadn't made a mistake. The killings were spread out, and random, but that was the killer's M.O. If anything, Buttweiler had done a excellent job of plotting the course which Hayden had taken. The surprising part was those murders spanned damn near a decade. They seemed to fall into particular time periods, and they were disjointed in direction. Some string of murders seemed to cease within a week, while others appeared to go on for twice that long.

Callahan was a great detective, but even he couldn't tell all the patterns that were present in this killer's action simply by looking at where they occurred, and when they happened on the surface. To get to the real answers at the heart of these cases, it was going to take countless hours of intense investigation. Searching for patterns was just a start. This would entail going through arrest records, and even cases which occurred in other jurisdictions because this killer was everywhere at some point. Callahan shared his thoughts with Buttweiler saying, "I don't see anything that leads me to believe you screwed anything up. This is one devious son of a bitch we're after, and he never appears to leave the hunt. What you have to ask yourself at this point is why do the murders start, and cease at some points. You got us a timeline, that's the most critical part. We're definitely dealing with a serial killer for sure, but you have to find the patterns no one else has discovered in order to get to who we're looking for."

Buttweiler understood most of what Callahan had said, but he had already established the pertinent pieces of the pattern using the method of assault, and the time and place of the murders. When he made mention of that, Callahan clarified what he was trying to point out, giving Buttweiler the most critical tool in a detectives arsenal other than his gun, and that was to spot the underlying patterns that weren't right in front of him to see. Callahan said, "you're not looking for what your information is telling you, you're looking for what it's not." He posed questions to Buttweiler like, "how long did he go between killing sprees? Where was he at the time in which they ended? What about some link to the times in which they were committed? I can tell you from the map this guy travels, and he doesn't have a day job, the time, and place which he kills are much too varied for that."

Buttweiler started to see Callahan's point. He now realized what a daunting challenge it would be as he responded to the detective saying, "I got it. So, we look for every pattern we can find using what can't be seen on the surface."

Callahan replied, "that's right, and that's going to take a

hell of a lot of work."

Buttweiler remarked, "we could really use more men on this, couldn't we." Callahan looked down at him with a concerned look on his face, and then he lifted his head up along with Buttweiler as they both turned their attention toward Henley. He was sitting at his desk eating his lunch perusing one of the case files in the stack which sat on the corner of his desk as he crunched away on some Doritos. He could literally feel Callahan, and Buttweiler staring at him. Cutting his eyes in their direction, he stopped chewing before questioning, "what?"

All Callahan had to say is, "we need you Henley." He put down the folder he was reading along with the chips he had in his hand. He was at their disposal once again, and this time it was doing real police work.

Chapter 21

The Search Widens For Hayden Keller

Callahan figured Henley could assist Buttweiler with the unsolved cases currently on his plate by expanding their records search into neighboring states. He instructed him to focus primarily on unsolved murders, and arrest reports. A gleam was present in Henley's eyes, and a confident tone was clearly heard in his voice when he contacted the other records clerks in neighboring states to request access to their records. When he told them who he was, and that he was working with law enforcement officials in an effort to catch a serial killer, he had no trouble gaining their support. They were all more than happy to assist Henley in the hunt.

Sister Lee's powers over Buttweiler made him a better investigator. He was driven to search for answers even when there were none, and that was the only way he could possibly discover what Sister Lee needed him to reveal to Callahan. Most cops would have stopped amassing data long before Buttweiler. Creating a timeline which spanned years is something they wouldn't even begin to consider being possible. Doing it would take more than some key search, and sort parameters punched into a keyboard. Used in conjunction analysis applications, it would prove fruitful though. That was the only way they would uncover the truth, and Buttweiler's computer skills were critical to say the least. She now had the junior investigator exactly where she wanted him, Henley too, for that matter. Over the next week, they both worked twelve hour days, hardly taking a break to eat. They were consumed with identifying the killer, something Callahan projected would take months.

Buttweiler's day didn't end when he left the office. He soon became accustomed to running on less than four hours sleep. He worked relentlessly well into the wee hours of the morning on discovering the hidden patterns Callahan spoke of given the information he and Henley extracted from the case files. In fact, he became quite good at it. So much so, that he truly started believing in himself for a change. That was the one thing he had always lacked since joining the force. The amazing part was he stuck it out this long.

The information he had uncovered brought them closer to solving a numerous number of cold cases. With eyes on he, and Callahan from their higher-ups, he felt pressure at first, but the more he worked the cases the less it affected his performance. For once, he possessed the one quality every good officer needs - confidence in his own judgment. No longer was he afraid to be criticized for his theories. In the past, he seldom bothered forming any, and when he did he never presented them to anyone. How do you solve a crime when you don't trust your own hunches? There's certainly no way you'd ever follow them. In Buttweiler's case, that had now changed since being teamed up with Callahan and Henley.

He actually started to believe he might make a pretty damn good detective someday. Callahan knew a hell of a lot more than him about being a cop, and Henley didn't know near as much. It was the perfect combination for Buttweiler, and the fact that Henley handed him a compliment from time to time, comparing him to Callahan on occasion when he stumbled onto something, definitely didn't hurt.

Henley possessed the ability to guide Buttweiler simply by making a casual comment of some sort. It often pointed him in the right direction causing him to focus on what was important. The epiphanies they were faced with stemmed largely from the connection Sister Lee had established with their subconscious thoughts, but it all seemed natural in their course of conversation. Henley never really thought about what rolled off his tongue, it just left his mouth with the help of Sister Lee prodding him to say something whenever Buttweiler seemed to be drifting off course.

When Buttweiler would mention something regarding the time period the killer went dormant, Henley would always say something like, "maybe you should focus on that. I really think you are on to something there." That was Sister Lee speaking through him of course, but they were her pawns though neither of them knew it. That's not to say they weren't extremely important pieces in the game. Without them, evil would never be stopped, with them, the world still stood a chance. That little bit of encouragement was usually enough to spur Buttweiler into pressing onward no matter what roadblock he faced.

It was 8:00 p.m., and it was long past time for Henley to lockdown the records room for the night, but he and Buttweiler had become quite accustomed to staying late going through stacks of paper searching for clues. Henley had spent the better part of the day viewing electronic files which were emailed to him from other parts of the country. The search for Hayden Keller now stretched across the country. Henley couldn't believe where some of the records were coming from. He had arrest records, and case files sent to him that went all the way from the east coast out to the west, and it was a hell of a lot of stuff to wade through. Buttweiler had already traced Hayden's path out west all the way to California, and back up the west coast to Seattle before following him across the central part of the country headed for New York. He had become intimately familiar with his travel patterns. It was only when he killed in large metropolitan areas that he lost track of him due in large part to the high numbers of murders taking place there all throughout the year, but he would always pick up his trail when he departed from the big cities.

Buttweiler had become quite adept at tracking him on paper using police reports. There were several times where he actually thought Hayden had been apprehended since the killing ceased, and didn't start up again in that region of the country, but what he found was they always appeared to occur in another part soon afterward. That part left him thinking hard about why the break in the pattern. He questioned if the killer was smart enough to hop a plane to another part of the country to prevent police from tracking him traveling along the highways, but that didn't seem plausible in his mind. Airline data was readily available should authorities believe that was his mode of transportation, and seldom did any murders take place near the airports. Again, he was brought back to the timeline for key answers to his killer's true identity.

When Henley felt like he had enough for the evening, he looked over at his partner asking if he was ready to call it a night. Buttweiler was hell bent on figuring something out that he knew was critical in some way to the cases. He held up his hand saying, "just a minute." Henley could tell he was in deep thought at that moment as he got up from his chair, and walked over to the table where Buttweiler was working.

Henley asked, "did you find something?"

Suddenly, it clicked as he told Henley, "have a seat." Pointing to a bunch of case files not yet entered into his spreadsheet he told Henley, "go through all those, and give me the D.O.D.s. I need the dates, and the times of death."

Buttweiler logged them in as Henley read out the date, and approximate time of death associated with each victim. Staring at the computer screen his eyes grew big. All Buttweiler said at that point was, "I think we just hit on something Henley."

The keeper of the records room still didn't know what the hell was up. All he knew was Buttweiler seemed satisfied, and somewhat eager to close up for the night. When Henley pressed him for details regarding what they'd discovered, Buttweiler promised to share his findings with him first thing in the morning. He just needed time to compare his theory to the other cases to see if it held true for each one. Promptly, shutting down his laptop he grabbed his things, leaving Henley behind to lock the doors behind him. His only concern was what the timeline had not yet revealed to him. This was the fact Sister Lee needed him to uncover. Callahan had to know this, and more before he would be willing to listen to her, and Henley still had to do his part.

That night Henley could hardly sleep, but he tried. He knew he had a long day ahead of him with many more records to comb through as he closed his eyes, and finally drifted off to sleep. Buttweiler didn't hit the bed at all that night. Instead, he worked for hours on end comparing dates using the internet to view old calendars of years past in his attempt to determine on which days of the week the killer committed the murders, and which days he did not. At two o'clock on the morning, he became convinced the killer never killed after midnight on Friday no matter what time zone he was in. There were a number of variables to consider, but he also determined for some strange reason he wouldn't kill again until twenty-four hours had passed. Whatever it was that prohibited him from killing centered around the last day of the week. It was a weird window of down time he took, but he never seemed to deviate from the unusual hiatus. He knew this was important even though he didn't fully understand what that time period meant for the killer. Unable to uncover the answer himself he figured Callahan might be able to explain it. He was certain it was an important factor in cases. It tied them all together, and weeded certain ones out.

Buttweiler's mind raced all night thinking about it before he finally laid back on the couch. He emptied the coffeepot, and started making more. His night of uncovering clues was far from over. He stared at his computer screen off and on for almost two hours as he rubbed his tired eyes. He couldn't help but wonder why that particular pattern existed. He knew it would be important in discovering their next clue, but he had no solid answer for the killer's behavior. Never bothering to finish off his last few swigs of coffee in his mug, he faded off to sleep.

When the sun rose that morning, Buttweiler woke from less than three hours of rest. He looked at the clock on his phone quickly realizing he was running late. This wasn't the first time, and it probably wouldn't be the last. The bright side was he didn't have to make roll call. His permanent attachment to the cold case investigations spared him from that for the time being. He rubbed his hand over his face feeling mentally drained. He was still half asleep, but the excitement he felt spurred him to sit up, and put both feet on the floor. He couldn't wait to share what he'd discovered with Callahan and Henley. They had planned to meet that morning to go over the list of cases they planned to reopen.

Less than two weeks into Callahan's new assignment, Captain Rollins was demanding a formal update of some sort. That meant he wanted to know how many cases

Callahan felt they could close within six months, and what was the likelihood of solving them given that timeframe. Those were hard statistics to give upfront, but Callahan could spit-out percentages, and numbers just like Henley. He based his best guess on evidence, and the passage of time since the crimes occurred along with his gut. In a way he was being asked to tell the future, but the Captain demanded much from him. Callahan had seen much of what was contained within the reports, and he was always conservative with his estimations. He had learned long ago if you're not, they often bite you in the butt, and he planned on walking out of there with his gold watch in hand when it was all said and done. He'd have to stick it out seven more years before he saw that day arrive.

Buttweiler climbed up off the couch, and made his way to the shower. The cold water splashing on his face woke him right up, and he was energized just as if he had a full night's rest. Trying to make up for lost time, he hastily put on his clothes, the ones he wore from the day before. He hadn't had time to do the wash. Normally, he at least had a bagel, and a taste of orange juice before heading out for work, but this particular morning he just shoved the papers he used to establish the hidden pattern into his computer case along with his laptop. The printouts of calendars from previous years were quickly crammed into a brown leather satchel, and he carried them with him as he walked out the front door of his apartment.

It was clear he was in a rush as he scurried down two flights of stairs with both hands full. He didn't even bother to speak with anyone on the way to his car. Tunnel vision had its hold on him, and he appeared to be more like Callahan than himself that morning. Fighting his way through traffic he became agitated. The congestion wasn't worse that day than it was any other, but he was running late with something extremely important to layout for the detective. That's what really bothered him most. He had traveled that same stretch of highway numerous times back and forth to work for the better part of two years. Now, he was kicking himself for not taking another exit. If anything, he should have been used to it by now. When he got right down to it, he had no choice really. He had to cross the bridge, or add another fifteen miles to his route in order to avoid it. His bet was that would take even longer. Sitting there in traffic did one thing other than make his blood boil. It gave him time to think. Stuck in a motionless sea of vehicles, something became quite clear. The stress he felt dissipated almost instantly upon his discovery. Suddenly, he understood why the killer seemed to spend a great deal of time right in the central part of the country, more so than other areas. It was all a part of his normal travel path no matter what direction he was headed in, he always had to pass through that part of the country to get to where he was going. It also stood to reason he would be back again real soon.

Buttweiler felt certain they had twice as good a chance of stopping him this time considering what they now knew. He was eager to share what he had uncovered with Callahan, and when the opening presented itself Buttweiler took advantage of it. He stepped on the gas, and quickly changed lanes. He was a cop with some place to be, and he made sure others knew it. Rolling up to the road-worker holding the slow sign he held up his badge, and lowered his window. "All he said was IMPD coming through." The rest of the way he was riding the express lane to the station.

Chapter 22

Critical Information Unsolved Cases

Henley was right on time as usual unlocking the doors to the records room just as he had done for nearly three decades. He couldn't wait to find out what Buttweiler now knew. As he stood there, he looked at the stack of case files he went through the night before. Callahan stuck his head in the door just to see how things were coming along. He not only had to oversee the cold case investigations, he also had three active cases he was working on too. When he asked Henley how it was going, he mentioned Buttweiler had stumbled onto something. "I'm not sure what it is exactly, but I think it's really important." A great deal of excitement was present in Henley's voice.

That, of course, peaked Callahan's interest as he asked, "have you seen him this morning? He wasn't upstairs at his desk."

Henley covered for him saying, "no, but I'm sure he'll be here soon." Hearing that, Callahan's lips tightened a little. Henley sensed some tension so he added, "I'm sure he was up working late. It was after eight when we left last night, and he took a stack of papers with him. He said he had to go through a bunch of stuff." Callahan nodded his head, and he looked around at the tables which were filled with files inside the records room. Something deep down in his gut told him Buttweiler had really stumbled onto something - he just wished he knew what it was prior to speaking to the captain.

When Henley told him he had gotten records sent to him all the way from California, Callahan's eyes opened a little wider. Callahan reminded him they weren't in the FBI. He was half-ass joking with Henley, but when he looked at the maps Buttweiler had used to chart the killings, he knew right then this thing stretched from one end of the country to the other. He was going to put the captain off until he had a chance to speak with his junior investigator.

Out of curiosity, the detective asked Henley, "How many pushpins you think I'm looking at on this map?"

Henley glanced at it, and then at his desk before responding, "one hundred eighteen, but we still have to add some that we went through last night. Buttweiler knows which ones, we ran out of pins."

Callahan now had plenty of questions, but he didn't doubt Henley's count for a second. Borrowing Henley's mathematical mind again he asked, "what percentage of cold cases get solve after lying dormant for three years?"

Henley educated Callahan once again, "less than ten percent prior to 1990. Once genome sequencing was introduced, the number more than doubled. I'd say it's now in excess of twenty-two percent." Henley then went on to add how many convictions were overturned as a result of the DNA evidence, but Callahan didn't really listen closely to that.

"That's interesting Henley." He was in deep thought as he brushed him off. It was safe to say he could tell the captain thirty cold cases could be closed within his jurisdiction if they were able to help apprehend one serial killer. Five a month would be damn impressive in anyone's book. Oddly enough, they could end up solving twice that number, but Callahan realized the guy they were after was the most elusive killer law enforcement had ever run across. He had to ask if Buttweiler's judgment might be to blame for so many cases being credited to this particular killer, but his new partner wasn't there to make his case for the moment.

111

Callahan thumbed through some of the folders Henley had mentioned before looking at his watch. That's when he said, "let me know as soon as Buttweiler gets here." Without question, Callahan was every bit as interested in finding out what Buttweiler had discovered as Henley was.

Taking a sip of his morning coffee, Callahan left Archives, and trotted upstairs to his desk on the third floor. Passing several officers on the way, he overheard one of them say something about a red pathfinder. The vehicle had been carjacked, and used in an armed robbery. Callahan believed it was also a part of a hit run case he was investigating. Callahan turned to Officer Barrett stopping him on his way out the door. He pressed him for a few details concerning the vehicle, and its whereabouts. All Barrett could tell him was it had been found abandoned on the southeast side of town. When Callahan asked where it was, Barrett said, "I'm pretty sure they got it in impound." Within less than two minutes Callahan was out the door to investigate it further.

Buttweiler pulled into the parking garage less than a minute after Callahan pulled out. The first place he went was to Callahan's desk. Detective Murphy sat right next to him, and as soon as he saw Buttweiler walk up he spouted, "you just missed him, Buttweiler. He flew out of here like a bat out of hell."
A disappointed look was present on Buttweiler's face as he asked Murphy, "can you let him know I was looking for him?"
Murphy shoved a fresh stick of gum in his mouth while crumpling up the wrapper to dispose of it saying, "yeah, I'll tell him if I see him."

Buttweiler checked his voicemail before making his way down to the records room. Even if Callahan wasn't there, he knew Henley would be, and he would most certainly want to know the newest piece to the puzzle. Buttweiler even figured with more time he and Henley may come up with something else worth having before presenting this critical timeline consistency to Callahan. He had no idea how on target he was. What he, and Henley would soon uncover would leave them all questioning - how on earth could it be possible.

Sister Lee had orchestrated this moment right from the very beginning when she brought them together to hunt for Hayden Keller. When Buttweiler opened the door to the records room, Henley looked up from his desk. He was already hard at work searching through records using his computer. Some of them were so old they were recorded on microfiche, and Henley's vision became blurred as he read through some of them.

Buttweiler could barely manage to say, "good morning," before Henley asked him if he had seen Callahan yet. When Buttweiler explained, "I tried to catch him this morning at his desk, but he'd already left," Henley couldn't wait to hear what Buttweiler had uncovered.

He wasted no to time in asking, "so, what did you come up with last night?"

Buttweiler grinned knowing it wouldn't take Henley long to ask that question. He even glanced up at the clock on the wall inside the records room taking note of the time. That's when he blurted out, "the killer, our guy, he takes off every Saturday."

Henley just looked at him not understanding the significance of that. A bewildered expression took hold of his pudgy face as he questioned, "is that it?"

Buttweiler laid his papers down on the table. He smirked a little as he looked at Henley. He tried to sell him on the fact it was a critical piece of the timeline even though Henley couldn't see the real relevance it had on the cases. He had heard Callahan mention the timelines importance when tracking a serial killer, but understanding what could be extrapolated from consistent holes in it didn't hold as much meaning for Henley as it did a real cop. What propelled Buttweiler to think in that direction initially was actually something he heard Henley say in passing conversation.

It was Sister Lee's words which Henley spoke that steadily encouraged Buttweiler to keep searching until he found that clue. Now, he wasn't willing to overlook it even if Henley couldn't see how important it was. He didn't have to recognize its significance, Callahan would put it together with a little help, and Buttweiler would use it to weed out crimes that didn't belong to their serial killer.

The statistics Henley threw out to Callahan should have served as an earnest reminder the bad guys don't always get caught no matter who's on the case, but he had no real understanding of what was required to crack cold cases. On television, they did it in less than forty-eight hours. Henley was damn near ready to help them haul the guy in that was responsible for all of the unsolved murders provided he was already handcuffed. He had seen it done that way countless times on TV, and never did it involve so much paperwork. In fact, they always caught the killer by interviewing someone that was around at the time the crime was committed. Henley was now starting to think they were going about this thing the wrong way, or those TV shows he had been watching for decades were a little far-fetched compared to reality. Either way, Henley was still in disbelief that's all they had after nearly a week's worth of work. All he could say was, "that's all we got out of it?"

Buttweiler jokingly remarked, "I guess you thought I was

going to hand you the name of the guy we're looking for."

Henley admitted, "something like that, but now that you mention it, I think that's what we should be looking for." Ironically, that was Buttweiler's next move. He figured he was now at the point where he could do just that with some degree of accuracy.

Henley had received a lot of arrest reports from all over the country. Buttweiler knew they could match a few of them to the timeline, perhaps where the trail seemed to grow cold. All they needed was a name match in several places along the timeline to account for the interruption in the killer's schedule. What may have seemed like an overzealous suggestion in an attempt by a novice to solve a string of murders was actually the proper step to take in this case. Buttweiler just assumed it was all a part of doing good police work. It was more than that though, it was Sister Lee's bidding. Buttweiler said, "a name huh. That's what I think I'll have you give me."

Henley looked a little confused as Buttweiler sat down, and pulled out his computer. He was also armed with a notepad, and these were the tools he planned to use to locate their killer. Firing up the computer, he was ready to get the show underway as Henley took a seat behind his desk awaiting his first order.

Buttweiler leaned forward observing the map for a moment. Taking his left index finger, he placed it on the central most part of the country tracing a highway that intersected the state of Kansas. He looked over at the list of murders which he had compiled paying particular attention to the dates. Buttweiler then instructed Henley, "give me the names corresponding to arrest reports from Kansas between June of 2009 to September that same year." As soon as Henley pulled up the names, Buttweiler started making his list. He was searching for any arrest reports with matching names, and that was the start of what should have been a long, and arduous process. Buttweiler knew it was all they had to go on for now. Hopefully, with time, it would yield the name of the killer. It was their only hope of discovering Hayden Keller's identity, but that too can be rather difficult when the man you are after changes bodies the way others change their clothes. Buttweiler, nor Henley were privy to that though. He had faith, eventually, they would uncover a duplicate arrest.

Hunting a demon offered its share of challenges, and Hayden Keller was one hard bastard to hunt down. He could be standing right in front of you, and you'd never even know it until it was too late. As Hayden neared the town of Chanceville, he was about to prove it once again. Sister Lee's concentration was broken by the evil presence she felt in the world of spirits. A cold wind was felt moving around her, and she knew the beast was close yet again. She feared for the people of Chanceville, and she knew why Hayden had returned. He wasn't coming for her just yet. He was in search of Ashley and Ben.

She held her hands over the large book resting on the altar as she chanted, "defendo nostrum animus." In the language of old that simply meant protect our souls. She performed this incantation to shield the townspeople of Chanceville from Hayden's bloody vengeance. They knew the hunter was close, and the only thing overriding his thirst for the blood of man was his desire to track down the one responsible for sending him back to hell.

Chapter 23

A Haunting Presence Returns

It was just before noon when Hayden passed the little green sign on the side of the road which read, welcome to Chanceville. He wasn't much on feelings, but he held a great deal of hatred in his empty heart for that little town. He could still remember everything that took place there as if it happened yesterday. He could almost smell the gas, and smoke from his burning clothes. It reminded him of hell even though he was no longer there. That little place on the map would forever serve as a reminder of just how close he was to residing there for all eternity. The mere thought of that pissed Hayden off to no end.

He tried to calm himself down as he stepped on the brake, slowing Ronnie's truck down to thirty miles per hour in order to stay under the speed limit. He recalled what happened last time he lost control of his temper behind the wheel. That's when he ran into Officer Danford, and while that was a once in a lifetime experience he didn't regret having at all, this was neither the time nor the place to pull such a stunt. Dead cops tended to draw lots of heat from all directions, and Hayden had business to tend to at the moment. He told himself there would be time for killing later, and when the time came he would wipe that place from the map. When he was done, no one would wish to live there, and all that were left alive would run in search of any place other than Chanceville to call home.

Hayden's black heart knew nothing other than vengeance. It was the one thing he took pride in stealing from the Lord.

The souls, they were Satan's, but the wrath, that belonged entirely unto Hayden Keller himself. The thought of him burning alive festered in his twisted mind as he vowed to find the son of a bitch responsible for his horrid demise. As he drove passed the stores which lined the main street, he tried to mask the detest he had for the place, but there was no concealing the venom in his eyes.

Hayden picked up the sunglasses he had swiped from Officer Danford, and he used them to cover his face when he noticed people turning their attention to the flashy ride he was sporting. He had been driving quite some time when he pulled into the parking lot of the diner just several blocks down from Sheriff Baker's office. They couldn't see Hayden through the thick tinted glass of the pickup he was driving. They all just knew they had never seen that truck before, and it was sharp looking.

Hayden exited the truck never bothering to lock it. His hand covered his left cheek as he rubbed it some when he entered the diner, and promptly took a seat which faced toward the window. The fresh looking scar on his cheek now faced the wall adjacent to him, and when the waitress came over to get his order, he knew exactly what he wanted. It was almost as if he had been there before, but she certainly didn't recognize him this time. He had passed up the chance to kill her once before many years ago. She was one of the lucky ones though she didn't know it. Hayden knew where to go in a small town to get answers. All he had to do was start the conversation, and keep his ears open for that which he was interested in. It would no doubt come his way sooner or later through the voice of someone in that diner that picked up on a little bit of gossip involving the murders, and the serial killer responsible for them. Hayden was famous in that town, yet he couldn't introduce himself to anyone just yet. All he wanted to know was the name of the guy at the gas station that caught his ass on fire, or where Ashley was now. If he could find her, he could find him, and Hayden was dying to torch his ass. He even told himself if all he got was a name out of that place, he would relentlessly hunt down every one with that name listed in the phonebook, and Hayden would undoubtedly do it.

He watched the goings on out on the street in front of the little diner. Not much changed in a little town like that. It somehow seemed like time passed it by in a way, but Hayden was unable to appreciate anything it had to offer in the way of nostalgia. He wasn't made that way. He only saw things with distaste. The truck parked outside was perhaps the only exception. Even the food he ate was unappealing for the most part, it was simply a necessary evil of keeping the body functional in order to live to kill another day.

When Stella brought his plate over, she politely asked if he wanted more water. Hayden never looked at her. He just kept staring out the window. He managed to communicate his wishes to her though as he touched the glass with the back of his hand, and slid it over toward the edge of the table. His hand formed a fist remaining stationary next to the glass. It took all his willpower to maintain control in social settings, but he was trying his best to remain stable even though blood was coursing through his veins. Stella could tell something was gnawing at him, but he didn't strike her as the kind of guy that talked to anyone about problems he faced. She didn't really care to hear them anyway. She had a few of her own to contend with. All that really mattered was him leaving a tip on the table. That's the only reason she asked, "is everything okay?" With the nod of his head he answered her question, and confirmed her assessment of him all at the same time.

With Hayden, it was always a tightrope act of sorts trying to quash his urge to kill was extremely difficult. He knew Satan relished this part the most for this was Hayden's eternal torment. He fought the rage he had inside him telling himself there would soon come a day. For the time being, he was in hell on earth unable to take another life for the moment with so many walking around for the taking. It was enough to drive a demented psychopath crazy.

As Stella filled his water glass, Hayden sat there thinking, *what a waste, so many lives to take - so little time to do it.* He made short work of the food on his plate, but he paused scarfing down what was in front of him to check-out the patrol car pulling up next to his vehicle. At that moment, the deputy inside the patrol car had his complete attention. Hayden played it off, of course, when he looked back down taking another bite of food to avoid causing suspicion. Still, he chewed slowly watching the deputy get out of his car. He didn't recognize Deputy Rately, but that was fair enough because Ratley certainly didn't recognize Hayden Keller. How could he ever imagine seeing him chowing-down on a pepper-steak inside the local diner? The last time he laid eyes on him, he resembled what was on his plate instead of the man seated in the booth devouring it. All Ratley had seen of him at that Marathon station was the charred remains of what was once a man. That image along with the severed body parts in the back of the black SUV were enough to make Ratley loose his lunch right there at the crime scene. He would never block those images out of his mind along with what he saw out at the Ferris Farm, but that case was now closed. Hayden's burnt body sealed the case for good, and Ratley slept well at night knowing that. It was all in the past as far as he was concerned, and he preferred not to think about it now. He certainly never allowed it to enter his mind right before he ate.

The sheriff, and his deputies just kind of put it behind them for the most part. They had finally come to face they couldn't fix the evil deeds done out on the Ferris Farm. It was an unpleasant moment in the history of the little town, but at least they were able to recover the missing girl before she was mutilated like the others they found. That, of course, would not have turned out that way without Sister Lee's help, but Ratley knew nothing of her. One thing's for certain, without her, Hayden's bloodthirsty rampage would have been far more extensive than Sheriff Baker, and his deputies could've imagined. Ben's premonition brought that to light. It's what caused Ben to alter his course of action, and change destiny, thereby, saving Ashley, and countless others, maybe even you, and me in the process.

The fact that Ratley didn't recognize him didn't matter to Hayden. He was cleverly camouflaged in the body of another person. His main concern was Ratley's interest in his vehicle. Was he admiring it, or was he checking it out for some other reason altogether? Hayden realized the truck was flashy. Hell, it turned heads even in Nashville, and that's saying something. There were few things Hayden liked, but he damn sure took pleasure in riding in that thing. Right then, though, he began to consider parting with it. It was just a fleeting thought once he was fairly certain the deputy had no idea what he was looking at.

After giving the truck the once over, Ratley turned to walk inside the diner to pick up lunch for him, and Singer. Hayden sat there thinking *damn dumb-ass deputy, even Barney Fife's probably got one up on this guy*. That was the only thing that allowed Hayden to attempt a smile. It always came across as a sick snarl of sorts, but with Hayden that was as close as one would get to ever seeing him grin.

As Ratley made his way to the counter, he looked over at Hayden. He knew he wasn't from anywhere around there, and that caused him to strike up a bit of conversation. Ratley asked, "is that your truck out there?"

Hayden pushed out his lips a little never looking directly at the deputy. He continued chewing a little as he took hold of his glass, and he raised it up off the table. Holding it up as if he were about to make a toast, he held it in the air a second before taking a long swig. Saying absolutely nothing, he then placed the glass of water back on the table. Ratley surmised from his response that he got asked that question a lot. Still, the deputy complimented him on it telling him, "I haven't seen one like it around these parts." Just then, Stella came to the counter to take his order, and Ratley turned his attention to her saying, "Hi Stel, I'm going to need two specials to go. I've gotta meet Singer over at the station."

Stella asked, "how you want yours?"

Ratley replied, "medium-well is fine, and if you would, throw a little extra gravy on those mash potatoes for me."

As Stella said, "I'll do it," Ratley gave her his old cheesy smile. When he started to tell her how Singer wanted his, Stella said, "oh, I know how Singer likes it." She then added, "but he's not getting it that way."

Ratley laughed a little as she walked away. Stella had a few years on her, but Ratley could see why Singer had a little thing for her. They would have probably made a good couple if it weren't for the fact that Stella got irritated just hearing his name being mentioned.

The deputy turned looking back at the truck through the window. His curiosity got the best of him, and he asked Hayden, "where on earth did you get it?" That's when Hayden proudly told the story of how he picked it up from a guy that had special ordered the thing, and he waited for almost a month just for them to deliver it.

Ratley listened as the diner started filling up with more people. He was impressed enough to ask, "so, how much do you have wrapped up in it?" Two more customers walked through the door, and Ratley greeted one of them calling him by name as he said, "hi, Dell."

Hayden answered him saying, "I don't have near as much in it as the guy I got it from, that's for sure." Seeing that goofy grin on Ratley's face, Hayden became bold enough to go right to the official source to get the information he came for. Hayden said, "I don't know, but you can probably tell me. Is this the place where that girl was found that police were looking for, sometime back?"

That grin on Ratley's face vanished quickly. He now had a question for Hayden as he enquired, "why do ask?" Ratley didn't figure him for a reporter. Hayden was much too reserved for that. He also didn't fit the bill for the last of those passing through town to get a glimpse of the scene where the killer was found, or where the murders occurred. Those people were a little more pumped up about hearing all the gory details even though some pretended as though they were shocked by it all.

Hayden responded, "oh, I just remember something about that taking place around here. I think there was some guy involved in helping police find the girl. I can't remember his name though. I don't guess you would know."

Ratley didn't feel compelled to share anything he knew with anyone regarding that situation. He was young, but he was smart enough to know when he was being baited. Clearly, Hayden was fishing for some reason.

The sheriff had stated in no uncertain terms what their stand was on talking to anyone about that entire incident. It was to never be discussed outside the sheriff's office, and only then for damn good reason. That alone, made Ratley unwilling to share any details of what happened, least of all with some guy just passing through. Telling him anything could only lead to more people catching wind of it. That's what Ratley figured anyway, and should that happen it would lead to more people coming with more questions. The deputy knew that wasn't what Chanceville needed. Just when it looked like they were moving beyond all the bad stuff that happened it never failed, there was always someone else asking about what happened there.

Ratley said, "we don't talk about that much in this town, mister."

Right about that time, Stella placed two boxes in a large paper bag, and she handed them to the deputy telling him, "that'll be eight ninety-six." Ratley's friendly demeanor was no longer present as he dug in his wallet laying a ten dollar bill down on the counter. As Stella went to ring him up on the cash register, Ratley told her to keep the change. He turned back toward Hayden asking him, "where are you headed?"

Hayden resisted the urge to sarcastically say nowhere at the moment. Instead, he went with, "the next town, I suppose. Wherever the road takes me, that's where I go." Ratley became a little more at ease hearing he wasn't planning on staying long. He was on the verge of asking Hayden what his name was, but he thought - *what does it matter as long as he just moves on.* Taking a peek inside the bag the deputy told himself maybe he was making a big deal out of what was nothing. Hayden didn't say a word as the young deputy headed for the door, and exited the diner. When he got in his car, Hayden even raised his hand in the air holding it in place for a moment as one would do when bidding someone goodbye.

Stella walked over asking him if he needed anything else. Hayden thought for a second before he requested a hot cup of coffee, and a large piece of chocolate cake. It brought back sweet memories of a little diner he visited down south that was no longer in business. That was, of course, due in large part to Hayden himself. As Stella removed some of the dishes from his table, Ratley pulled out of the parking lot heading back toward the sheriff's office. Hayden watched the taillights on the deputy's car as he drove away.

Stella looked out the window to see what had Hayden's interest. That's when she said, "oh, don't mind him. He's harmless." Hayden voiced his thought at that moment saying, "I didn't mean to upset him. I was just trying to recall the name of that guy. You ever get something like that stuck in your head? You know, like a question you have to know the answer to, or you just never get any peace until you do."

Stella replied, "oh yeah. I think everyone has at some time or another. He didn't mean anything by it though, but that guy you were talking about, I don't even know his name, and I hear everything that goes on in this little town believe me, most of it right here in this diner." Hayden believed it. That's why he stumbled in there, that, and Vincent's stomach was beginning to growl a little.

When she brought Hayden the piece of cake he ordered, he finally asked, "did they ever discover the identity of the guy that committed the murders?" Stella's eyes lit up a little. That, she did know the answer to, and she didn't mind sharing that juicy little piece of information with him seeing as Deputy Ratley was no longer around to keep a lid on things.

She lowered her voice a little as she said, "yes, everybody around here is familiar with that name. The way I first heard it was through Patricia Horvath. Her son Bruce, well he saw the whole thing you see, and while he's not the brightest bulb in the bunch, he told her the guy's name was Hayden

Keller. At first I thought it was some kind of sick joke or something. I mean, can you imagine a better name than that for a serial killer, come on."

Hearing that, Hayden twisted his head slightly as he confessed, "no, I can not."

Now the whole damn town knew his name. There were few times in history where Hayden had allowed his name to surface to anyone other than those he was about to take under. He guarded his identity until just the right moment, and then he proudly enlightened them to who was stealing the precious gift God had bestowed on them. That was his favorite part. One of the gentlemen seated one row back started talking to the other man seated across from him about the whole incident. He obviously overheard Stella's vocal whisper. That opened up a course of conversation which happened to be a hell of a lot more interesting than what the weather was supposed to be like the next few days. Just about that time, a man outside the diner held the door open for several women before following them inside. They were chatty long before they entered the restaurant. The gentleman that ushered them in took a seat at the counter. The women chose a table close to the window which happened to be near Hayden. He just looked over at them babbling like blooming idiots, and he questioned in his mind if any of them heard what the others were saying. Listening to them was enough to give Hayden a headache, but it didn't take them long to pick up on the current topic of conversation.

Hayden looked back out the window as he listened while finishing what was left of his coffee. He couldn't help but think *for a town that doesn't talk about that whole incident, these people obviously didn't get the message*. Fragments of various conversations could be heard as Hayden sat there partaking of the dessert. Overhearing someone mention how terrible it was what happened to the Ferris,' Hayden got a warm feeling inside, it wasn't from the coffee Stella had brought him to help him wash down his cake. Hayden found moments like that priceless. There was a little talk of what was found at the crime scene, but not much of it accurate according to Hayden's recollection. He found it amusing how people could get it so wrong, but who was he to straighten them out. He was nobody just passing through town. The only thing that did peak his interest were the pieces of conversation he heard concerning the gas station where his chard remains were discovered.

One of the women said, "well, if you ask me I say he deserved a whole lot worse after what he did to the Ferris,' and that girl's family." One of the women agreed with her, and the other had a hard time imagining a more painful way to die than being burned alive. Hayden knew of ways, countless in number, and it was all he could do to contain his temper. Nevertheless, he kept his vengeance in check long enough to hear someone say, "I'm not sure where that girl is now, but I heard the only living relative she had was her grandmother who lived in Peoria. Inez, Ilene somebody."

Hayden got up to pay the check when he heard one of the women seated near him say, "what kind of animal could kill that girl's entire family. I couldn't begin to even imagine."

He stood there looking down at the table with a serious look on his face. Slowly, he turned facing the women, and the scar he had on his face startled them to the point that they stopped speaking. Hayden sternly said, "I'll tell you ladies, he's one you don't want to mess with."

One of the women seated with her back toward Hayden said, "well, he's dead now. Sheriff Baker, and his boys saw to that."

Hayden left them with food for thought as he reached down snatching a piece chicken off her plate. Devouring it in one bite he remarked, "or so they'd have you think." Silence fell over the diner as he handed Stella the check along with the money to cover the ticket. Just as Ratley had done, he said, "keep the change," and he turned to walk out the door. Everyone inside the diner eventually returned to their topic of conversation with the exception of the three women Hayden addressed before walking outside to get into his hot pickup truck.

One of the women mentioned the scar which crested Hayden's left cheek when she asked, "did you see that guy's face?" Repulsed by it as well, the one seated next to her replied, "how could you miss it?" That's when they agreed to talk about something else altogether as Hayden hit the road headed for Peoria. With his destination charted, that's where the road would soon take him. He only planned on making one more stop before leaving town, and that was to have a face to face interview with Bruce Horvath, the store clerk at the Marathon station where it all went down.

Singer and Ratley were having lunch at their desks unaware the killer had returned to Chanceville. Singer's only concern at that moment was why Ratley always seemed to get larger helpings than him as he said, "it never fails. You always end up with more food than me even when we order the same thing. I don't get it. Look at all that gravy they gave you."

Ratley just smirked saying, "yeah. I'm just lucky, I suppose."

The sheriff called Singer on the radio as he watched Ratley stuff his face full of food. None of them had any idea their luck was about to run cold.

Chapter 24

Tracking Down A Serial Killer

Several hours into their attempt at finding a matching name using police reports, and intermittent breaks in the timeline as their guide, no matches were made. That seemed odd given all the background work Buttweiler had put forth to get to this point, but he told himself to just be patient. He then reminded himself of what Callahan said just days earlier. He made it clear to Buttweiler that this whole thing was going to be grueling, and tedious, but if he stuck with it they would identify the killer. Those certainly weren't the most encouraging words Callahan could have delivered, but it was the truth.

It was now lunchtime, and still no sign of the detective. That was unusual. Even on days when his caseload required him to be out in the field the better part of the day, he always managed to check in on them about midday to see if he could offer any assistance, or at least get an update on how the investigation was going.

Henley read off another name on a police report. The tone in his voice changed a little as he spoke the name out loud. That name was Hayden Keller, obviously. Buttweiler even had time to look up from his notepad to see the expression on Henley's face as he read the name out loud. When that name slowly rolled off Henley's lips, Buttweiler could tell he was puzzled by it. The name was one Henley had stumbled over some time back while reading through one of the archived files on his lunch break. That was how Henley passed the time in the records room. He randomly read through everything in the place whenever he wasn't busy. Archives was like his own personal library in many ways. Henley couldn't place quite where he had encountered it before as Buttweiler asked, "what is it?"

Henley just paused looking at the name, and he shook his head rather slowly as he thought. This was the first he had seen of it on any police reports which were sent to him from other parts of the country. He couldn't piece it together at that moment, but the first time Henley ever ran across that name was in a case file created almost thirty-two years prior. It now sat in the back of the room in a box along with hundreds of others. Henley admitted it sounded vaguely familiar for some reason as he said, "I don't know. Something about that name, seems like I read it somewhere before."

Buttweiler became hopeful that this was the name of the guy they were looking for, thinking they would soon match it with a name found on another arrest report, if it wasn't already on his list. Buttweiler began flipping through pages in his notepad. He scanned over the names that he had compiled on his computer which made up a fairly extensive list at that point. He clearly had hopes of finding it somewhere on one of the pages, but Henley was sure he hadn't spoken that name out loud more than once. If he had he would've certainly remembered it. That name was very distinct, and something about that stuck with him even though he continued reading names off other police reports.

When it came time to take a break, Henley eagerly asked Buttweiler if he wanted to check to see if Callahan was back at his desk. The up and coming investigator was still paging through the list of names he had compiled somewhat perplexed that they hadn't run across a match yet.

He dismissively replied, "no, he's not there."

Henley asked, "how can you be sure?"

That's when Buttweiler explained, "if he was back, he'd be here." Then Buttweiler mumbled, "I just wish we had the name of the killer we could share with him." Looking over in Henley's direction, Buttweiler finally offered, "if you want to check, and see if he's at his desk you're welcome to, I'll wait here."

Henley never left the Archives Department unless he stepped out to use the restroom or get a drink of water. Even then, he was only a stone's throw from it, and he would always lock the door behind him if he was ever out of eyeshot. This was his chance, for once he could do it. With Buttweiler there minding the place, he wasn't about to miss the opportunity to go upstairs, and rub elbows with the big boys as he often referred to them in conversations he had with those not a part of the police force. Henley got up from his chair saying, "well, he said he was interested in what you discovered. So, I'm going up there if you got things under control here."

Buttweiler found that somewhat amusing even under the current circumstances. He raised his head with a blank expression on his face for the most part. Just to have some fun with Henley he said, "I'll try, but God help somebody if they come down here looking for something, cause I wouldn't know where to tell them to start. Both he, and Henley looked at the files that seemed to cover the three large tables inside the records room. It looked like total chaos. To most, it would appear the room was in disarray, but Henley still knew where everything was even under present conditions.

Locking eyes with Henley, Buttweiler remained seated at his post never flinching a muscle, and that's when Henley smiled big as he said, "yeah, God help them, alright. I'll be back, don't worry." With that Henley took off upstairs, and Buttweiler started to laugh his ass off. It was the comical break he needed at that moment, but reality was sobering as he looked back at the growing list of names he had in his hand. Now, he felt he was no closer to uncovering the killer's identity than when he started. He knew nothing of Sister Lee, and the hold she had on Henley's subconscious.

The psychic palm reader was in a deep meditative state. She was unable to communicate with Henley while Hayden was still in close proximity. While he combed Chanceville for answers to who actually killed him, she had to focus all of her attention on the townspeople which encountered the evil one. She could not allow another massacre to take place within Jefferson County, and she had to make certain he didn't discover Ben's identity. Erasing Ben Goodman's name from Bruce Horvath's memory was critical at that point as she channeled all of her energy clouding the details of that event in Bruce's mind forever. She had seen the evil yet to come. She knew Hayden would kill again, and who his next victim would be. There was nothing she could do at that point to prevent it.

Hayden had already found Bruce Horvath standing outside the Marathon station where he burned to death nearly a year earlier. Bruce was taking a smoke break since the store was empty, and Hayden took that opportunity to ask him a question or two. She knew that conversation would not end well for Bruce. The only thing she could ensure was Ben's whereabouts, and name would remain a mystery to Hayden, thereby concealing her from him as well. Bruce's death would serve as proof Hayden Keller was back. Without it, her claims would never be taken seriously, with it the sheriff of Jefferson County would soon come to believe in her gift of sight. Moreover, he would recognize he needed her in order to track Hayden down.

Chapter 25

Tell Me What You Know

As Sister Lee focused on stalling Hayden Keller through the spiritual realm, Henley's focus was on finding Callahan. That wouldn't be easy though. He was right in the middle of interrogating a suspect as he slammed a folder down on the table in front of him. Detective Willis stood near the door of the room with his arms folded staring at the tattooed gang member as Callahan tried to get him to talk by stating, "we know it was you Julio. So, why don't you just save us both the trouble." He stared into his eyes when he added, "there's nothing to be afraid of, just admit you stole the car."

The young gang-banger on the other side of the table sat there with ill contempt, and it was present in his voice as he replied to Callahan's accusation saying, "I don't know what you're talking about, and my name ain't Julio. It's Jose."

Callahan shrugged off what he said cause it in no way sounded like a confession. "That's funny, cause you look like a Julio to me, and I know scared when I see it. That's you Julio." The old detective knew how to push buttons. The young punk turned his head away breaking eye contact with him. All he said was, "I don't fear you. I don't fear nothing!"

That's when Callahan replied, "I guess that's why you joined a gang. Huh?" Jose scoffed at his words. He let out a heavy breath of air through his widening nostrils as the muscles in his face tightened. His fuse was growing shorter by the second as he listened to Callahan say, "you weren't tough enough to stand on your own, but that gang isn't going to protect your ass now Paco." The young street thug became incensed hearing Callahan's condescending words.

He raised his voice in anger shouting, "my name is Jose mother fucker, and don't you forget it!" He locked eyes with Callahan, and all the detective saw in them was hatred. He knew it was there masking the young man's fear, but there was no denying the seasoned gang member on the other side of the table sat there despising everything Callahan represented.

Detective Willis continued observing the suspect trying hard to restrain himself from jumping down his throat as Callahan said, "looks like we have something in common Josie." Obviously, the irate remarks the inked-up punk made had no effect whatsoever on Callahan. The detective was simply focused on getting the information he needed when he said, "you don't like me or anything I stand for. That's okay, cause I sure as hell don't like you, but none of that matters. You see, you're going away for a long time. Hell, you'll be lucky to see the light of day outside a prison when you're as old as me. Your whole life is about to go bye-bye if you don't start talking, and you think it's tough on the streets, wait until you're in the joint."

Even though Jose tried to act aloof, Callahan had his complete attention when he said, "somebody's going to have to pay for shooting the clerk in that convenience store." Callahan lifted his hands up off the table making the point, "it might as well be you Eladio."

Jose was thoroughly disgusted. Sitting back in his chair, he threw his cuffed hands up before slamming them down hard on the table yelling, "what is it with you? I told you my name, and you still don't know who I am. How the hell are you going to put me away for something I didn't do?"

Callahan revealed a pirates smile using one side of his mouth. He informed Jose he had everything he needed to make his case. His words to him were, "you better get used to answering to a lot of names cause they're going to have plenty of them for you in lockup. Isn't that right detective?"

Willis now had the opportunity to press Jose's buttons as he said, "yeah, I think he looks more like a Francis. You better get used to that one for sure, cause all the boys will be calling you that in the shower room."

Jose came unglued as he yelled, "fuck you, mother fucker. You don't know who you're talking to."

Willis started to move toward Jose as he shouted, "are you trying to say you're somebody?!"

Callahan held up his hand to keep Willis from coming any closer to the suspect. He informed Jose, "I know exactly who you are, or you wouldn't be here. Your name, it means nothing to me until you help us catch the guy who did this. I happen to believe someone else shot Jeremy Layton in that store. I think you just boosted the car, but until you give me a name, everything points to you."

Jose was adamant when it came to keeping his mouth shut. All he said was, "I ain't telling you shit." That actually told Callahan a great deal. He knew the tension between Jose, and Detective Willis had become a barrier to him getting the information he was after. He also knew Jose feared the shooter more than he feared police. It was clear he wasn't ready to talk.

Callahan suggested Willis grab them something to eat as he said, "why don't you leave me, and Mr. Guerra here to hash this out in private? I'm sure we can get to the bottom of this in several hours." He turned toward Willis saying, "if we haven't made some headway by then, I'll let you continue the interview." That was intended for Jose to hear, just so he understood this wasn't something that was going to end quickly without him talking. What Willis understood it to mean was leave me alone with the suspect, and make sure no one disturbs me while I'm conducting the interview, even if it takes hours before I step foot out that door.

Callahan turned his attention back to Jose saying, "I want the name of your partner, and I want it now." Willis placed his hand on the doorknob as he stood there a second observing Jose's militant demeanor. Jose jerked his head rather aggressively as he pushed himself away from the folder resting on the table. That's when Callahan threw out, "twenty-five to life, that's what you're looking at if you don't come clean with me." Jose wasn't buying that though. He figured it was all a bluff, and whatever Callahan had, he could never make it stick, at least that's what he hoped as he sat there motionless.

Outside the interrogation room it was another typical day inside the IMPD. There was lots of noise, and the entire third floor had a unique aroma all its own. It was a subtle blend of disinfecting cleaner, cheap aftershave, and copy toner, mostly. Phones seemed to ring continually, and they were only muffled by the voices of the officers fielding the calls. The third floor was a busy place. It didn't resemble the records room at all. Henley could feel the tension in the room just looking around at the faces of the officers as they moved about talking to one another. Several of them were working at their desks doing a variety of things he knew little about from researching phone records to verifying the whereabouts of witnesses, and suspects. If they weren't busy examining evidence, they were filling out reports. There was plenty of energy in the room, a welcome change of pace for Henley no doubt. It was obvious he was out of his element, that's why one of the officers asked if he knew who he was looking for. When Henley said, "Detective Callahan," the officer just raised his hand pointing toward his desk on the right side of the room. Henley grinned thanking him as he meandered off in that direction taking in the sights as he passed the interrogation rooms.

Eventually, he saw the nameplate marking Callahan's desk, but before he could reach it, he was cut off by Detective Willis hastily leaving one of the nearby rooms. Carrying a stern expression on his face, he wasn't nearly as friendly as the other guy Henley bumped into. Failing to acknowledge his presence, he just kept walking shaking his head as he said, "that guy sure as hell ain't talking." He sounded rather pissed as he directed his comment toward Detective Murphy who happened to be on the phone.

Henley noticed Callahan's desk was right beside his, and he figured if anyone knew where he was it would probably be that guy. He stood there waiting patiently looking around trying to spot him, but there was a sea of officers moving about the floor. He figured it would just be a matter of time before Murphy got off the phone, but he continued listening to someone on the other end of the line with an exasperated look plastered on his face occasionally, taking notes.

Henley cleared his throat as Murphy spoke into the phone saying, "yeah, I understand, but this guy has gang ties." Murphy continued listening to the voice on the other end of the line as he covered the lower portion of the receiver with his hand. He was now looking at Henley, and all he said was, "yeah. What is it?" Henley cut his eyes toward Callahan's desk, and then he looked back at Murphy asking where Callahan was. Annoyed by the interruption, and the captain's voice in his ear, Murphy uncovered the phone, and pointed toward one of the interrogation rooms. Henley turned looking in that direction, and he looked back at Murphy raising his hand a little trying to thank him, but the detective was now getting an ear-full through the phone. His attention was no longer on Henley as he marched off toward the door Murphy pointed to.

Just about the time Henley reached the door, Detective Willis looked up noticing he was about to walk right into the room where Callahan was conducting a heated interview. Willis stood up from his chair asking, "who the hell is that?" Murphy looked up not believing what he was seeing as he yelled out, "hey, you can't go in there!" It was too late though. Henley already had his head in the door. He didn't hear a word Murphy said. It was hard to hear anything over Callahan's voice, and the profanity spewing out of the guy's mouth which he was grilling. For a moment, Henley wondered what the hell he had walked into.

Jose shouted, "you don't fucking scare me." He sounded just like Tony Montana right out of Scarface.

Henley's eyes opened a little wider as Callahan said, "it's not my job to scare you, but you better deal with me Jose, cause you don't want to deal with my partner there. He doesn't make deals with guys like you."

Callahan had no idea it was Henley that entered the room. He just knew he never liked being disturbed when he was questioning a suspect, and this guy was bad news. Callahan glanced over his shoulder at Henley as he told Jose once again, "I want a name, and you're going to give it to me."

Henley stood there in the doorway, looking at the gang tattoos covering both arms of the guy wearing the handcuffs, and he didn't look happy to be sitting in that chair. Henley was more than a little intimidated by him, but he just stood there almost frozen as he tried not to show it. Callahan was obviously surprised to see him there, but he figured he would use him to scare the hell out of Jose, hopefully to the point of making him come off the name of his accomplice. That's when Callahan said, "Henley, go ahead close the door. Why don't you tell Jose here what my

138

conviction rate is for those pleading not guilty on murder charges in the past eight years."

Henley knew that off the top of his head as he confidently blurted out, "ninety-two point eight percent."

Callahan smiled at him, and he looked directly at Jose saying, "those aren't good odds for you Jose." Never taking his eyes off his suspect he said, "now tell him the average sentence handed down for those convicted."

Henley's eyes moved upward as he thought for just a second. He promptly said, "the average is twenty-five years to life without parole, but I've seen a lot of cases where they got the death penalty."

Callahan just shook his head slowly with a serious look on his face. He couldn't have planned this any better. He told Jose to think about that for a second, and he turned walking over to Henley placing his hand on his shoulder. Callahan quietly asked him, "what brought you in here?" When the king of record archives started to apologize for interrupting, Callahan said, "that's okay. What do you got?"

At that moment, it started to come together for Henley. Maybe it was that scar Al Pacino wore on his face in that movie that Jose's voice reminded him of. Sister Lee was no longer in a trance. She was now tapping into Henley's thoughts. The name that was so familiar to him, the one he read on that police report, he now realized where he first saw it. His face lit up as he said, "I think we know the name of the killer."

Suddenly, Callahan became extremely eager to get down to the records room. Jose was looking like a small fish, and his ass was already caught. He told Henley to hang on a second. The detective turned back to Jose telling him any deal he hoped to have with the prosecutor was off the table as soon as he left the room. Callahan added, "stealing a car is one thing, killing somebody - that's a whole other story, and if you don't talk - we can't help you."

All Jose could think about was the death penalty for jacking a damn SUV. He broke his code of silence as he shouted, "I didn't kill that dude man. I wasn't even there."

Callahan just looked at him. He turned walking toward the door saying, "a name Jose, give it to me."

Suddenly, Jose couldn't seem to keep his mouth shut. He passionately confessed, "Hector and Carlos pulled that job. I just got them the wheels. That's it, I swear."

Callahan nodded his head telling him he did the right thing. Then he said "I guess, I can count on you to give your statement to the detective that was in here earlier, in exchange for me putting in a word with the DA on your behalf." Jose nodded his head with a defeated look on his face. All he requested is that he not be sentenced to the same prison where Carlos and Hector were to serve out their time. Callahan confidently said, "I'm pretty sure we can arrange that," as he, and Henley exited the interrogation room.

Willis and Murphy along with several other officers looked up from what they were doing seeing Callahan follow Henley out of the room. They were all expecting to see some fireworks, but when Callahan threw his hand on Henley's shoulder he said, "Willis, forget about grabbing something to eat. Why don't you get in there, and take Jose's statement. I want to see the entire transcript when you're done. I believe he's ready to talk now, thanks to Henley here."

Murphy turned his head grinning a little at some of the other officers as one of them boisterously said, "well, alright." A round of applause slowly engulfed the room in Henley's honor as he, and Callahan departed for the records room. Henley hardly knew what spurred the appreciation. He simply thought he could get used to rubbing elbows with the big boys up on the third floor, especially if he was treated like a celebrity.

Chapter 26

Man On Fire

Hayden was in search of information himself, and there was nothing he wouldn't do to extract it from Bruce Horvath. He needed another life to pay the devil his due, but in Bruce's case he also needed to know what he knew prior to sending him on his merry way.

It was late in the day as Hayden Keller ventured out of town destined for Peoria. He had Bruce handcuffed in the seat next to him as he drove down Highway 80. Bruce could remember seeing the burning man moving toward the gas pumps as he searched for the fire extinguisher inside the store. He would never forget the severed arm which fell out of the back of the Tahoe when Ratley, and Singer opened the door. Beyond that, and the name Hayden Keller, the rest was all a blur for the most part. He did remember details about the beamer Ben drove. When pressed for answers, Bruce described Ben's BMW in vivid detail as he said, "I think it had a Delaware plate, and it read "GOODMAN." Hayden's spine tingled just hearing it. In his sick mind, he questioned if he had ever met him before.

Sister Lee knew he'd gained a useful piece of information which put him one step closer to finding Ben. Bruce had said too much. She was left with no choice but to leave Bruce with virtually no recollection of what happened the night Ashley Pennington was found at the gas station. She turned her attention to a chart which held the secrets of the constellations. The moon was now in its waning cycle, and with its diminishing power it brought with it a decrease in

Sister Lee's mystical abilities.

Hayden drove down the highway with Bruce Horvath bound inside the pickup. Hayden forewarned him saying, "I'm only going to ask you one more time. Are you sure you don't know the name of the guy at that gas station the night that girl was found?" Bruce was petrified as he shook his head no.

He could barely speak as he said, "I don't know, really. I swear."

Hayden grinned as he casually said, "I believe you, Bruce. It must have been something to see that guy on fire there next to those gas pumps. You don't see that every day I imagine." Bruce shook his head no, wondering what the hell Hayden was going to do with him next.

Hayden calmly pulled over to the side of the road saying, "I guess I'll let you out here if that's alright with you." Bruce was certainly ready to part company with him. He actually believed Hayden was going to simply let him out there in the middle of nowhere. He was halfway between the town he hated more than any other, and Justice. The spot even looked familiar to the serial killer from hell. As he exited the cab of the pickup to let Bruce out, he pulled a gas can out of the bed of the truck.

Walking around the rear of the vehicle, he never took his eyes off the prize even though he couldn't see Bruce through the thick tinted glass of the rear window. Bruce could see Hayden though as he approached the passenger door. When Hayden lifted the handle to open the door, he held the gas can where Bruce couldn't see it. Taking one hand, he grabbed Bruce's shirt near his shoulder, and he pulled him out of the passenger seat. Now, all of a sudden, exiting the vehicle didn't seem so appealing to Bruce. All

Hayden said was, "well, you're free to go. If you walk, you might make it back to town before sundown, but you should probably run."

Hayden slammed the door to the truck shut as he raised the gas can pouring the flammable fuel all over Bruce's body. He tried to move to avoid being dowsed with gasoline, but in hindsight that merely helped Hayden. Bruce looked up in horror, his eyes were opened wide until the gas hit them. He clinched them shut as he yelled out in pain. His eyes stung like hell as if they had been swarmed by bees. He couldn't see shit at that point. Fearing the worst, he took Hayden's advice, and started to run with his hands still cuffed behind his back. He, of course, stumbled, and fell within thirty feet from the truck, and Hayden took that opportunity to help him to his feet. Pulling the key from his pocket, Hayden retrieved Danford's handcuffs before setting Bruce on fire with his own lighter.

Hayden watched him as he ran down the road screaming, "oh God, fuck man." Before he could say anything else, the flames had overtaken him. Hayden turned his head as he looked at him, flailing his arms over his chest, and shoulders in an effort to keep the flames away from his face. Within seconds, Bruce was consumed by the fire as he staggered over the pavement. Hayden watched him fall to the ground before walking back to get in the truck. Before climbing in he couldn't help looking back over his shoulder at what was left of Bruce. Thanks to him, he now had something to go on to help him answer the burning question which plagued him ever since enduring his last stint in hell, and the man on fire had seconds to live. Hayden appreciated the irony in that when he climbed back into what was no longer Ronnie's truck.

Taking in the view of Bruce burning there in the road, Hayden began counting backwards starting with the number six. The flames covering his body flickered as the wind caught them, and Hayden's lip curled a little as he cranked his pickup. Shifting it in gear, he was off to grandma's house. "Who's afraid of the big bad wolf?" That's what he grumbled looking in the side view mirror as he pulled back onto the road. Locking that image away in his mind of his victim lying motionless, he glanced down at Bruce's wallet tossing it into the center compartment next to his seat.

The road to Peoria was long, but Hayden deemed it a trip worth making. He had a man with two lives to kill, and he couldn't wait to get his hands on Ashley. Scanning for something worth listening to on the ride, he fiddled with the radio. Turning up the volume he soaked in the lyrics to "Hotel California." Hayden felt alive listening to the Eagles sing, "they stab it with their steely knives, but they just can't kill the beast." He even sang along to the final lyric of the song, but he grew silent after uttering the words, "you can check-out any time you like, but you can never leave." It reminded him his time on earth was borrowed, and one day he would return to hell no matter who, or, how many he killed. His attention became focused on finding Ashley, and Ben at that point to make certain they got there long before him. Misery does tend to love company, and Hayden knew firsthand hell had plenty to go around for everyone. He was simply the soul collector. Hayden had been the man on fire more times than he could count. Now, it was Bruce's turn to experience the heat for himself. Hayden held out a worse fate for Ben. He couldn't wait to deliver it to him personally. For now, he found it fitting to leave something in Jefferson County for folks to remember him by. He could picture Ratley's face when he found that little surprise. Hayden looked at it as his personal calling card.

Chapter 27

The Missing Piece

Sister Lee had enlightened Henley to a point. The rest was up to him to discover on his own, but Henley was smart enough to piece it all together. As he, and Callahan walked downstairs to the Archives Department, Henley explained about the name he had read off of one of the police reports. He told Callahan they had yet to match it, but that's when he said, "I knew when I read it, I had seen it somewhere before." He looked up at the detective adding, "at first, I couldn't figure out where I encountered it, but it hit me when I was talking to you upstairs. I came across that name while reading over one of the old files in the records room."

Henley was excited, Callahan could tell by the tone of his voice. He believed him when he said, "Hayden Keller is the guy we're after. I just know it. It may take me a while to find that file, but I'll do it partner." As they walked into the records room, Henley assured the detective he could count on him. Buttweiler was trying to narrow down the next place to search for records when he overheard their voices. It caused him to look up from the map he was studying. He was somewhat surprised to see Callahan, but glad nonetheless. Finally, he could show him what he had uncovered. Before he uttered a word though, Henley said, "you were right, Hayden Keller is our guy." That aside, Henley was certain they had identified their serial killer. All his extracurricular reading had paid off.

Callahan allowed Henley his moment in the sun. He listened to him inform Buttweiler he had come across

Hayden Keller's name once before. Looking around the records room, Henley then said, "now, all I have to do is find that file."

Callahan looked at Buttweiler saying, "it sounds like you fellows have been doing some work." He knew they had been going at it for nearly a week without much rest, and they finally had something to show for it. He eagerly asked Buttweiler about his discovery, and he looked over the old calendars with him that were used to record the killings. He was damned impressed when he slapped his young partner on the back telling him, "that's first class police work."

Buttweiler's response was, "yeah, well maybe I'll make the grade next time I try for detective."

Callahan earnestly replied, "don't sell yourself short. Only a real detective could uncover what you did. I don't care what your badge says."

Buttweiler was seldom handed a compliment, but that one was well earned. He confessed he hadn't figured out why the guy never killed on Saturday. "It's weird. I can't make sense of it," he said. Looking at the calendars, and back up at Callahan, he continued with, "I was hoping you could help me figure it out, but this guy will be back this way again soon, that I do know."

Callahan asked where the record came from that had Hayden Keller's name on it. Henley pulled it back up saying, "Winnebago County, it looks like. That's Rockford, Illinois." Callahan looked down at the map pinpointing the location.

Buttweiler stated, "it looks like at that point he was headed toward Madison, but he didn't make it there." Pointing to another spot on the map, he said, "here is where I lost track of him. It's like he just up, and disappears at times, but I always find another string of murders in another area that matches our guy's MO. What do you think, is it Hayden

Keller?"

Henley printed off the report, and handed it to Callahan. Buttweiler observed the expression on his face as he read over the report. Callahan started to nod his head a little. He said, "they picked him up in a stolen vehicle. I wouldn't be surprised if he is our guy. Why don't you see if the body of the vehicle owner was ever discovered." Buttweiler realized the killer dumped bodies all over the country. If Hayden Keller did kill the owner of the Jeep Grand Cherokee he was found in, there was no telling where the body may have been uncovered, but it was start.

Even though the detectives had their reservations at that point, Henley was sure. That report was over five years old though. Callahan addressed Buttweiler when he asked, "have you worked both ends of the timeline?"
"Yeah, see." That's when he handed Callahan a list of places and corresponding dates, showing where, and when he had lost track of the killer. They spanned a period of seven years, and the most recent date on the list was eleven months earlier.
The place was Chanceville, and Callahan looked at it asking, "where on earth is this place?" Buttweiler pointed to a small dot on the map. Neither he, nor, Callahan had ever heard of it. Callahan found it odd that Buttweiler lost the trail there. It was a small town, too small for Hayden Keller to get lost in the shuffle. He was actively killing right up until that time. Callahan was thoroughly familiar with all of the other places on the list. They were all notable cities of some size much like Indianapolis.

Cities with populations in excess of two hundred and fifty thousand tended to have their share of murders. The greater that number, the harder it was to weed through all the killings to find Hayden. Still, the question Callahan had at that point was why the break in the pattern for such an extended period of time. He didn't believe for a second he just up, and stopped on his own accord. Callahan knew he could never stop killing, not unless someone stopped him. That's what went through his mind as he stared down at the map. Looking at the town of Chanceville, he said, "this guy killed religiously according to this schedule. Six kills each, and every week without fail, and he always refrained from taking the seventh victim on Saturday. Why is that?" Both he, and Buttweiler were somewhat confused by Hayden's unusual behavior, but he was a serial killer, little had to make sense as to why he committed the murders. It was a compulsion regardless of the pattern, but the pattern held a secret clue as to who was behind the vicious murders, the detective understood that. He focused on the number of kills when he asked, "what's the significance of the number six for this guy?"

Henley listened as Buttweiler said, "I don't really know."

He scrolled over several pages on his computer looking at the column of the weekly kill totals. Six filled that space without fail for what seemed like week after week with no end. The tally of six murders a week went unbroken, regardless of where the kills took place. The victims were random, but the pattern remained constant, and that one numeric value representing the number of murders ran the length on the page. Callahan verified the count was correct randomly checking at various intervals. Underscoring that number, he knew of no significance six held. Seven on the other hand seemed to be considered lucky by most people. He was looking at the invisible number in the equation. The question which entered his mind was why no seventh victim on the seventh day. Callahan had taught him to look for what couldn't be found using only the eye. Buttweiler said, "perhaps seven holds the key not six. Maybe seven holds some kind of sacred meaning for him, and that's why he doesn't kill a seventh victim on the seventh day." Callahan could certainly appreciate that train of thought. He started to buy into that notion as he continued looking at Buttweiler's computer screen. He pulled out a small notepad he kept inside his coat pocket, and he briefly made some notes.

Henley felt compelled to share his knowledge regarding the number seven as he said, "you know the number seven is considered to be the perfect number in the bible. In fact, it's used there seven hundred times, and while many people believe it symbolizes good luck, mathematically it's the largest single digit prime number."

Callahan interrupted Henley telling him to hold that thought. Something registered with him as he asked Buttweiler to take a look at his notepad. Seven was a sacred number. Six, six, six was another biblical number, and Callahan recognized it as he underlined the number six, two more times. Things look different on paper don't they?" Buttweiler nodded his head in agreement.

The killer continually spelled out that number, week after week, without fail with the body count of his victims. They didn't share their discovery with Henley, but they could easily see the significance of the pattern. There was no denying the murders were beastly in nature, and when looking at the number six in that light, it appeared they may be dealing with someone promoting Satan through killing random innocent people. The practice of satanic worship wasn't uncommon when it came to serial killers, but they needed more than that to go on.

When Buttweiler asked, "what are you thinking?"
Callahan just shook his head as if it were nothing. He

admitted, I'd be interested in finding out if anything took place in Chanceville that offers up an explanation as to why the trail seemed to stay cold for so long." Callahan looked at all the information Buttweiler had compiled seeing a considerable number of murders committed in Des Moines, IA. Following the trail of dead bodies out of town, it did appear the trail ended somewhere near Rockford. The detective told Buttweiler he wanted him, and Henley to concentrate specifically on the name Hayden Keller. "I want you to find everything you can on him, and I'm going to contact someone in Des Moines about these unsolved murders." Buttweiler assured him they would do it. He was just glad they had a name to go on though. Callahan then said, "if you get a hit on him anywhere within a hundred miles of Chanceville let me know."

Chapter 28

Following A Lead

Callahan placed a lot of trust in Henley's memory. In the short time he'd known him, he had never been wrong when it came to instant recall. "You must be hell playing Trivial Pursuit." That's what Callahan casually muttered when Henley mentioned some of the details contained inside the case folder where he first found Hayden's name almost nine months ago. The good news was those details seemed to match their killer's M.O. Henley just had to determine where that folder was now. They had already delved as far back as ten years, but Henley was willing to bet the folder was twice that old.

Callahan needed to know for certain if Hayden Keller was indeed the man they were after. He stressed that to his partner before informing him he had to get back upstairs to handle something urgent. He had plans to pull a set of prints on their newest suspect when he told Buttweiler, "let me know if you two need help with something." He made a few quick notes jotting down the names of the victims, and the dates which the murders occurred. Callahan tore the page out of his notepad, and he stuffed it in his coat pocket as he told Buttweiler to stick with it. Promising to get back with them as soon as possible, with a serious tone in his gravelly voice, Callahan turned to exit the records room saying, "well done, keep him straight, Henley."

They were now more motivated to hunt down the man they believed was responsible for the heinous murders than ever before. Henley started looking through old cases from more than twenty-five years prior, and Buttweiler walked over to Henley's desk to use his computer. While Henley searched through countless boxes of files, Buttweiler searched for any records he could find on Hayden Keller using the internet. Typing in Hayden's name, and the town of Chanceville, he watched as the computer slowly did its thing. It took nearly a minute just to show one green bar at the bottom of the screen. Buttweiler looked over at Henley asking, "is this thing always this slow?"

Henley glanced over his shoulder as he continued rummaging through files saying, "yeah. Sometimes it can take a while. I filled out the 211B." Buttweiler just looked at him as Henley said, "you know the requisition form for a new computer." Buttweiler nodded his head as though he was thoroughly familiar with the form like he kept track of that kind of crap in his mind.

Henley's ability to remember massive amounts of stuff others could never manage to retain was amazing, but Buttweiler found him amusing most of the time as did Callahan, but that's what made the junior grade investigator buy into the fact Henley was right about the name of the killer. He didn't forget shit, Buttweiler knew that. Looking back at the screen, one more green bar was present as the computer continued searching for Hayden Keller.

The search for records seemed as though it would take forever. Buttweiler literally went mind-numb staring at the screen. Figuring he could make better use of his time, he got up from Henley's chair, and walked to the back of the room to see if he could help him. Buttweiler said, "it looks like you could use a hand. You want to tell me where to start?"

Henley directed him to a stack of shelves next to where he was standing. "You can start there. I know it's here somewhere," he said.

There was no concealing Henley's excitement as he opened another box in search of the file. It was as though he were a kid on an Easter egg hunt. Buttweiler perused the contents inside some of the folders. The cases were dated 1980. He looked at Henley in disbelief. He never imagined Henley meant old to be damn near thirty years, or more. He thought to himself, *this can't be right.* If this were the case, the guy they were looking for was drawing social security by now. That certainly wasn't factored into the profile. He pointed that out to Henley, but it didn't slow him down. Henley was adamant insisting, "the file is here, I know. It might be older than that." Buttweiler became a little disheartened as they continued searching. Combing through records, he began to lose faith in the fact that Henley was right about the name of their killer.

Henley moved to another shelf which contained files that were older than the ones Buttweiler had grumbled about examining. Henley wasn't deterred in the least, even though Buttweiler stood there motionless holding folders in his hands nearly as old as him. It was apparent based on the expression on his face, he'd become exasperated looking at plenty of paper without the name Hayden Keller printed anywhere on it. He looked back at the computer, figuring it might hold something of value on it by now, he hoped anyway. Sitting the box he was sifting through back on the shelf, Buttweiler said, "I'm going to leave it with you, and see if that search gives us anything." Henley never looked up. He just kept pulling one folder after another out of the box he was working through.

Buttweiler made his way back towards Henley's desk while Henley continued running his finger down the page of the file he was reading over. On the surface, it appeared promising. Buttweiler had barely made it halfway across the room when Henley enthusiastically announced, "this is the one." Buttweiler stopped where he stood as he turned around to face him. He couldn't believe it. He thought to himself, *if the file's that old what does that mean.* Maybe this wasn't the guy they were looking for at all. Maybe the name was simply a coincidence.

Henley read through the file as Buttweiler walked toward him. There were consistencies in that case that matched the killer's M.O. just like Henley had shared with Callahan. Buttweiler realized that right off the bat. Henley handed him the file when he asked to see it. Reading though the entire thing, he looked at Henley not knowing what to say exactly. The report showed Hayden Keller was believed to be the killer in a double murder investigation. Gerald Pruitt had given that name to police. He was the one who discovered the bodies in the park, and that was the name he claimed Roderick Gower gave him shortly before dying. Along with that name, Gerald relayed a description the victim had given him of the attacker. The description itself was a bit unusual in nature. There was no mention of height, weight or even skin tone. Gerald told police, "all he said was he had a huge scar on his left cheek, and crazy eyes." The other victim's name listed was Tamara Ward.

The violent deaths occurred one Friday evening decades ago. Gerald had discovered the bodies while walking his dog. Their IDs were missing, and robbery appeared to be the motive according to the report. Reading Mr. Pruitt's statement of what he found, Buttweiler could envision the last words Mr. Gower spoke in his final breath of life. The face of his assailant had made a serious lasting impression on him, and he obviously didn't live long enough to be treated by medical personnel. Pruitt was questioned in connection with the murders, but never arrested.

No one had ever been charged with the crime. Buttweiler didn't know what to make of it. No one had looked at that case in over twenty-five years except for Henley, of course. He was eager to get Buttweiler's take on it as he put the rest of the files he had waded through back in their proper place. Buttweiler desperately wanted Henley to be correct about the name they had given Callahan. The only thing that stood in his way of believing it was possible, was the timeline he had constructed thus far. He had trouble believing this guy had been at this for over thirty years. The sheer victim count alone would be staggering to even estimate. He pointed that out to Henley as he said, "the guy we're after kills six times each week. That's a lot of bodies to account for Henley. It's a lot of time too."

Henley couldn't argue with that, but things were fairly simple in his mind when it came to possibilities. Henley had been at the same job for almost thirty years, as Callahan had pointed out when they first met, and he saw no reason why the killer couldn't have been doing his thing that long. Henley made his case saying, "well, some of those files you were working from were seven years old. If he killed seven years ago, why not thirty."

Buttweiler replied, "cause that's thousands of bodies Henley." Henley lowered his head doing the math in his mind. Buttweiler stood there looking at him wondering if he was alright. He tilted his head lowering it some, and he could see the look of concentration occupying Henley's face.

Just as he was about to say something, Henley looked up with a stunned expression on his face. He promptly informed Buttweiler, "that's a little more than ten thousand actually." Henley was talking victims, he had even factored in an additional week to account for leap years. Ten thousand victims in thirty-two years was nearly impossible for either of them to imagine, but that's what the math worked out to be. Buttweiler certainly didn't question it. All he said was, "well, maybe we'll find something else on him. That was his subtle way of saying nice try, but this can't be the Hayden Keller we're looking for.

He handed the file back to Henley, and walked over to the computer to see what his search for Hayden Keller had revealed. Buttweiler jokingly remarked, "maybe this cutting edge computer of yours can tell us something we don't know."

Henley ambled along behind him reading through the file he had in his hand. He thought about the time that had elapsed, and he started to doubt himself. He looked up at Buttweiler who stood there staring down at the monitor on Henley's desk. His eyes were now open wide as he read over the information on the screen. Hayden Keller was believed to be the name of a man found burned to death in the town of Chanceville nearly a year ago. He immediately thought that would certainly explain why the trail went cold. Few details were given regarding his physical appearance since his body was virtually destroyed by fire.

Using the mouse, Buttweiler clicked on one of the other listings on the search page, and Henley couldn't refrain from asking, "did you get anything?"
Buttweiler said nothing as he read over that report. He then looked up at Henley with intent concern in his eyes. His expression was deathly serious as he nodded his head yes. The report he read described a man in his late thirties with a scar on his left cheek responsible for a string of killings in the Midwest along some of the most widely

traveled highways in the country. He clicked on something else as he said, "Henley, make sure you hang on to that folder."

Henley peered around the edge of the desk to get a look at the computer screen. Another article showed a picture of the man some identified as Hayden Keller. He had a scar on his left cheek just as was described in the other reports Buttweiler had read, but this man was nearly ten years older than the man in the previous report. What made it more disturbing was the article was printed in 1963, twenty-six years prior to the previous report, and eighteen years earlier than the case they had on file which Henley was holding in his hand. Those weren't the only hits they got on Hayden Keller. One record gave an account of a convicted murderer that had been hung for his crimes back in 1909. The man's name was, of course, Hayden Keller, and the scar was present there as well.

Buttweiler had a chill run up his spine as he read over another report that had Hayden's name all over it. Details of the murders were disclosed in the report, and the manhunt that ensued in an effort to catch him. Henley was amazed by how much information they had on the screen in front of them. He pointed to something else questioning, "what's that one say?"
Buttweiler was damn near afraid to open another one. This shit was getting too fucking weird for him. He turned the mouse over to Henley saying, "here, click on it, and print all that stuff off. Callahan needs to see this."

That last item mentioned Hayden Keller as a suspect in the killing of several college students at a campground in Scott County. It matched one of the breaks in Buttweiler's timeline, but the man that was ultimately tried, and convicted of the crimes was someone by the name of Curt Sevier. Buttweiler didn't know all the details regarding that case including the forensic evidence found at the crime scene, but he felt certain the wrong man stood trial for those murders. The way those college kids were tortured, and mutilated, there was no doubt in his mind it was the same guy he had been tracking for almost three weeks. Now, he had to reason how any of this was possible.

The name Hayden Keller seemed to be synonymous with brutal killings, and he had records to prove it dating back over a hundred years. Henley asked, "what's all this mean," as Buttweiler stood there asking himself the same thing. How in the hell was he supposed to piece all this together? Other than the scar on the killer's face, and the M.O. of the killer himself, nothing else fell into place.

He replied, "I don't know Henley. Maybe the guy we're after is a copycat killer. Maybe he's modeling himself after one of these men." Buttweiler didn't believe that, but it was the only logical explanation he could come up with at the moment.

Henley continued printing information off as Buttweiler tried his best to assimilate it. They now knew more about the killer than they did when they walked through the door that morning, but with that knowledge came many more questions.

Chapter 29

The Invisible Killer

Callahan's thoughts remained trained on catching the invisible serial killer as he read over Jose's statement which Detective Willis had just taken. He had found it sitting on his desk when he returned from downstairs. It contained everything necessary to get arrest warrants issued for both Hector Herrera, and Carlos Garza.

Jose was no longer in the interrogation room, Willis had taken him back down to holding. Callahan figured he would assist him by verifying some of the information concerning Carlos, and Hector's whereabouts. After doing that, he made the call to have the warrants issued. The whole time he couldn't help but wonder if Henley, and Buttweiler had uncovered something worth finding.

Placing the statement, and the locate verification on Willis's desk, the only thing left to do was haul their asses in, and write up the reports. Invariably, they would share in those duties, but Callahan couldn't wait to put them in the hot seat, and bring about some justice for the wounded store clerk. Returning to his desk he found Murphy standing next to it with a stack of papers in his hand. It was apparent he was waiting on the rest of the story, but Callahan said nothing. Murphy had to ask the question. A sly grin surfaced when he looked over at Callahan. "Now, how did you get that guy to confess?" Callahan held back a smile as he searched for the number to the Des Moines Police Department via the internet. There was someone there he desperately wanted to speak to. Murphy prodded him a little saying, "come on, I got to hear this one."

Callahan replied, "oh, I don't know. He must have overheard something he didn't want to hear. It must have upset him a little, I guess."

Murphy knew that was all he was getting out of Callahan when he remarked, "you're not about to tell me what that would be are you."

Callahan picked up the phone dialing the number to the Des Moines Police Department as he shook his head a little saying, "if I told you, you'd never believe me Murphy, but Jose there was looking long and hard at the death penalty for jacking that car by the time we walked out of there. He really didn't a have choice but to talk." Callahan listened to the operator on the phone as he took in Murphy's facial expression which he found priceless.

As Callahan asked the operator to transfer him to homicide, Murphy said, "you do know no one was killed during that robbery."

Callahan sarcastically played dumb saying, "oh really, I didn't know that." He added, "I'm pretty sure Jose didn't either, but what the hell. What he doesn't know won't hurt him, will it?"

Murphy was almost at a loss for words as he hit the top of his desk with his fist saying, "son of a bitch. I love it." He and Callahan were old school. It reminded him of some of the interviews he conducted with him in the past. They would take turns playing good cop, bad cop, but nobody played the hard-ass better than Callahan. There was more than one occasion when false information fed to the suspect led to them spilling their guts about everything they knew, but this was the first time a desk jockey like Henley had been used to get a confession. Murphy just started laughing. He turned swiveling in his chair as he jerked his head in the direction of his desk saying, "that's why you're the best. There, I admit it."

Callahan wasn't about to argue with that, but his attention was focused elsewhere as he spoke into the phone saying, "yeah, this is Detective Callahan, I need to speak with someone regarding an unsolved case."

Officer Neely listened to Callahan as he looked across the room at Sergeant Gant. He was the officer in charge at that moment, and he more than had his hands full. It was a madhouse as usual inside the Des Moines police station at 25 East First Street. Sergeant Gant was busy shuffling papers while fielding calls. It was late in the day, and he hadn't even taken lunch yet. The last thing he needed was something else added to his plate. When Officer Neely yelled, "hey Gant, you have a call waiting."
He brashly responded asking, "yeah, who is it?"
Neely replied, "I don't know exactly. Said his name is Detective Callahan, something about an unsolved case. It might be Dirty Harry himself for all I know." Gant found little humor that. He was overworked, underpaid, and too damn tired, not to mention hungry, to even begin to appreciate the sarcasm the other officer provided with that humorous remark.
Gant said, "oh really, well put him through."

Gant thought to himself, it better not be some kind of prank call by one of his fellow officers, because he was in no mood for it. Suppressing his agitation for the moment, he picked up the phone, and pushed the button for line two, then he said, "this is Sergeant Gant. How can I help you?"
Callahan looked down at the notes he had made regarding the unsolved murders in Des Moines. He introduced himself saying, "Sergeant, this is Detective Callahan with the IMPD, and I've got something I think I should make you aware of, hell it might even help you close a case or two." This was by no means the typical call Gant received each

161

day. Seldom was anyone ever calling to assist him with solving a case. He was the one that did all the calling for the most part. Normally, he had to do a considerable amount of investigative work in order to gather any information worth having, and this sounded a little too good to be true right off the bat.

Gant replied, "Well, Detective Callahan, I'll be, why don't you go ahead, and make my day."

Callahan paused a second before saying, "well, you know that's not the first time I've heard that one." His tone made it clear to Gant he was who he said he was. Gant took his words a bit more serious at that point as he said, "no, I bet not. What do you have for me?"

Callahan responded saying, "the name of a killer for starters, a killer I believe is responsible for several murders that occurred in your jurisdiction."

Now, he had Gant's attention which caused him to ask, "what makes you say that? Don't tell me you got a confession out of him."

Callahan said, "no, not exactly. We haven't caught him yet, but this guy will be back this way before long if the past is an indicator of the future. I happen to believe he might be headed your way too."

Gant's curiosity was raised another notch when he asked, "what cases are you referring to exactly?"

Callahan read off the names of several victims, and the dates when the murders occurred. Gant immediately realized he was talking about cold cases, and he didn't have a suspect in custody. He needed another wild goose chase like he needed more paper on his desk. He simply wanted to end the call as he told him, "I'm sorry, I'm not familiar with them." He had plenty of pending cases to investigate, and he knew what the chances were of solving a cold-case from five years ago. They weren't good, especially when you considered the odds of catching a serial killer that had managed to avoid capture that long.

Confident in Henley's memory, and Buttweiler's research, Callahan still asked him if he'd take a look at those cases, and get back to him as soon as possible. He threw out the name Hayden Keller stating that he believed this was the man responsible for the violent unsolved murders. Gant didn't say it, but he was thinking to himself, *Hayden Keller, huh. Yeah, this just keeps getting better, and better.* He started looking around the room questioning if he was on Candid Camera. All he said was, "yeah, that's quite some time back, but I assure you, you'll be the first to know when I put my hands on them." Callahan knew what that meant. He didn't have much to go on other than a well-defined M.O., a historical travel pattern, and a suspected name. He couldn't even give Gant an accurate physical description of what Hayden Keller looked like.

With no eyewitnesses to speak of at that point, the killer might as well have been invisible, and hunting down an invisible killer is as hard as it sounds. Callahan understood that, but he also knew it was only a matter of time before they had a face to put with the name. He never imagined how many faces Henley and Buttweiler would uncover baring that name. Once that was made known to him, his world would change forever. No longer would he be able to fool himself into believing that supernatural forces were not at the heart of the evil deeds of men. Never again could he simply pretend nothing existed beyond the life we live. In fact, it would cement in his mind that everything he feared as a child was real, even the devil himself. Acknowledging that, Satan's role in the murders would take on new meaning.

For now, the strong belief which he had that Satan played a part in the killer's motivation was merely a way of profiling Hayden Keller. Callahan had no understanding of how accurate that assessment truly was. Either way, he didn't feel it was time to share that part of the profile with anyone, not until he had more answers.

Everyone faces demons in life, but Callahan would soon be confronted with one sent straight from hell. Only with Sister Lee's assistance would he ever succeed in stopping him for good. Callahan knew nothing of her though, nor what took place in the town of Chanceville. As he combed through several pages of notes, Sister Lee walked over to the phone which sat on a small table next to the window in her parlor. She knew there would soon be a call placed by the detective, and he would certainly want to speak with her given what she knew. That call would be made to Sheriff Baker's office though, and she had to arrange a way to get there.

Chapter 30

Piecing It All Together

Callahan's phone rang as he attempted to find the number to the Sheriff's Office in Jefferson County. He answered it only to hear Buttweiler say, "we need you down here right now." It was clear by the tone in his voice something he found was unsettling.

Callahan asked, "what's the matter?"

Buttweiler replied, "you just have to see this for yourself. I can't even begin to explain it." The sense of urgency never wavered as Buttweiler spoke, and that alarmed Callahan enough to tell him he was on his way. Quickly taking a pen, he jotted down the number to Sheriff Baker's office on a post-it note, and shoved it into his coat pocket before leaving his desk. His computer screen still displayed the numbers to the Jefferson County Courthouse as he walked toward the stairs.

McDermott passed him as he trotted down the steps, and he asked Callahan, "where the hell are you headed in such a hurry?" Callahan didn't bother looking back when he replied, "hell, I don't know. Thought I might see what's going on in the records room." That was the last place McDermott expected him to be headed. Evidently, the Archives Department held more than he gave it credit for, and that was soon proven.

Buttweiler and Henley had amassed a pile of information on Hayden Keller, none of it made for a comforting read. Callahan had wasted no time in getting there. Buttweiler looked at him admitting, "this is some scary stuff we dug up on him Callahan."

The detective walked over to the table where Buttweiler was standing. He looked at the articles, and reports which Henley had printed off. His mind raced as Buttweiler pointed out dates, and ages of the killer at the time of the murders. Henley was still clicking through stuff on his computer screen as he said, "don't forget about the scar," as if Buttweiler could ever overlook the mark of identification. It was the one thing that was consistent about the killer in all the cases - that damn hideous scar on his left cheek.

Speaking with authority, Buttweiler said, "give me that folder Henley." When he opened it, he read through the file Henley had found there in the records room with Hayden Keller's name listed in it.

Callahan paid close attention to the details surrounding that case before he admitted, "it sounds like the guy we're looking for." That's when Buttweiler shared with him the date in which those murders occurred. Callahan's first thought wasn't that's not our guy - it was more along the lines of, how in the hell is it possible.

With nearly a dozen official reports or newspaper articles with information on Hayden Keller being sought for in connection with, or convicted of, unspeakable crimes, Callahan couldn't ignore the evidence. Like Buttweiler, he too wanted to find a logical reason as to how these cases could possibly span more than a hundred years. He didn't have that answer though, not until Buttweiler asked, "how in the hell does this guy keep coming back?"

Callahan certainly didn't like the answer which popped in his mind. It was a crazy thought he couldn't even begin to process. It was both bizarre, and unconventional. Neither of which were the norm for Callahan. The facts were all he was ever interested in. Callahan's theories were derived from sound logic, and visible evidence. They never centered around the supernatural, and the thought of reincarnation had never seriously been a consideration in his mind until that very moment.

The continual numeric pattern the killer made with his weekly kills brought Callahan to the point of questioning if demonic possession was truly real. Could an evil spirit be behind something so terrifying? It made him uneasy just thinking about it. He had encountered a lot of strange things in his years in law enforcement, but nothing like this. There was simply no way he could share that possibility with Buttweiler, or Henley, not until he spoke with someone that knew a hell of a lot more about the afterlife than he did.

Callahan only knew of one expert knowledgeable enough to answer his questions concerning spiritual matters, if that's what it could be called. That was his priest, Father Tomas at St. Michael's Cathedral. Truthfully, Callahan felt uncomfortable discussing that possibility with anyone, including him. Still, nothing else offered a valid explanation for the murders occurring for over a hundred years, all of which were credited to the same marked man wearing different faces as he killed randomly in different places all across the country. It was like something right out of the movies, but it was real.

Initially, he preferred to lend support to Buttweiler's alternate explanation of a copycat killer conducting the murders. Those murders did seem to cease upon Hayden Keller's chard corpse being found just outside of Chanceville. As Callahan read over that report, Buttweiler asked, "you want me to contact the sheriff in Jefferson County?"

Callahan immediately told him, "no. I'll take care of that. I was looking up the number to the sheriff's office when you called me."

Buttweiler was at a loss as he asked, "so, what do you want me to do now?"

"I want you looking at current cases that match our guy's M.O., and if you find any, you let me know," Callahan replied. That made no sense to Buttweiler. The killer was obviously dead, end of story. The conclusion unfolded in Jefferson County eleven months earlier. He had no expectation of finding more murders matching the ones he had been tracking. Callahan felt otherwise, and he feared Buttweiler would have to make that call confirming his most dreaded suspicions which revolved around satanic spirits with the ability to inhabit the bodies of men.

As Buttweiler stood there trying to understand Callahan's thought process, the detective said, "just humor me. You've done a great job. This is just part of it. We have to make certain that the body discovered near Chanceville was our guy, and not the body of one of his victims." Callahan added, "there's no better way to prove it than to confirm he's no longer operating anywhere in the country. It might take some time, but we have to do it."

Buttweiler understood that much as he nodded his head. Using an old saying he heard growing up he said, "yeah. Well, I guess we can't have him playing opossum can we."

Callahan never made eye contact with him when he agreed, "no, we certainly can not."

He made it clear to both Buttweiler, and Henley that no one outside of that room should be made aware of the progress they had made thus far, not until they had concluded their investigation, and Callahan had a chance to review the findings with them. When the detective turned to exit the room, Buttweiler asked, "where are you going?"

Callahan muttered, "oh, I just have to see a man about a dog. That's all." Henley took Callahan's statement literally. Buttweiler knew it meant he had business to tend to that probably entailed a meeting of some sort.

As Callahan walked toward the door, he paused looking over at his partner, and that's when he said, "you did good Henley." Just before stepping out the door, he glanced back at Buttweiler saying, "that goes for you too."

Seconds later, Henley directed his comment toward Buttweiler as he said, "I never knew he liked dogs, but he's a baseball fan you know." Buttweiler found Henley amusing as usual. He didn't bother to explain about the dog, he had other pressing matters to tend to. Henley, on the other hand, was glad the investigation was still on. He enjoyed the excitement it brought through the doors of the records room. He was going to miss it when it was all over, and he knew it would all end soon.

Even Buttweiler felt they were close to solving countless murders all over the country. He paid little attention to the concerned look Callahan had on his face as he left the room. He chalked it up to Callahan's conservative professional nature. He tried to emulate him in some ways, but Callahan never seem overly excited about much, and this definitely wasn't the first major case he ever oversaw. Buttweiler, on the other hand, had never been such an integral part of any investigation during his career, and this one would top them all if Hayden Keller was proven to have killed all those people which were charted on the timeline.

Working under the assumption he was indeed a copycat killer, the number of victims could be as high as several hundred. That was much more fathomable than thousands.

Following protocol under Callahan's direction, he and Henley did their due diligence as they searched for any open cases throughout the U.S. which matched Hayden Keller's M.O.

The time was at hand, Callahan had to give Captain Rollins a status report on where he, and Buttweiler were at in the cold case investigations. When he returned to his desk, Murphy informed him, "the captain is looking for you." Callahan was fully aware of what he wanted. He shut down his computer, and grabbed some things from his desk telling Murphy, "you haven't seen me."

Murphy just muttered to himself, "seen what," as Callahan fled down the hall, and out the building. He could always count on his old partner to cover for him in a pinch. Callahan didn't wish to share any of their latest findings with him. The Captain always liked things in a nice neat package, and this was anything but that. In Callahan's view, it had come completely unwound. What appeared to be a jagged string of run of the mill brutal slayings orchestrated by a rampaging serial killer turned-out to be a nationwide hunt for a madman with multiple lives, and thousands of victims. Maybe it was a secret order of some type, a collective group of satanic followers passing on the torch. Try sticking that in a report to your superior. Callahan wasn't about to do it. He needed answers before he said word one to the captain.

Tossing a battered outdated laptop in the passenger seat of his car, he climbed in cranking the ignition. He only wanted to get out of there before someone else spotted him leaving. He had barely driven a mile down the street from the station when he reached inside his coat pocket for his cell phone. It was Captain Rollins calling. He was determined to track Callahan down. The first words out of the captain's mouth were, "you know why I'm calling. "Where's your report?"

Callahan paused not knowing what to say other than, "I'm following up on a lead as we speak, and I'll have it on your desk first thing in the morning."

"That's what I want to hear," Rollins barked, and with that he hung up the phone. Callahan couldn't stall him forever.

When he placed his phone back in his pocket, he withdrew the post-it note with Sheriff Baker's number on it. He stared at it a second as he sat at a traffic light several miles away from a place he seldom visited except on special occasions. This occasion was unique, but "special" would not be how Callahan would've described it. He placed the number in the cup holder next to his seat, and he continued making his way through the congested downtown streets as he drove towards St. Michael's Cathedral. It had been months since he stepped foot in the place.

Chapter 31

Searching For Fatherly Advice

The wind began to gust as Callahan pulled up in front of St. Michael's Cathedral, a storm was brewing. He looked up at the bell tower, and then at the lavish windows of the church which were overshadowed by the grand steeple. It had been a number of months since he had seen the inside. He wasn't figuring much had changed in that length of time, but something weighed heavy on his heart as he questioned if he would find the answers he was looking for through those doors.

Admittedly, to himself, part of him feared to know the answers. Was there something after death? Really, was there another life to live, or a place to go to? Could some demonic spirit take over the body of another human being? How do you combat that which you cannot see? Does this kind of stuff really occur? All of these were questions in his mind, and until that moment he had never really pondered them much at all. Sure, he was brought up in the church as a kid. His grandfather made sure he went every Sunday for some reason. He even made his grandson promise to never turn his back on the Lord. Those were some of the final words he spoke on his death bed at the time Callahan was fifteen years old. Now, here he was thirty-two years later questioning if he had let his grandfather down. He brushed aside that feeling of guilt telling himself that's what the church is all about. Yeah, they preached a good game about forgiveness, but they never let you forget you're a sinner, and how much you owe the Lord.

Callahan was smart enough to see through some of the facade of the church. He never blindly followed something. He couldn't, it wasn't in him to do that. He was a cop, and within every cop is a doubting, at least in the great ones like Callahan anyway. He never made excuses for his lack of faith, he just recognized the cynical side he had, and realized the church used guilt to fill the offering plates. Callahan shook off any feelings of guilt he had before he walked through those doors, because he was there on official business in his mind. Other than answering the questions he had, it really didn't matter what the priest had to say.

Entering the cathedral, he was overwhelmed by the number of people attending afternoon mass. Other than the overabundance of parishioners filling the pews, he was right, the church itself never seemed to change. Callahan looked around as he walked over to the back pew, and he knelt down lowering his head as he began to pray.

Father Tomas was finishing up the service as he calmly announced to everyone, "go in peace." That was an odd thing for Callahan to hear, he was a cop for God's sake. The only peaceful part of his life was when he made it home at night without encountering something unpleasant in the course of his day that would keep him from being able to enjoy watching the ballgame. He thought to himself, perhaps he should go in peace, but something told him to stay. Just at that moment, Father Tomas walked over to him placing his hand on Callahan's shoulder. With a friendly smile he said, "now there's a face I haven't seen in a while."

Callahan looked up at him, and Father Tomas could sense something was wrong. As Callahan stood, he symbolically gestured with his hand moving it from the upper part of his head vertically down below his chest, and then horizontally across his chest from one side to the other as he drew an invisible cross with it. The priest nodded his head as he extended his hand to Callahan. Then he made the comment, "you should have been a priest. You know that don't you?"

Callahan replied, "that's probably what my grandfather wanted me to be."

As they shook one another's hand, Father Tomas said, "well it's never too late, but it's not about your grandfather. It's about what God wants. Isn't it?"

Callahan felt the weight leave his shoulders with the words the priest spoke. He knew his purpose in life. He knew why God made him a cop as he said, "well, He knows best I guess, cause I would have made a lousy priest."

Father Tomas smiled a little as he said, "I would have made a not so good cop, I imagine, but we do have something in common you and I."

Looking for some kind of common ground, Callahan replied, "yeah, what's that exactly?"

Father Tomas replied, "St. Michael, he's the patron saint of both the church, and the police officer. We both have him watching over us."

Callahan couldn't help but find that ironic as he admitted he never knew that. If there was ever a time he needed someone watching over him it was now. A calm look was present on Father Tomas's face as he asked, "to what do I owe the pleasure?" Callahan looked around at the other parishioners inside the church. He didn't really know how to go about asking Father Tomas if he believed in reincarnation. He didn't want him to think he was crazy, and he certainly didn't want anyone else to hear him pose that question to the priest. Callahan simply started out by saying, "I have a few questions I need answers to."

Father Tomas could tell he was uncomfortable in the company of those around him. As the priest turned to walk toward the confessionals, Callahan walked alongside him. A more serious look formed on the priest's face, but he kept the mood light by saying, "a cop with questions, imagine that." Callahan confessed that his questions were a little out there. The priest nodded his head once as he listened closely, and he said, "well, you're in the right place. People come to church all the time to get the answers which they seek. God has them all, I assure you."

Callahan admitted he, and God hadn't been talking a lot lately. "I have to confess it has been a while since I've been in the church."

Father Tomas immediately said, "I'm not worried. I knew I'd see you before the start of the season." Callahan looked at him with surprise. Father Tomas cocked his head a little as he looked toward Callahan. That's when he said, "oh, you don't think you are the only one that prays for the Indians to have a great season do you."

Callahan smiled a little saying, "no I guess not."

Bringing the topic of conversation back to why he was there, Father Tomas said, "so, you are searching in your heart for what you already know to be true. This, I already know, regardless of your questions."

Callahan made an attempt to clarify his position before broaching the subject of demonic possession with the priest as he said, "this isn't some kind of search for confirmation. That I assure you."

The priest responded with, "then what is it exactly. You seek the truth. So be it, for most truth is what you see."

Callahan could identify with that. He listened to every word Father Tomas had to offer before he asked the first question. When he was given the chance to speak, he chose to lead with a question that brought up the topic of exorcism. Callahan asked, "where does the church stand on that?"

Father Tomas found that question coming from Callahan rather odd, but he answered saying, "the church has no official position that I'm aware of regarding exorcism. However, there are those that believe in the practice of casting out spirits. They are a small group within the church, but well respected. I know of one such priest. Perhaps, you would like to speak with him regarding this matter."

Callahan hardly felt comfortable speaking with Father Tomas, and there was no one within the church he trusted more than him. Callahan quickly declined that offer saying, "no, that's alright. Father Tomas asked, "why do you ask? Have you encountered someone you believe is plagued by an evil entity of some sort?"

Callahan replied, "I'll get to that in just a second. So, what you are saying is it's possible for demonic possession to occur."

Father Tomas confessed of personal knowledge he had of those that had encountered demons. He also pointed out there were numerous examples in the Bible of people that were possessed by spirits. Callahan looked gravely concerned as Father Tomas pointed out our bodies are simply vessels which God has given us to move about the earth. When he said, "we all choose that which we allow to enter us," Callahan latched onto the fact that only a willing candidate could be inhabited. Father Tomas said, "to the contrary, sometimes the participant is willing, but more often than not, they are powerless against inhabitation."

Callahan wanted to gain a deeper understanding as he asked, "can you explain why?"

Father Tomas nodded his head as he spoke explaining, "for some, their spirit is weak, and susceptible to being overpowered by stronger spirits, if you will. For them, it simply isn't a matter of choice, but of inability to defend themselves against more powerful forces. Sometimes, it's even a matter of someone simply letting their guard down long enough to be inhabited." The priest's words brought much to light before he asked Callahan, "what's going on? Can you tell me that?"

Callahan looked around to make sure no one could overhear them talking. That's when he told Father Tomas about the pattern of the killer, how he consistently killed six victims each weak, but never did he kill on Saturday. Father Tomas recognized that day to be the Sabbath, and he pointed it out to Callahan as he asked, "do you believe this killer you're after is tied to a particular faith?" Callahan gave the priest a general idea of the wrath the victims endured, and he pointed out he saw no way for there to be any connection between him, and any church. That's when Callahan questioned the priest about Saturday being the Sabbath. Father Tomas responded with, "the seventh day is the true Sabbath according to the Bible, that will never change. It was in fact Constantine, and the Catholic Church itself, which moved the Sabbath to the first day of the week in order to retain its pagan followers. That is why you, as most believe, Sunday is the Sabbath, but your killer knows different."

Callahan thought about that as Father Tomas asked, "do you wish to tell me anything else about the man you are searching for?" Callahan revealed the fact that multiple killers had been discovered bearing the same name. He also explained they had occurred over an inconceivable amount of time, and the only thing the men had in common other than the method of killing was the scar they all carried on their left cheek. He left it at that.

Father Tomas showed some sign of concern as he offered an explanation for the scar, and its particular location on the killer's face. "It could be the mark of the beast," he said reluctantly. When Callahan pressed him for more information the priest said, "there was a time when those found guilty of worshiping Satan were marked prior to being put to death. That mark was usually a sizable scar of some type placed on the left side of the face either through laceration or branding."

Callahan recalled some of the images of the men wearing that mark he saw in the records room. He wanted to know the purpose behind the mark they wore. It was something dark and sinister, that much he knew for sure. He also believed Father Tomas knew more than he was revealing regarding the mark of the beast as he referred to it. Callahan questioned him saying, "the branding, what was the significance?"

Father Tomas looked over his shoulder before speaking. He wanted to make sure he wasn't overheard as he said, "it was put there to identify that individual as a follower of the devil prior to them being burned at the stake." Callahan found that insightful, and alarming all at the same time. Still, he could see no real purpose it served if it was administered right before death, unless they feared that person would return someday. Only then would the mark be of value labeling that individual as property of Satan himself.

Rephrasing the question, Callahan grilled the priest as he asked, "what purpose did that really serve?"

Father Tomas slowly shook his head as he said, "it was simply referred to as the mark of the beast in the book I read. I can't tell you much more about it. I can't even tell you the name of the book where I ran across it. I will tell you it was placed there to warn others to stay away from the marked individual. I'm sure it also served as a form of public humiliation prior to execution."

Callahan saw an opportunity to asked Father Tomas about

reincarnation as he said, "you don't think they placed it there to mark the person in case they ever became reincarnated do you?"

Father Tomas refused to answer that. He just looked at Callahan as he asked, "what do you believe?" The grave concern in Father Tomas's face provided Callahan with some clue as to how on target he was with that theory. Hoping the priest would elaborate, Callahan replied, "I don't know. I've never seen anything like what you, and I are discussing right now."

Father Tomas looked into Callahan's eyes saying, "what we believe is what is yet to be seen. You understand what we believe is our version of truth."

Callahan couldn't believe Father Tomas's candor as he said, "this comes from a Catholic priest."

Father Tomas realized Callahan wasn't ready to hear the truth, but he would come to face it on his own. All he said was, "you must understand this in order for me to answer your question. Man is only limited by his ability to perceive. Through the eyes of God, all things are possible, and forget not, Satan once believed he was superior to the one we worship. That said, all things are possible, including that which you have mentioned." The priest added, "that wasn't the answer you were wishing to hear, but you know in your heart it is true or you wouldn't have asked it to begin with."

Callahan questioned him, "how do you know that?"

Father Tomas fired back with, "you're a cop. Cops seldom ask questions they don't already know the answers to when it comes to determining truth."

Callahan looked around the magnificent cathedral saying, "now who's playing cop?"

The priest began to walk toward the rear of the church as Callahan strolled along beside him. Father Tomas said, "you asked, and I have told you all things are possible, without exception. Now, understand it's those things we fear we simply choose not to believe. Most men do not seek truth, only their version of it. If it is truth you are searching for, you will face demons, but only through faith will you defeat them. Remember that."

Callahan hadn't been much on faith since he could remember. He relied more on instinct, and he had to ask, "faith in what?"

Father Tomas looked at him once again. This time he said, "that too, is for you to discover for yourself. God put you here for a purpose Callahan, and it is my belief he has called on you to serve as a guardian to those who need protection."

Callahan looked out the open doors of the church as he asked, "and who would that be?"

The priest replied, "the one He brings to you. Oftentimes, the ones that need protecting never seek it out. Instead, they go unprotected, and eventually they fall to one such as you have described. I will pray for you, and my prayer is that God will guide you, and you will know without question in your heart when you meet those God has chosen for you to shield. Trust me, when the time comes you shall know it." Callahan didn't have to ask if there was something beyond this life. He had his answer. He carried it in with him when he walked through the doors of that church, and now it was time for him to go. Father Tomas bid him farewell as he said, "God bless, and God speed. I expect to see you back in here before the start of the season."

Callahan looked out the door for a second time, the weather was growing increasingly turbulent, and Father Tomas assured him he was never alone. Reminding him of something important, he told Callahan, "I know you have a job to do, but you remember what we share, and who is watching over us both."

Pulling the collar up on his coat, he nodded at the priest one last time as he prepared to step out into the cold. For the first time in a long time Callahan felt what it was like to possess faith. He knew someone more powerful than Satan himself was watching over him. Leaving the church, he knew he was in his priest's prayers, and he glanced up at the name which adorned the cathedral reading the name of St. Michael. It now held new meaning in his eyes.

He stood there just a second thinking about what Father Tomas had shared with him about the patron saint the church was named after, and the role he played in the lives of priests, and police officers. He couldn't help but think, *I sure as hell hope you can help me pull this one off.* With that, he turned making a b-line for his vehicle in an effort to stay ahead of the storm which was fast approaching.

Chapter 32

A Sobering Thought

The sky grew darker as Callahan got into his car. Maybe the weather foretold of danger yet to come, but he preferred not to connect the two in any way. His meeting with the priest left him with much to think about. What he had to process in his mind wasn't easy to accept, not by a long shot. In fact, it would no doubt require a stiff drink just to swallow, and he preferred to ponder life's mysteries in a place he visited quite often, at least twice a week on average.

Buchanan's was practically like his second home, and although some might think a bar is an odd place to travel to after leaving church, it made perfect sense for an Irish cop with no family to call his own. Father Tomas would have understood. It was the kind of place where he always felt welcomed even on dismal days like this one. More often than not Callahan's thoughts revolved around more of a personal nature, but that's where he stumbled upon answers most of the time. God knows he needed them now more than ever. Either way he had a great deal to consider, and he usually did his best thinking with a shot-glass in his hand.

He looked down at Sheriff Baker's number, and he checked the time on his watch. He figured if he didn't make that call soon, he'd most likely not reach him. It was late in the day, and the sun could no longer be seen thanks to the clouds which had moved in abruptly. The wind itself blew so hard it actually shook his blue Crown Vic as he gripped the wheel with one hand while occupying the driver's seat.

Watching the street signs flip back, and forth as if they were made to do so, he held respect for the power of Mother Nature, and as heavy rain pelted the windshield of his car, he fumbled in his coat pocket for his phone. Just his luck, the damn battery was low. "Damn it," was all he said before putting it away. There was no way he was making that call, not until he got some place where he could charge it.

With the rain hammering away on the hood, and roof of his car, it would have made it difficult to hear anything over the sound of the pounding rain, and roaring thunder. He could hardly hear his own thoughts, much less carry on a conversation with someone at that point. Callahan's cynical side took over as he thought, *so far St. Michael doesn't seem to be tending to his end of the stick*. He flipped on the windshield wipers before pulling back onto the street, and he set a course for his favorite tavern on the corner of Westside, and New York Street.

Usually, when he entered the doors of his favorite pub he was off duty. Today, however, that wasn't the case. His thoughts centered on work related matters, a massive number of unsolved murders, Hayden Keller's past lives, and the chance he would ever meet him face to face. In addition to that, there was the matter of what to include in his report to the captain. If he wanted to keep holding his badge it went without saying there could be no mention of supernatural forces behind the deaths of countless people. That kind of shit would put him in weekly sessions with a psychiatrist, and eventually in front of a review board. Little made sense in his world at that moment. He knew only one thing for certain, the killer had to be stopped, sent back to the depths of hell from which he came, and Callahan replayed Father Tomas's words over in his mind as he questioned if he were the man to do it. Sometimes, we all look for signs, he was about to encounter his soon enough.

Thankful to be out of the elements, Callahan shook off the rain from his coat when he walked through the door. He could see Sean standing behind the bar filling a frosted mug full of ale for one of the other patrons. Noticing Callahan out of the corner of his eye, he looked up with a friendly smile on his face, and greeted him saying, "another hard day at the office I see." Callahan just twisted his head a little thinking, you have no idea my friend as Sean asked, "what will it be?"
Callahan looked up at the television overhearing some of the sports scores as he said, "scotch on the rocks, and make it a double." Pulling his phone from his pocket, he laid it on the counter along with the charger asking, "you have some place to plug this in." Sean quickly nodded his head sharply just once, and Callahan pointed to his regular table. Placing the detective's drink on the counter, Sean informed him, "always good to see you."

Callahan sat down pulling out his laptop, waiting for his phone to charge as he watched ESPN on the big screen which was mounted on the wall next to the bar. Everything that once held importance in his world now seemed less significant. When Grace set the plate of food down on his table where Callahan was seated, she smiled saying, "hard at work I see." Callahan never even bothered to look up at her to see her pleasant expression.

The detective was in the process of wading through information when his phone started ringing. Sean's attention was drawn to it as he wiped down the bar. Looking over at Callahan, he yelled out, "hey, looks like you have a call."
Callahan stopped what he was doing to walk over to the bar in order to catch it. Hoping not to miss it he told Sean,

"go ahead and take it for me."

Sean picked up the phone saying, "Callahan's office." It was Buttweiler, and he was somewhat stunned to hear someone's voice other than Callahan's, but Callahan knew who it was before Sean unplugged the phone from the charger handing it to him. He knew Hayden Keller was back, and he desperately needed to get a hold of that sheriff in Jefferson County. When Callahan said, "tell me what you found."

Buttweiler said, "a string of murders in the Southeast that match our guys M.O. I'm sending them to your email." Callahan paused. Buttweiler questioned if he heard him. There was plenty of noise coming from the bar in the background, mostly jeers from enthusiastic football fans, and the sound coming from the television.

Callahan responded saying, "yeah, I heard you. That's what I was afraid of."

Buttweiler asked, "does this mean our guy didn't die in that fire like we thought?"

Callahan replied, "I can't say until I take a look at what you're sending me. I'm about to call the sheriff, and get some answers from him. I'll know more when I see you in the morning." More noise was heard in the background as Callahan walked away from the bar, and back toward his table.

Out of curiosity Buttweiler asked, "where are you, anyway?"

Callahan didn't want to answer. It was after hours. The fact that he was in a bar really didn't matter. He just kind of kept that place to himself, that's all, but his young partner had done a hell of a job proving to Callahan he had what it takes to make a great detective. He needed to go over some of the details in the case with him anyway just to make sure they were on the same page before he issued his report to the captain. He said, "I'm having a bite to eat down here at

185

Buchanan's. It's on New York Street. You know where that is?"

Buttweiler said, "no, but I can find it. How about I meet you there."

Callahan informed him, "there's no rush. I'll be here whenever you get here."

At that point, Buttweiler let Callahan in on something else of great importance. He said, "by the way, there's something else you need to know Callahan."

The detective said, "yeah, what's that?"

"It looks as though those murders are headed straight toward us." The tone of his voice carried with it a high level of concern which was warranted under the circumstances. As Callahan ended the call, he knew he was going to have to try to explain something even he couldn't fully comprehend. Just how much he could share with Buttweiler remained to be seen, but he knew he had best do it sober.

Sitting back down at his table, he asked Grace for a glass of iced tea. Callahan immediately logged into to his email. He scanned over the dates, and places where the murders occurred. They certainly fell in line with the pattern established by Hayden Keller even though authorities suspected a man by the name of Vincent Russell for several of those murders. The other thing he noticed was Buttweiler was right. The killer was headed their way.

From the path the killer seemed to be taking, if it was indeed the same man as both he, and Buttweiler suspected, he would no doubt reach that small dot on the map called Chanceville long before hitting Indianapolis. Within days he would be in Des Moines just as he had predicted in his heads up call given to Officer Gant. Callahan had no doubt this was the case. How could he put this in terms Buttweiler could accept? Some of the words Father Tomas spoke ran back through his brain as he finished off his scotch.

Callahan had a rare opportunity placed in front of him, one he had never encountered before. He could put to rest a lot of old cases with the charred body that was discovered in Jefferson County eleven months earlier. In fact, he could help close cases all across the country going as far back as one could possibly imagine. In order to do it though, he'd have to reveal only what was necessary to those above him, and even his counterparts to close the files for good. It was a dream, and a nightmare all rolled into one. There was no warrant to be issued, no indictment process to go through, and no trial necessary to bring closure to the families of those Hayden Keller had murdered. Callahan knew what the best course of action was to take at that point, even if it meant skewing the truth a little.

Father Tomas had pointed out truth for most people is what they see. He knew it was within his power to limit what they saw, thereby, tailoring the evidence to fit their preconceived notions, and he wasn't beyond doing it. It would require a degree of secrecy to be kept between he, and Buttweiler, Henley too, for that matter, but that was doable. Pulling out the sheriff's number for a third time, he looked down at it. It was time to make the call.

Chapter 33

A Strange Sequence Of Events

The storm which raged in Indianapolis first brewed somewhere west of Chanceville within minutes of Bruce Horvath falling dead against the pavement, his body still covered in flames. Sister Lee knew of what was to come. She had managed to catch a ride into town with Mitchell Bonner, one of the few people she ever spoke to, and even then it was on an as needed basis.

Seeing two patrol cars parked next to the side of the old building near the center of town, she raised her hand for Mitchell to stop the truck. He immediately pulled over next to the curb in front of the sheriff's office to let her out as he asked, "are you sure you don't want me to wait on you Ms. Lee?" Sister Lee looked at him as she closed the door to his truck. That's when he said, "no, I guess not." For a moment, he had forgotten who he was talking too. Sister Lee never changed her mind about something at the last minute. She was the most decisive woman Mitchell had ever met. He liked that about her. It compensated for the strange nature she displayed, and the odd way she spoke at times. The last thing he said to her was, "I hope there's nothing wrong." Maintaining her stare, Sister Lee said nothing as Mitchell reached over to close the passenger door.

Mitchell Bonner knew Sister Lee well enough to know everything she did, and said was deliberate. He had even gotten used to her over the years to the point where she didn't strike him as weird anymore, just different. That's what he thought anyway. She could tell him who was going to win the Super Bowl every year even though she never watched football. In the seven years he had known her, she was never wrong. Mitchell did a little handiwork for her from time to time, and he would occasionally run an errand for her when she needed groceries or something, but Sister Lee had never asked him to take her into town until now.

When he asked, "so, what made you decide to take the tour of Chanceville?" She had simply told him she had business to attend to at the courthouse. As far as he knew, this was the first time she had ever stepped foot in town. As he drove away, all he could think is *of all the places to request, a lift to the sheriff's office is a little beyond weird.* Whatever her reason for going, she wasn't sharing it with him though.

Sister Lee turned to walk up the steps to the door of the sheriff's office, and the people of Chanceville tended to stare a little. She paid them no mind as she opened the door walking inside. It was there where she saw a familiar face leaning up against the filing cabinet. It was Deputy Ratley, and he appeared just as she had seen him in her vision, the one she shared with Ben Goodman eleven months earlier. Ratley, of course, didn't recognize her at all. How could he? He had never consciously seen her before, but there was a dream he had eleven months earlier. The memory is short though in the minds of the weak. Sister Lee knew that to be true. She held the wisdom of ages in her mind yielding her great power, power only she knew how to use, power neither Singer nor Ratley could ever begin to understand. Nevertheless, they would eventually be given the chance, even if it wasn't of their own choosing.

Sister Lee calmly took a seat on the bench next to Sheriff Baker's office. She could see through the window he was busy talking to Singer. Ratley turned around asking her, "can I help you with something?" It was obvious he had no idea who she was.

Sister Lee stated, "it is I that am here to help you."

Ratley was a little lost as he questioned her saying, "help with what exactly?"

Sister Lee replied, "I am waiting for a call. It's very important. When it comes, I will tell you." Now, Ratley was really puzzled. It was time to knock off, and here he was stuck talking to a crazy woman that just happened to make it inside before they locked the doors to the office.

Ratley told Sister Lee, "unless there's an emergency you'll have to leave."

Sister Lee boldly announced, "I'm not going anywhere, not unless you take me." Ratley had no clue what spurred her to say that.

He was caught off guard by her defiant remark as Singer walked out of the sheriff's office saying, "alright, I'm going to call it a night, and see you in the morning." Closing the door behind him, he looked down at Sister Lee, and then over at Ratley. Singer had to ask, "what's she doing here?"

Ratley replied, "I don't know. She said she's expecting a call or something." He knew Singer would set her straight.

The senior deputy took the liberty of informing her she was in the sheriff's office as he asked Sister Lee for her name. When she told him, he looked over at Ratley asking, "does that name ring a bell?" Ratley shook his head no as Singer placed it. He said, "you're that palm reader that has the little place across from that café near the county line." Sister Lee nodded her head, and Singer said, "well, we haven't had any calls for you, and we're about to leave for the night. So, you'll have to come back some other time."

Ratley picked up his keys informing Singer, "I already told her that, and she said she wasn't leaving." Just at that moment, the phone rang.

Singer looked over at it as Sister Lee proclaimed, "they wish to speak with me."

Singer turned to Ratley saying, "what the hell, go ahead and answer it."

Both deputies found it rather odd to get a call coming in that late in the day, but he answered it saying, "Sheriff's Office, this is Deputy Ratley." It was Callahan's voice he heard on the other end of the line. Eager to get some answers, he announced who he was before requesting to speak with the sheriff. Ratley promptly asked, "can I tell him why you're calling? He was as nosey as he was thorough.

Callahan said, "it's regarding a case I'm working, which I believe you may be able to shed some light on."

Ratley said, "hold on just a minute."

Ratley walked over to the sheriff's office cracking the door slightly. He leaned his head in telling the sheriff he had a Detective Callahan calling for him about some case he was working. The sheriff nodded his head as he reached over to pick up the phone. When Ratley closed the door, Singer looked toward Sister Lee saying, "well, it looks like you were wrong, and now it's time to go home."

Sister Lee said, "Detective Callahan will wish to speak with me."

Ratley started to grab his coat as he informed her, "he asked to speak with the sheriff."

Sister Lee then informed him, "soon, he will ask to speak to me."

Singer was now tired of her games. It was no longer amusing. He was tired, and hungry. He let go of a deep breath saying, "yeah, what for?"

"He will wish to know everything there is to know about Hayden Keller," she retorted. The mention of that name took both deputies by surprise.

Singer responded saying, "you knew him personally, I suppose."

Sister Lee replied, "I know him better than anyone. I have seen him in my visions."

Singer confidently said, "that guy is dead lady. I assure you. Isn't that right, Ratley?"

The young deputy nodded saying, "yeah, there's no doubt about that."

The younger deputy did find it odd that Sister Lee should bring up Hayden Keller's name. The guy he met in the diner that afternoon driving the flashy F-350 had brought up what happened eleven months earlier as well. Now, here she was demanding to speak with someone who asked to speak with the sheriff claiming she knew more about the case, and Hayden Keller himself than anyone else in the room. It was a strange sequence of events for sure.

Sheriff Baker was now slowly pacing the floor as he spoke with Callahan. Ratley looked at him through his window. The sheriff turned making eye-contact with him. He motioned with his finger for him to come into his office. Ratley did just that as Singer said, "well Sister Lee, I'm afraid I'm going to have to show you out."

Sister Lee said, "the man he is after has already come this way. I know where he is headed, and only I will recognize him."

Taking her by the arm, Singer patronized her a little when he said, "yeah, well I'll get your number, and have him call you." Sister Lee raised her voice a little saying, "I know about the scar."

Singer paused, no one knew about the scar. That information was only privy to those that had access to the file. Ben and Ashley were the only people left alive who had seen it before Hayden Keller caught fire. The flesh had burned from Hayden's face by the time he, and Ratley arrived at the scene. The charred remains which were present were impossible to identify visually. Even the gas station attendant at the scene couldn't describe what Hayden looked like, by the time he discovered him he had burst into flames.

Inside the sheriff's office, Ratley stood there struck with awe as Sheriff Baker said, "get me the file we have on Hayden Keller." Ratley looked stunned as he asked the sheriff, "is that what Callahan is asking for?"

The sheriff said, "no, I'm the one asking for it, and if you don't mind, I'd like to have it before tomorrow." The sheriff had a way of grabbing his deputies' attention when it was called for, but this time Ratley remained motionless. He was thinking about every weird thing that had taken place since Sister Lee walked through the door. The sheriff told Callahan to hold on just a minute as he asked Ratley, "what's wrong?"

The young deputy looked the sheriff in the eye with disbelief covering his face as he said, "there's a woman out there that claims she knows all about Hayden Keller, and she said Callahan would want to speak with her."

In Ratley's mind, he had to ask himself how on earth she knew the sheriff's discussion with the detective centered on information about Hayden Keller. Ratley didn't even know himself until that moment, and he's the one that answered the phone. He started to mention that he ran into some guy passing through town that afternoon, and he even had a question or two regarding what happened at that gas station where the girl was found.

The sheriff glanced out his window seeing Singer walking Sister Lee toward the door. That's when he ordered Ratley to bring her inside his office as Callahan said, "I just need to know one thing sheriff. Did Hayden Keller have any identifying marks at all on his face."

Sheriff Baker honestly said, "I can't even tell you what he looked like detective. He was burned to a crisp by the time I arrived."

Outside the door to the sheriff's office, Ratley called out to Singer saying, "wait, the sheriff wants to speak with her."

Sister Lee turned her head as Singer asked, "about what?"

Ratley replied, "Hayden Keller, I guess," as he walked over to the file cabinet pulling out the file which contained everything they had on the serial killer which also happened to be Ashley's abductor.

Singer followed Ratley, and Sister Lee back inside Sheriff Baker's office. When Ratley ushered her through the door to see the sheriff, Singer volunteered, "she knows about the scar, and she says that's not all." His loud voice was overheard by the sheriff, and Callahan himself.

The sheriff held the phone next to his ear asking Callahan to excuse him for a moment. Ratley introduced Sister Lee to the sheriff, and Singer elaborated on who she was by saying, "you know that palm reader out near the county line. This is her sheriff. She claims the guy that the detective is looking for already passed this way, and only she knows what he looks like."

The sheriff took her claims a bit more seriously than Singer did. Sheriff Baker even said, "perhaps, I should let you speak with the detective then," as Callahan requested that he put her on the phone. Handing her the phone, Sheriff Baker took the folder from Ratley reviewing all of the information which was inside it starting with the forensic reports. Reviewing the statements given to him by Ben, he listened to every word which left Sister Lee's lips. Everything she said was completely accurate. She might as well have been reading straight out of the file the sheriff now held in his hand. She even had details neither the sheriff nor his deputies knew anything about which she shared with Callahan.

The sheriff tilted his head a little trying to gain a clear understanding of where she acquired all that information. He looked over at his deputies, and they both had concern on their faces as Sister Lee described a man fitting Vincent Russell's appearance. Ratley confessed he had seen that man in the diner, and he had even spoken with him. Singer even remembered Ratley mentioning the flashy truck he saw earlier that day. They were left damn near speechless by what they heard come out of Sister Lee's mouth, and still there was much she had not revealed. She divulged only what the detective needed to hear.

Callahan had no doubt Sister Lee was truly gifted when she said, "his face will change before you meet up with him, but rest assured you will face him in time. It is your destiny, and only I can guide you to the evil one which you seek. You can no longer depend on Buttweiler or Henley, only me." He had to question how she knew of his partners.

Callahan's breath was halted by her ability to see things no man could see. Father Tomas had enlightened him though. He had told Callahan he would not defeat the demon he would face without faith. Callahan now placed his faith in Sister Lee as he said, "I believe you. Listen to me. I want you to say nothing about this to anyone. From now on, you only speak with me." Looking up at the clock on the wall inside the bar, the detective added, "I want you here immediately."

The detective believed wholeheartedly in everything she said. Days earlier he would've had a hard time believing a word which she spoke, but thanks to Father Tomas, Callahan now understood all things were possible. Truthfully, though, he didn't really believe that until he spoke with her. His world changed immediately, and although Sister Lee seemed quite capable of taking care of herself, he would soon come to see her as the one Father Tomas spoke of, the one needing his protection.

Callahan started to make a request, but two words left his mouth before Sister Lee cut him off saying, "you will not need my number. Soon we will meet."

He was left in awe of her intuitive capabilities when he said, "I think you're right about that. Let me speak with the sheriff for just a second if you would." That's when Callahan asked the sheriff if he could take Sister Lee to the nearest airport.

As he began looking up flight schedules on his laptop, Sheriff Baker informed him, "the nearest major airport is almost an hour and a half away." Sister Lee began shaking her head saying, "I do not fly. It is much too dangerous."

Ratley and Singer simultaneously looked at one another. This was getting weirder by the second. Sheriff Baker informed the detective, "she says she won't get on a plane." Ratley couldn't blame her. He had never been on a plane himself. That was probably the only thing they had in common though, but he didn't share that with anyone else. The sheriff suggested the Greyhound Station saying, "the nearest one's about forty miles from here. My guess is it leaves out tomorrow morning."

Callahan said, "that's too late, I need her here ASAP. Could you have one of your deputies transport her?"

Sheriff Baker wanted to help, but Callahan was two hundred miles outside his jurisdiction. He replied, "no detective. I'm afraid I can't do that."

Callahan labeled Sister Lee as a witness in an effort to compel the sheriff to give into his request, but it had no effect. Sheriff Baker said, "I'm sorry, but without an extradition order, I simply can't do it."

Callahan needed the gifted palm reader there desperately. He had a window of opportunity which was closing fast. If he allowed this killer to slip away, it would no doubt lead to a massive number of additional murders. More than anything, he believed Sister Lee when she told him the killer would soon change his face. The sheriff, and his deputies, had no real understanding of that. To be honest, they didn't get Sister Lee whatsoever, but Ratley tried as she reached for the photo of the sheriff's daughter which sat on the corner of his desk.

The sheriff started to tell her to leave the picture alone. He didn't like anyone messing with it, but Ratley interrupted him saying, "I think she's having some sort of vision sheriff." Placing both hands on the picture, her eyes became intense as she raised it closer to her face staring down at the photograph. It resembled Ashley Pennington greatly. The sheriff and his deputies were fully aware of that as Sister Lee said, "if we don't get him in time he will find the girl again. This time she won't have Ben there to save her." She knew those words would spur the sheriff to see to it that she made it to Indianapolis long before morning.

Caught off guard by her words, the sheriff didn't quite know how to take her interpretation. "That's my daughter," he said, looking into Sister Lee's eyes.

The gifted woman with the power of the cosmos informed the sheriff she was aware of that. Then she said, "Rebecca is safe, it is Ashley who is in danger. Now, it is up to Callahan, and I, to save her."

Suddenly, this was no longer a game of secrets locked away inside a filing cabinet in his office, and the ramblings of a weird woman he had never met. Was Hayden Keller still alive? The sheriff didn't know for sure. It could have been anyone's carcass they recovered at that gas station along Highway 80, but he trusted Ben, and Ashley's statements. Still, the sheriff, as well as his deputies, had to ask themselves several questions. How in the hell did Sister Lee know about Ben, Ashley, and Hayden? How did she know the sheriff's daughter's name when he had never laid eyes on her before? The sheriff had a question he had to ask of Sister Lee, but he chose to do it when they were alone. He looked at Ratley, and Singer as he spoke into the phone telling Callahan, "I'm going to make sure I get her there tonight. One of my deputies will find out where you want her delivered." Callahan thanked him as the sheriff placed him on hold.

Sheriff Baker instructed Singer, "get the location from him, and give yourself plenty of time when figuring the E.T.A. I want her there tonight, and you back here by morning. Understood?"

A beleaguered expression was present on Singer's face as he asked, "what about Ratley?"

"He's going with you," the sheriff said. "Now, give us a minute." He motioned using his head directing his deputies to step outside his office. Singer just nodded closing the door behind him.

By the time Singer made it over to the phone to speak with the detective, the sheriff had closed the blinds hanging in his window. The question he had for Sister Lee was serious indeed. "Is this man, the one in search of Ashley, the same man that killed her family?" Sister Lee did as Callahan instructed. She said nothing, but she did nod her head. The sheriff then asked, "and the body of the man that was recovered that had burned at that gas station, are you telling me that wasn't Hayden Keller's body?" Truthfully, it really wasn't Hayden's body, just one of many he took possession of to carry out his evil mission. Sister Lee could have nodded once again, but that would have only led to another question, and she would never make it to Indianapolis in time to assist Callahan.

Instead, she chose to assure the sheriff he would have his answer soon enough, and he would not have to take her word for it. Sister Lee said, "when I reach Indianapolis you will know without question."

To the sheriff, it sounded as though it all rested in the hands of what she, and Callahan would uncover, but reality was he would discover it for himself with the help of the burning man found in his jurisdiction. A phone call, and a déjà vu experience would make Sister Lee's powers all too real for the sheriff. He, like Callahan, would come to believe in her abilities, and trust in them without exception.

Chapter 34

Déjà vu

The sheriff had instructed his deputies not to waste any time in getting Sister Lee to Indianapolis. "You take her straight there, and don't stop for any reason until you've turned her over to Callahan," he said firmly. Just before they reached the door leading outside the building, the sheriff added, "you call me as soon as you get there. You understand?" Singer led Sister Lee out the door as he had tried to do earlier, and Ratley compliantly nodded his head saying, "sure thing sheriff."

Even though they were unaware of what was said privately between Sister Lee, and the sheriff behind the closed door of his office, it was apparent he felt it was urgent that they get her there immediately. With Sister Lee secured in the backseat of the patrol car, Singer closed the rear door shut, still in disbelief he had been tasked with this assignment. He braced himself for the nearly eight hour roundtrip ride to the big city before climbing into the driver's seat. Ratley, of course, took shotgun. The perturbed expression on Singer's face said it all, but looking over at Ratley, he had to ask, "how in the hell do we always seem to get mixed up in shit like this."

"I don't know. You heard the sheriff, he wants her there A.S.A.P. You want me to drive?" Singer didn't even bother responding to that question. He just turned the key cranking the car as Ratley remarked, "that's what I thought."

Anything that took Ratley some place other than Jefferson Country was almost welcomed including a midnight run to, and from Indianapolis. He didn't care if it was three o'clock in the morning when he saw his pillow, but the same couldn't be said for Singer. Typically, he was waking up at that hour. Under normal circumstances, Sister Lee would have found the two of them amusing, but little could distract her from doing what was necessary to stop Hayden Keller.

Unfortunately, in the meantime, they were all stuck with one another. Singer was irritable cause his stomach was growling. It was well after 6:00 p.m. with no dinner in sight, just a lot of desolate miles ahead, and here he was acting as taxi driver for the strangest woman he had ever heard of or seen. *It was all because she had a fear of flying*, he thought. Sister Lee read his mind, and she voiced her position stating, "I am not afraid. So, do not think that is the case."

Ratley looked over his shoulder at her, and Sister Lee clarified who she had directed that comment toward. There was a displeased tone present in her voice when she said, "not you, him."

Ratley looked at Singer as he put the car in reverse in order to maneuver out of the parking space. An annoyed expression dominated Singer's face as he defiantly said, "don't look at me. I didn't say a thing." Ratley continued looking at Singer as he slowly cut his eyes toward Sister Lee. Taking the main road out of town, Singer adjusted his head slightly peering into the rearview mirror for a second. He remained silent before glancing over his shoulder in the direction of the backseat. "What," Singer questioned in a rather perturbed tone.

Ratley replied, "she just read your mind, didn't she?"

Singer started moving his head denying that she could tell what was going on in his head. Pressing down a little harder on the accelerator he said, "don't listen to her. Whatever she says is all just some sort of trick. It's vague and cryptic."

Sister Lee took offense to that remark, and to put Deputy Singer in his place she said, "you are the one who is afraid."

Singer cut her off saying, "yeah, well why don't you tell me what I'm afraid of then."

Sister Lee replied, "you fear the dentist, and that is why your teeth hurt. I can sense it."

Ratley started to laugh, but he refrained as he blurted out, "she did it again." Then he admitted, Singer had been nursing a bad tooth for almost two weeks.

Singer retaliated, "that doesn't prove anything, lots of people don't like going to the dentist."

Ratley shook his head saying, "no. I'm not buying that. Now, I know why you haven't gone to get it fixed." Singer mumbled something about not having the money or time to do it, but that's when the young deputy turned to Sister Lee asking, "so, what else is he afraid of - going bald or maybe losing the use of a lower extremity?"

Singer was insulted as he raised his voice some saying, "that's not funny Ratley." Sister Lee found it mildly humorous though you could not tell it by the stoic expression she carried on her face. She was reminded of why she liked Ratley, he was open with very little to hide, unlike Singer. Her face was emotionless as usual when she responded candidly to Ratley's question openly saying, "all of the above." That, of course, was strictly to give Ratley a laugh because she knew it was going to be a long ride to Indianapolis. Singer believed that as well.

To make matters worse, Singer was forced to listen to Ratley ask Sister Lee numerous questions, one after another. He was now quite curious to know more about her. Questions that didn't revolve around her unique ability to see into the future were concerning the man he saw in the diner, and of course, Hayden Keller. He had no idea he was talking about the same demonic spirit. He simply assumed he was a man, like any other.

When the patrol car neared the county line, a strange feeling came over Ratley. Flashes of lightening appeared as the wind picked up under fast moving cloud cover. It was eerie how the storm just kind of rolled up on them, but there was no rain anywhere in sight, just lightening, and heavy thunder. An uncomfortable chill touched Ratley's bones at that point. He ceased talking as he observed the turbulent sky. Singer was also experiencing the same kind of feeling. They both felt they had been down that road with Sister Lee once before, but that was impossible. They knew nothing of her up until the point she walked through the door. That didn't stop Ratley from asking the question though. Glancing at Singer he asked, "do you get the feeling we've done this before?" Singer just looked at him. He was thinking the same thing, even though he would never admit it.

Sister Lee coldly commented, "only in a dream, and nothing more." That added another layer of bizarre to the already uncomfortable ride they were taking to Indianapolis.

In Singer's mind, there was simply no way for things to escalate in terms of weird, and unexplainable. Every time she opened her mouth, it tended to send a shiver down his back. He avoided admitting Sister Lee freaked him out a little. Instead, he pretended he had heard enough stupid questions to last for the remainder of the trip, and he instituted the childish rule of no more talking. In the place of Ratley's endless stream of questions, silence overtook the vehicle. Soon enough though, Singer was treated to the eerie sound of Sister Lee chanting under her breath as she meditated focusing all of her energy on locating Hayden

Keller.

Ratley fought the urge to ask another question figuring it would only set Singer off, but there was no question about it, Singer was in absolute hell, even with Ratley's lips buttoned. He had over two hours left ahead of him before they reached Indianapolis. He so wanted to flip on the blue lights, and floor the gas pedal, but here he was stuck driving a clairvoyant know it all that pried into his mind at will, with Ratley riding next to him questioning if Sister Lee really had the gift of seeing into the future. He pulled out his lottery ticket taking a look at the numbers, and Singer couldn't help but notice Ratley's intent interest in the power ball ticket. He sarcastically said, "put that damn thing away. Staring at it all day sure as hell ain't going to make you any money."

Ratley started to speak as he looked toward the backseat. "I was thinking maybe she could help me improve my chances."

Annoyed once more, Singer shook his head giving a slight groan before pointing out, "she can't tell you what the power ball number is, much less what all the other numbers are."

Sister Lee tried to maintain her focus, but she found it difficult with all the chatter taking place inside the squad car. She shushed them somewhat sternly, and gained their complete attention. Ratley lowered his voice as he spoke saying, "I think she's doing something."

Singer replied, "yeah getting on my last nerve."

Sister Lee responded bluntly questioning, "what part of shush do you not understand?"

Singer replied, "it's Ratley's fault. He thinks you can pick winning lottery numbers for him, and I had to explain to him you couldn't." Ratley was left speechless holding his power ball ticket in front of him.

Sister Lee's eyes remained shut as she spoke in a rather curt tone saying, "I could, but I have more important things to do."

Singer scoffed at her saying, "I told you she couldn't figure out that damn power ball."

Sister Lee took a little offense to his blatant denial, and in order to see to it that silence was all that was present in the car for the rest of the trip she volunteered, "you won't win with 35 as your power ball number. You would do much better with 15." That was all the information she left them with regarding their chances of becoming millionaires.

Ratley stared at his ticket with a questioning look on his face. Thirty-five was his power ball number. How in the hell she knew, he didn't know. Her eyes were closed the whole time he had it out. Singer looked over at the ticket as Ratley held it out for him to see. All Ratley could do was chalk Sister Lee's knowledge up to powers beyond what he could understand just as she had said. Singer, on the other hand, couldn't wait to drop her off with Callahan, but he made a mental note of 15 being a good power ball number bet. He planned to make it his next stop before finding a greasy-spoon of some sort to grab a double cheeseburger.

Chapter 35

Questions Answered

It was approaching 11:00 p.m. when Sheriff Baker reached for the remote to change the channel on his television set. He planned to catch the news that was worth hearing before letting Blue out in spite of the old bloodhound's protest. "Hold on just a damn minute Blue. Whatever's out there will be there, I assure you." His gruff remarks to the dog stifled his loud bark long enough for the sheriff to toss his plate in the sink. Rinsing off the dishes, he listened to the upcoming highlights of the news broadcast along with the weatherman touting some unusual storm activity seen in the area.

Old Blue whimpered a little, and the sheriff glanced over at him as he sat patiently by the door. Something outside had his attention. The sheriff looked at the phone hanging on his kitchen wall expecting it to ring at virtually any moment. In his mind, he started to question what was taking Singer and Ratley so long. *How damn difficult could it be to deliver a witness*, he thought.

Hearing the rumbling sound of thunder outside, he decided to open the backdoor, and let Old Blue tend to his business. The dog was filled with as much curiosity as his owner at times, and that nose of his could usually manage to sniff out trouble. Blue was on the trail of something though, and he paid no attention to the sheriff when he hollered, "come on Blue, get your ass back here. We don't have time for this shit." Lightening reflected off the clouds as the sheriff stood on his back porch still keeping an ear out for the phone to ring. He could see his dog's tail disappear into the trees as the lightening lit up the ground in front of him. Growing more impatient as he stood there, he started to yell for Old Blue once more, but he was interrupted by the sound of an incoming call.

Stepping back inside the house, the sheriff picked up the phone saying, "well, it's about time. What took you two so long? I said call me as soon as you get there." Clearly, he was expecting to hear Singer's voice on the other end of the line, but to his surprise it was someone else he hadn't spoken to in quite some time. Thrown-off by Sheriff Baker's words, Cal Milner stammered as he spoke, "ah, sheriff?"

"Yeah. Who's this?"

"This is Cal Milner. Look, I just ran over something in the road a few miles back, and well ah."

"Well, what?"

"It's bad sheriff - I think you need to see this for yourself."

"What the hell did you hit Cal?"

"I didn't hit him sheriff, but I think I ran over one of his arms. He was just sprawled out in the road. I couldn't stop the truck in time." On the surface it sounded like a case of vehicular death until Cal added, "he was dead when I found him sheriff. It looked like the poor bastard was burned to a crisp before it started raining."

The sheriff listened as Cal tried not to lose his whopper combo he'd devoured an hour earlier. This wouldn't be the first chard remains the sheriff had seen in his jurisdiction, and just as Sister Lee had said, he now had his question answered. The one which remained was whose body was lying in the road torched beyond recognition. He never would have guessed it to be Bruce Horvath. Knowing he was going to have to call the county coroner, and he would

207

most likely miss the call from his deputies, Sheriff Baker said, "tell me where you're at, and I'll be there as soon as I can."

Hanging up the phone, the sheriff was fairly certain Sister Lee had made it to Indianapolis. Listening to part of the newscast, he picked up the phone to dial Fred Hicks to ask him to meet him at the crime scene, he heard mention of a string of recent murders taking place along the Ohio, Indiana border. He didn't stop to question who was behind it, he had troubles of his own. His concern for Ashley Pennington's safety was at the forefront of his mind though as the county coroner answered with a groggy voice.

"Fred this is Sheriff Baker. I hate to wake you, but we've got a mess it appears off of Route 9."

"Alright, sheriff. I'll meet you there."

"Very good. Oh, and Fred."

"Yeah?"

"You probably want to make sure you bring a shovel."

Fred just groaned as he hung up the phone thinking if the sheriff knew one thing it was how to paint a pretty picture. He could hardly wait to see this one.

Chapter 36

Joining Of Forces

When Singer made the turn onto Washington, Ratley started digging in his pockets for his cell phone. They were almost in front of the hotel where Callahan had agreed to meet them. Unsuccessful in his search, he looked over at Singer. "What," he muttered.

Ratley displayed that "we're screwed" smirk, and Singer immediately knew he didn't have his phone on him. "I must have left it back at my car, or maybe in my desk drawer."

With a degree of disgust, Singer reached inside his coat retrieving his phone saying, "here use mine. I guess it's a good thing one of us remembered."

Ratley flipped the phone open only to find the screen pitch dark. Pressing several buttons he saw no sign of life in the electronic device, and that's when he remarked, "I hope you brought a charger for it."

Singer quickly said, "give me that," as he snatched the phone out of Ratley's left hand. "What did you do break the damn thing?"

"I hardly touched it."

Sister Lee had heard enough. "Give it to me," she demanded. Singer pulled over in front of the La Quinta Inn, and he snidely questioned, "you plan on fixing it?"

"If it is power which is required, there is plenty within reach." Holding the phone in the palm of her right hand, she instructed Singer to turn on the phone, and dial the number. To his surprise the screen lit up, and he was able to place the call to Callahan. He, and Buttweiler were waiting inside the lobby for them, and within less than sixty seconds, he was out front relieving Singer, and Ratley of Sister Lee. The communication between Callahan, and the deputies was kept short. Singer was glad to get rid of the palm reader, and they were pushed for time. The detective, and his partner on the other hand were eager to find out everything she had to share regarding Hayden Keller's appearance, and whereabouts. The meeting between the fortune teller, and the detective wasn't awkward in the least. It was almost like they knew one another in some way prior to ever meeting. Callahan focused his attention on her as Buttweiler thanked Singer, and Ratley for getting her there safe.

"Don't mention it," Singer said with a grin. "Handing her over to you is our pleasure." Ratley got his inside joke, but Sister Lee paid him no attention as usual. As Callahan escorted the gifted psychic to the front doors of the hotel, he made a final request of the deputies. "Please tell Sheriff Baker thanks for me. You guys have no idea how helpful you've been." Singer took the compliment as he went to place the call to the sheriff. He planned on informing him the package had been delivered, but curiously, he found his phone without power once again.

Ratley suggested, "why don't you give it to her again. Maybe she can do what she did last time." Singer was far too stubborn for that though.

Just before entering the hotel, Sister Lee turned to him saying, "it's no use to call him now. He will not answer."

That was last prediction they heard her make right before turning the car around to head back to a place few wished to ever see. Ratley looked down at Singer's phone asking, "how did she ever get it to work?"

Singer's explanation was simple, "dumb luck, I tell you. Come on, let's get something to eat." That, of course, set good with Ratley. Truthfully though, he was going to miss Sister Lee.

Buttweiler could only guess what Sister Lee was like based on the information Callahan had shared with him. Her curious persona didn't disappoint though. She was precise in her words, particular in tastes, and all-knowing in matters most couldn't comprehend. His first impression was she, and Henley would make quite the pair, but he and Callahan agreed not to divulge any information about her to anyone. In a way, she was their best kept secret. She would be what they referred to as an unconfirmed source from that point forward, and no mention of her would make any report.

Sister Lee wasn't much on formal introductions. She knew everything she needed to know about both men. Once she was seated at a table away from the front desk, she openly said, "ask what you wish." Callahan gave a head nod to Buttweiler, and they immediately got down to business. Buttweiler held a number of case folders which he had managed to convince Henley he'd return first thing in the morning. Laying them out on the table, he showed Sister Lee a few of the photos. She was able to provide a great deal of information neither he, nor Callahan, could extrapolate from the crime scene pictures. The fact that she knew names without seeing them in reports gave credence to every word she spoke. She quickly whittled down the cases to the ones Hayden Keller was responsible for.

When Callahan went to check her in, she informed him, "I need no room because I'll be staying with you." That immediately grabbed Buttweiler's attention as Callahan said, "that's not going to work, I'm afraid."

"Of course it will, and there is little you fear," she said in haste. "Where you go, I go."

Callahan barely broke his stride as he told Buttweiler, "see if you can explain things to her."

Not knowing where to start, Buttweiler said, "look, Sister Lee - Callahan doesn't really, ah. Well, what I'm trying to say is it's just not how things are done."

The stoic expression on her face forced Buttweiler to ask, "you with me?"

She instantly replied, "silly question. I'm sitting right in front of you, but I will remain with him until the one you seek is stopped."

Buttweiler could see she was determined. In an attempt to sway her, he assured her, "look, you'll like this place. I promise. The rooms are nice, and they even serve waffles for breakfast."

Sister Lee's retort was, "do you wish to have my help or not?"

Buttweiler explained, "yes, but Callahan likes his space."

"That will not be a problem," she said. "Seldom do I sleep during the night, and he has a spare room which I shall use." The young officer tried to make his case heard, but Sister Lee prevented him from interrupting her. "I require a view of the stars to determine the evil one's next move, and I will not do it here. If you want me to tell you where you will find him, I suggest you explain that to him."

Buttweiler promptly stood calling Callahan by name as he waited for the desk clerk to hand him a key. The detective confidently asked, "you explained things to her?"

Picking up the folders, Buttweiler walked toward the counter as he said, "yeah. About that, she says you have a spare room of some sort that has a perfect view of the stars which she needs in order to help us find this guy."

"Forget it she can look at the stars here."

"She says she won't help unless she remains with you for some reason."

Callahan looked over his shoulder at her. Her persistence led him to a revelation of sorts. More of Father Tomas's words now made sense. To Buttweiler's surprise, Callahan told the guy behind the counter to keep the key. "We won't be needing it," he said. Instructing Buttweiler to get the car he added, "well, it looks like she'll be staying with me."

Chapter 37

Important Information

Sheriff Baker was reminded of the scene at the Marathon station nearly a year ago as he checked for identification on the burned corpse. The smell was brutal, and the sight of the body itself was grotesque just as Cal stated on the phone. Shining his flashlight over the roasted remains, he held it steady paying particular attention to the head, and upper torso. Prior images flashed in the sheriff's mind. He couldn't be certain, but he had his suspicions as to who it was. He didn't voice it though. There was no abandoned vehicle anywhere close by, and that alone told the sheriff this guy didn't get there on his own.

Except for the cleanup, the coroner got off easy. He certainly didn't have much guesswork to do coming up with a cause of death for that victim. "He died by fire aided by accelerant," he claimed. "Possibly dumped here. Picking away at the skin around the hands, face and neck, that's buzzards."

"Good to know Fred." The sheriff was sarcastic when he said it, but Fred never noticed. "Can you give me a time of death?"

"I'd say a couple of hours before he ran over him. You mind giving me a hand with this? The rain tends to make 'em a little slippery at times."

The sheriff pitched in giving Fred a hand as he said, "I can tell you more in the morning. Two burned bodies, a year apart, what are the chances of that?"

"You keep this one under your hat Fred."

"Okay, but word tends to travel fast around here, you

know that." Fred was looking toward Cal as he spoke.

"I'll take care of him, don't you worry." The sheriff sounded like he meant it too. After helping hoist the body into the meat wagon, he turned his attention to Cal Milner. He was standing next to his truck waiting to hear word from the sheriff.

"I've got one thing to say Cal, and I expect you to listen."

"Yeah, sheriff."

"You say anything to anyone about this, and I'll know who it came from."

"Okay."

"I guess that means I can count on you to keep this between us for right now?"

"Sure, Sheriff. Whatever you say."

"Alright, you're free to go then, but remember what I said."

"Yes sir."

"Very well, get this thing out of here."

Cal climbed up in his rig breathing a little easier as he turned the key to crank it. He left that scene with no intention of mentioning a word of that night to anyone. In fact, that would be that last time he ever took that road home. Route 9 was forever tainted in his mind. As rough as things were back in Jefferson County, Sheriff Baker, and the coroner weren't the only ones losing sleep. Ratley had taken the seat behind the wheel for the return leg of the trip, and the deputies still had three more hours of two lane in front of them. It would 4:00 a.m. by the time they made it back. *Just in time to start another day*, Singer thought as he closed his eyes. He had no clue what that day would entail, but the eight o' clock call from Bruce's mother concerning her son's whereabouts would confirm soon enough that the sheriff was right about the blackened body found out on Route 9. Singer would just be the lucky soul to take it.

Sister Lee, and Callahan remained awake until the wee hours of the morning. She had specific information she needed to share with the detective, and she did her best to put it in terms he could understand before mapping out Hayden's travel path for him. She was quick to point out he was headed for Peoria, but she assured him he wouldn't be there long.

Buttweiler was tasked with completing the report the captain had ordered. It wasn't fun, but it was necessary. The upside was Callahan had done the bulk of it for him. The conservative estimate he, and Callahan had come up with was thirty-five cases would be solved once the serial killer was caught, and that was just in their jurisdiction. Buttweiler had no true understanding of what would be required to stop Hayden Keller for good. The cost would be painful, and deadly. Sister Lee used those words only in Callahan's presence. She knew he would not shy away from his responsibility.

The detective's place could've certainly used a woman's touch, but Sister Lee was no interior decorator. Oddly, she felt as comfortable seated at his small dining table as she did the one in her parlor back home, but when Callahan offered her some coffee she declined saying, "I only drink water, juice, and goat's milk."
Callahan just looked at her remarking, "now that's a wicked combination."
She took what he said literally, informing him, "there is nothing wicked about it." Callahan could honestly say he had never met anyone like her. When he asked about the mark on her hand, she simply said, "it is the sign of power, and knowledge." Pointing to the one on the underside of her wrist, she informed him, "this mark represents the balance between good and evil."

"And, why is it there?"

"To remind me of my purpose, I suppose. It was given to me long ago." Sister Lee refrained from sharing her age with the detective. It was not unimportant. All that truly mattered was his role in stopping Hayden Keller before he found Ben Goodman. She now knew she couldn't shield Ashley Pennington from him. He was mere hours away from her grandmother's house, and soon he would find her in Des Moines no doubt. She would do what she could to keep her alive, but much was in the hands of Callahan concerning that. As he sat across the table from her, she asked for his hand. When he questioned what for, she said, "indulge me. I wish to see the right one."

"You want to see what secrets I have?"

"You have none from me."

She looked at his palm without tracing the lines which ran across it. She stared at it a second before looking up into his eyes. "Give me your other hand," she requested. Normally, she gave orders, but she knew him well enough to know which tone to use when speaking to him. The only demand she had made was to remain at his side until evil was halted. Callahan did just as she requested. Taking both his hands, she held them for a brief moment. Uncertain what was taking place he asked, "so, what do you see?"

Her earnest response was, "a great man, nothing less." She looked at his hands no more as she informed him, "it's late. Time for you to get some sleep. We have another long drive ahead of us." She stood, and turned walking toward the spare room, and Callahan started to say something, but she interrupted him with, "I know juice is in the icebox, glasses to the left of it, and bathroom at the end of the hall. I'll be okay. You go to sleep." Callahan took her advice somehow, appreciating the company of the oddest woman he had ever met, but he was on guard concerning his thoughts when in her company. There was no getting around that.

Chapter 38

Start Of A Hard Hump-day

Morning came quick. For Singer, it was just a grueling continuation of the previous day virtually uninterrupted. He was a creature of habit though. Without fail, he could be found each, and every morning eating breakfast at his favorite diner. It was the one where Stella worked, that's part of what kept him coming back, the ham and cheese omelet wasn't bad either. That's what he had almost every morning along with a healthy portion of bacon, and wheat toast.

This morning was a little different than most. Singer actually had something to talk about worth listening too. He planned on chatting up the waitresses by mentioning the overnight run he had made to Indianapolis, the one that brought him back in town just a few hours ago. It was guaranteed to make him the center of attention without him uttering one worn-out joke. The truth was, he loved throwing out a detail or two for them to chew on while he ate his breakfast. Leaving them asking him probing questions about his official business made him feel important. The best part was telling them he couldn't share pieces of information with them. He liked to use the phrase, "that's classified" a lot. That plan faded away in an instant though.

When the deputy went to pull into his usual space next to the restaurant, he found something he didn't expect. The sheriff had beat him to it. Parking alongside him, Singer suspected he was there for a particular reason, and he assumed it was to confirm the palm reader had been turned over to the detective without incident. Normally, the sheriff never did breakfast at the diner. He usually cooked it up himself, and shared half of it with Blue before leaving for the office. His being there meant something was up, and Singer felt certain he was there to meet with him personally.

It was 7:24 a.m. when Singer strolled through the door. All he had to do was raise his finger, and the young waitress at the counter greeted him saying, "a hot cup of coffee coming right up." He caught a glimpse of Stella carrying plates to one of the tables, but he locked eyes with Sheriff Baker almost upon entering. He carried a serious looked on his weathered face, and Singer could tell immediately he wasn't the only one working on little sleep.

The sheriff raised his coffee cup motioning for the deputy to come join him, and neither man said a word until Singer took a seat across from him. The sheriff first addressed him saying, "I see the big city hasn't changed you."
Jenny put on a fresh pot of coffee for Singer as he replied, "yeah. You probably want to know she made it there in one piece." Singer started to elaborate on the fact they tried to call, but the sheriff cut him short acknowledging he was certain of one thing.
"I know she's there," he said firmly. "It's what we've got here that concerns me, and I'll tell you right now they're connected in some way."
Singer looked lost as Stella made her way over to the table. The sheriff's serious look softened some as she said, "I told you he'd be here. You ready to order now sheriff?"
Singer promptly asked, "what about me?"
"I know what you want."
"Maybe I changed my mind."
"Really?"

"No. I'll just have my usual."

Stella shook her head. "I can't believe you work with him. You want something besides coffee sheriff?"

"Just give me what he's having."

"Two heart attack specials it is."

As Stella walked away, Singer remarked, "she's got a way about her, doesn't she."

The sheriff nodded his head once agreeing with him, yet he said nothing. Singer was as interested in hearing what the sheriff had to say as he was in watching Stella walk to the kitchen to place their order. The sheriff sat idle waiting for her to put some distance between herself, and their table before speaking another word though. Reaching for his coffee, he offered in a suppressed voice, "I got a call last night about a John Doe in our backyard, and no one needs to know about this other than you, me, and Fred."

"What about Ratley?"

"I'll tell him later."

"Sounds like you had more excitement than us."

"Yeah, that J.D. was found burned on Route 9 with no vehicle present." The sheriff looked around to make certain no one was close enough to overhear him before adding, "that scene looked familiar, and the guy's billfold was missing."

"Who called it in?"

"Someone who agreed not to talk to anyone about it. I won't have this town put in a panic over this until we have answers, and even then I want a lid on it." Singer nodded his head slightly in agreement.

"You think it has anything to do with that guy Ratley ran into yesterday?"

"He was here, wasn't he."

"What do you want me to do," Singer asked.

"If you get any wind of someone missing, you let me know first, and you don't breathe a word to anyone else.

Understood?"

Singer uttered, "sure," and cleared his throat as the young waitress brought over his cup of coffee fixed just how he liked it.

Breakfast was eaten in haste. The sheriff was eager to conduct some research of his own, and meet with Fred. Singer had the chore of answering the phone until Ratley crawled in later that morning. "Hell of a way to start a hump-day," Singer commented after wiping his mouth, and tossing his napkin in his plate.

"This thing's just gotten started," the sheriff added as he dug in his pocket for his wallet. Pulling it out to pay the check he was reminded of all the IDs Hayden Keller had amassed when they found what was believed to be his body just about a year back. He didn't say anything else to Singer regarding that though.

As the sheriff made his way to the door of the diner, he asked Stella if she had seen a guy driving a flashy truck the previous day. She looked at him saying, "you mean the guy Ratley spoke to? He was sitting right over there." She pointed to an empty booth close to where they had been sitting.

"That might be the one. What can you tell me about him?"

"Not much, he seemed kind of strange. Tall, short dark hair, he had a really nasty looking scar on his face. I didn't notice it until right before he left." That was enough to grab the sheriff's attention. Stella could see it in his eyes when she said it. "Is something wrong," she asked.

The sheriff quickly thanked her as he headed out the door.

Singer stepped up to the cash register blocking her view as he explained, "that truck might be stolen, that's all. Probably nothing though. You know how it is around here." He even left her an extra dollar to distract her, but Stella's curiosity was peaked when Singer remarked, "well, I better get to work, have a good day."

Buttweiler had a mission of his own to tend to. He'd arrived at the station early that morning hoping to put the report on the captain's desk without being seen. Luck wouldn't allow him to do that though. Captain Rollins made it in at seven sharp that morning. He had a scheduled meeting with the Chief of Police in less than one hour, and when he returned from the men's room, he found Buttweiler opening the door to his office with the lengthy report in hand.

The young officer left the report in the center of his desk on top of several others where it could easily be found, and he hastily turned to make his escape only to hear the Captain yell, "Buttweiler, you have something for me?"

"Just a report, I placed it on your desk. Callahan said you requested it." He never stopped walking as he spoke, hoping to make it back to his desk.

The captain growled, "yeah. Well it's about time. Come on in. Let's take a look at it. This should be interesting."

Buttweiler practically froze as Captain Rollins placed his hand on the door of his office. "Get your ass in here. I don't have all day." The captain's gruff demeanor rattled him some whenever he was in his company. Being pitted in the same office with him wasn't the first place he would've preferred to be, but that's where he found himself when the captain cornered him.

"It's all right there for you to read sir."

The captain said nothing as he walked over to his desk picking it up. It was thicker than any report he had seen Callahan submit. It also wasn't riddled with typos. He reviewed the first page briefly, scanning over it. Flipping to the next page he barked, "Callahan didn't write this. I know cause there are no misspelled words. Did he have you type this up for him?"

"It was a collective effort based on investigative research. You can see by the case count it took a little while to compile all of the needed information."

"I see where it says thirty-five cases. You expect me to believe that? Better yet, you think I'm promising Chief Cielinski anything based on these numbers?" Buttweiler had no clue what to say. "You think this assignment is some kind of joke don't you? Well, I'm here to tell you it's not." The captain checked the time on his watch. He knew nothing about the serial killer they were after, or how extensive their search had been regarding the cold cases. It all just seemed unfathomable in his mind when he said, "no wonder he sent you in here to deliver this. Frankly, I don't know what the hell either one of you are thinking." The captain had finished with his rant. A brief pause hung in the air before he said, "well what do you have to say for yourself?"

For the first time in his professional career, Buttweiler mustered the gumption to speak staring Captain Rollins right in the eye. "I know the information contained in that report is accurate. I know the evidence in each of those cases points to one person, and the timeline fits. We're tracking his movements at this very moment, and I also have it on good authority we stand a high probability of catching the guy responsible for all these murders based on the network of law enforcement agencies we're currently working with." The words flew out of Buttweiler's mouth faster than he could recite the alphabet.

When Buttweiler finished, the captain took a seat in his chair, and only the sound of pages turning broke the silence which filled the room. He'd taken the time to actually read through the first few pages of the report. His tone changed as he asked, "you have other police departments you're working with?"

"Listed on pages ten through twelve."

The captain turned to it visually taking in the vast number of police, and sheriff departments currently involved in finding the serial killer. Voicing his thoughts he remarked, "that's good work. You two let me know if you need something." That was Buttweiler's cue to exit, and he did, without hesitation, leaving the captain to his reading. Making his way through the squad room, he walked a little taller than he did before he entered the captain's office. For once, his chin was raised just like his mentor's, and he felt like he was made to carry his shield. He could hardly wait to discover what their unconfirmed source had divulged to Callahan.

Chapter 39

Suspicions Confirmed

Sheriff Baker had told Singer he'd meet him back at the office. He wanted a better look at the body of his John Doe. He also wanted to speak with Callahan, and Sister Lee. Soon enough, his suspicions would be confirmed though. Singer had barely stepped foot inside the door when the phone started ringing. Needing to hit the head, he wanted to ignore it, but knowing what he did, he postponed the call of nature long enough to answer it, "sheriff's office."

The woman's voice seemed weakened, and concerned when she said, "my son is missing. This is Mrs. Horvath."

Singer calmly stated, "okay Mrs. Horvath. I'm sure he'll turn up." He even lied convincingly when he said, "there's no need to worry. When did you last see Bruce?"

Patricia Horvath informed Singer she hadn't spoken to her son since yesterday around noon. Giving the deputy a description of what he was wearing, her intuition was telling her something bad had happened to Bruce. Not sure of what to tell her, Singer made mention of the fact that he hadn't been missing for twenty-four hours. "That's usually a good thing, he's probably with a friend, but the sheriff, and I will look into it for you." His promise to do his job did little in the way of easing her anxiety over the matter, but it ended the call without her asking any questions. Singer needed to hit the can, and radio the sheriff pronto in just that order.

Elsewhere, Hayden Keller had found the home of Ilene Vandershamp with the helpful information he gathered back in Chanceville, and the assistance he was given from the operator when he dialed 411 from Ronnie's cell phone. Hanging onto the truck longer than he should have, he found it difficult to part with, the damn thing was comfortable, and spacious, but filling up with trash quick. Parked on the same side of the street a few houses down, he watched the old woman back out of her driveway as he sat inside the pickup. She was alone, and easy for the taking, but not the one he was after for the moment. Still, the last living relative of Ashley Pennington was hard to pass up, but Hayden was on a tight schedule.

Her trip to the store saved her life, yet she had no idea it was in danger of being taken from her. Fortunately for her, Hayden didn't need the old lady to find the prize he was searching for. The younger version of her would serve him quite well. He was looking forward to a one-on-one encounter with her granddaughter. Hayden was certain she'd be surprised to see him again after the way they parted last time. He had no doubt she would remember him even with his new look. *Everyone appreciates a good change every now and then*, he thought as he salivated anticipating the pain he would soon inflict on her. That aside, the scar on Hayden's left cheek, and the vengeful stare he carried in his eyes always remained the same, no matter whose body he possessed. Glancing at his reflection in the rearview mirror, he knew Ashley would recognize him in a heartbeat without him uttering a single word.

Armed with nothing but a wicked desire to terrorize the girl, and extract the information he was after, he got out of the truck. Planning to put Danford's handcuffs to use for a second time, he walked to the front door. Never bothering to knock, he twisted the handle to see if it turned. He quickly learned Ashley's grandmother was cautious enough to secure the house before leaving. How long she would be gone, Hayden couldn't be sure, but it didn't matter. If she came back too soon she'd pay the price in the end. It was no skin off Hayden's back, just his victims. He still had his quota to fill, and Ilene Vandershamp would have been perfect to help him out with that.

Courteous behavior went against Hayden's grain, but as much as he hated doing it, he knocked on the door, and waited for someone to answer. A few seconds passed, and he decided it was time to take matters into his own hands. Walking around back, he saw no sign of a dog, and he unlatched the gate thinking, *she should get one*. Hayden approached the backdoor confident he would gain entry. He busted one of the glass panes in the door closest to the deadbolt, and reached his hand inside unlocking it.

Silently, he slipped through the backdoor closing it shut behind him. Stepping on the broken glass, he refrained from uttering a word. He so wanted to call out Ashley's name, and inform her he was home, but instead, he carefully searched the place until he was satisfied she wasn't there. Planning to wait for her to return, he ventured back to the kitchen which he passed on his way in. Looking around the place, he found her mail lying on the edge of the kitchen counter. It was piled high right next to a cookie jar, and next to it was the coffee maker. Hayden took the liberty of sampling the contents of both as he pulled open several drawers in search of sharp knife he could use for cutting.

Slicing open several envelopes, he determined her exact location in no time. It was clear she was away at college, and wouldn't return anytime soon. The list of numbers her grandmother kept handy on the frig were helpful as well. Hayden thought to himself, *could she make it any easier*.

He pulled a picture of Ashley out from under the magnet that was attached to the side of the icebox. Staring at it, he reflected back to when he first met her, and he grew angry seeing the cross still hanging around her neck. His big regret was not being given the time needed to break her.

Obstacles, he had plenty of them. The girl, and her faith were just one of them, but Hayden aimed to rectify that. Killing her family was only the start of her nightmare. Facing him for a second time would cement her fear of evil forever. Eventually, he would take her life once she had given up hope, and brought him to the man he longed to kill. He blamed her for his most recent demise as much as he did the man with two lives - the only difference was he knew where to find her.

Just before leaving, he opened the refrigerator swiping some items to take on the road with him. The selection was slim, but he made do as he said to himself, "who says stalkers can't be choosers?" Grabbing a plastic bag from under the sink, he filled it with the essentials - some cut fruit, some apple juice, and a large Tupperware container full of leftover pot roast, cooked carrots, and potatoes. It was everything a thirsty serial killer needed to keep his strength up once he finished off the milk leaving the empty carton resting sideways on the counter. He had to have something to wash down the Oreos, Vincent's taste buds couldn't seem to get enough of those. He went out the backdoor, which he left standing wide open. Hayden wasn't concerned about covering his tracks. He planned on making it to Des Moines in record time to pay a visit to his favorite college student, and find himself another vehicle.

When Sheriff Baker received word from Singer that Bruce Horvath was reported missing, he knew immediately it had something to do with what went down at the gas station where they found Ashley Pennington. Speaking with the coroner, he was handed an approximate time of death. It would have to do given the condition of the body. Sheriff Baker had no idea how to explain it to Bruce's mother. He didn't want her to see what was left of her boy, and he knew he couldn't face her until he could assure her the son of a bitch responsible was going to pay for his murder.

There was no fixing this. The reality was he couldn't guarantee that, and the town itself had already suffered enough. The loss of the Ferris' sent a number of people packing. The stories that would circulate about this would never end, and the sheriff knew it. The words truth, and justice ran through his mind along with a host of other thoughts. He knew Hayden Keller, or someone seeking revenge for his murder, was long gone out of his jurisdiction, but if he wasn't caught he'd probably come back at some point. None of that was adequate to share with Mrs. Horvath seeing that her boy was all she had.

Staring down at Bruce's chard remains, he looked across the examining table at his old friend Fred asking, "does this look like something that could have taken place inside a burning vehicle, initially anyway?"
Fred just looked at him saying, "I can write it up anyway you want, but what about that guy driving the semi?"
"He won't talk, but if he ever does, the body was found right where you picked him up on the road a short distance from a totaled vehicle."
"There was a vehicle?"
"Yeah, a black Ford Ranger. You mean to tell me you didn't see it?"
Fred made some notes as he calmly said, "well it was pitch dark sheriff. Besides, you were the one with the flashlight.

My primary concern was the body, you know that."

"I understand. After looking at it in full light what have you found?"

"Says right here death was the result of an auto accident along Route 9, see. Body is that of an unknown male between the ages of twenty, and forty."

"You're a good man Fred. Don't let anyone tell you otherwise." The sheriff paused before adding, "we both just have nasty jobs at times."

"Somebody has to do it sheriff, that's what I keep telling myself every morning."

Sheriff Baker started to head for the door as he placed a hand on Fred's shoulder saying, "I think you can cover him up now." Pausing before he opened the door, Sheriff Baker questioned, "this one stays?"

Fred never turned to face him as he answered in a monotone of sorts. "Under my hat." The sheriff nodded, their backs facing one another. That's when the truth usually surfaced between them in matters such as this one, and that's when Fred asked, "does your hat ever get full sheriff?"

In a dreary sounding breath, the sheriff professed, "God, does it ever," as he opened the door leaving Bruce in the capable hands of the longtime medical examiner.

Chapter 40

Race Against Time

The sheriff's mounting concern for the girl's safety dominated his thoughts on the drive back to his office. Given time, all he could do was place a call to warn her grandmother that she, and the girl might need to relocate temporarily. It sounded crazy to even try to explain, but the sheriff's gut seldom lied, and he had a strong feeling Ashley Pennington was next on the list, followed by Ben Goodman.

Knowing what he did, the sheriff placed a call to Singer. He felt it was urgent, and he needed to give him a heads up. As soon as the deputy answered the phone, the sheriff informed him, "this is important. I need you to pull the file we have in the bottom left drawer of my desk. I want you to give me the phone number we have for the girl's grandmother."

Singer dropped what he was doing, and went straight to his office as the sheriff told him where he kept the key hidden. He could hear Singer opening the drawer when he added, "that case I ran by you this morning has officially been ruled an accident, nothing more. For now, you know nothing about it, and that goes double for Ratley. You just investigate that missing person case as you would any other, and I'll be the one to break the news to Bruce's mother when it's time."

"Got it Sheriff."

"Good give it to me."

Singer read off the phone number to the sheriff along with Ilene's name. Quickly jotting it down, Sheriff Baker made a point to ask for Detective Callahan's number as well. Singer was curious to know what he wanted it for, but he didn't bother asking. He knew the sheriff well enough to know he had his own reasons for doing things, and he sure as hell didn't have to answer to his deputies. Besides that, he also felt the less he knew the better. He got little sleep at night as it was. The last thing he needed to hear was Sister Lee was right, demons were real, Hayden Killer couldn't be killed, and he'd eventually make his way back to Chanceville to pay them a little visit.

The deputy understood, when he hung up the phone, his job was to follow normal protocol, and drag his feet a little. The sheriff needed time to put the necessary pieces in place to make Bruce's death appear like something other than murder. Putting the file back where he found it, he locked the drawer placing the key in the appropriate hiding place. Seconds later, he heard Ratley shuffle in through the front door, and Singer quickly exited the sheriff's office.

Looking at Singer, Ratley removed his coat as he asked "what's going on?"
Singer walked over to his desk picking up his keys ready to leave the office in Ratley's hands as he said, "I've got work to do, and you've got phones to answer."
Ratley still looked exhausted when he said, "I can hardly wait. Sometimes, this is the most boring place on the planet. In fact, I'm convinced of that."

Singer just stared at him a moment without saying a word as Ratley meandered over, and fell into his chair. Irritable, and sleep-deprived, the young deputy questioned him saying, "what?"
"Oh, I was just thinking you really missed out on your beauty rest."

"Very funny. Maybe I can grab a few winks here before the sheriff gets back."

"You can try," and with that Singer was out the door. He had plans of finding a shade tree somewhere out of town, out of sight, and testing out that new seat massager he got for his birthday. All he had to do was listen out for the radio in between catnapping. Leaving Ratley in the dark was easy at times, especially when he was half asleep, and hungry.

The Sheriff dialed the number he was given in an attempt to contact the girl's grandmother, but he received no answer. Images he had personally seen of Hayden Keller's victims raged through his mind as he tried once again hoping she would pick-up. Growing more panicked, he pulled over to the side of the road. Looking up at a sign in the distance, he was pointed straight for Peroria, but it was a long haul to get there, and the guy responsible for Bruce's demise had a tremendous head-start. Sheriff Baker was convinced he had already come and gone. If that were the case, he didn't want to see the carnage left from his wrath. He just wanted the son of bitch to fry, and never be given the opportunity to venture back into Jefferson County.

Looking back down at his phone, he had to realize it was now out of his hands, just as Sister Lee had said in essence before leaving for Indianapolis. It didn't make the event that took place under his watch any more palatable, but he now depended on the all-knowing fortune teller, and the big city detective to set things right. He debated about calling them or trying Ilene one last time. Thinking about his own daughter, whom Ashley resembled in so many ways, he dialed her grandmother again. This time she answered, but her voice was shaken. Glad just to hear her on the other end of the line, Sheriff Baker forewent the normal pleasantries. First thing out of his mouth was, "Ilene, this is Sheriff

Baker. I believe we have a problem, and I'm concerned for you, and your granddaughter's safety."

Already startled by what she was looking at, Ashley's grandmother was thrown off by the sheriff's keen sense of looming danger. She said nothing as she stared at the ransacked condition of her kitchen. The groceries she held in her hand fell to the floor when the sheriff said, "something tells me you're both in danger. Is Ashley there with you?"

"No," she cried. "What's happened here?" She looked around realizing the place had been broken into, the backdoor standing wide open, and the glass covering the floor just feet from where she was standing. The sheriff questioned her, "are you alright? Where's Ashley?"

"Ashely's away at college, and my house has been broken into."

"Listen to me. Are you sure no one is still in the house?"

That question raised Ilene Vandershamp's anxiety level even higher. She had barely made it into the kitchen. She couldn't be sure who was elsewhere in the house. "I don't know," she responded in a frightened tone.

"Look, you need to get out of there now. Get in your car, and go to a public place. You can call police from there. Do not re-enter that house even after they clear it. Get a hotel room if you have to, I don't care."

"What's this break-in have to do with Ashley?"

"I'll explain later, just get out of there."

Panic-stricken, she managed to say, "okay sheriff," but Ilene never bothered hanging up the phone. The receiver just hit the floor with a hard thud as she made a hasty retreat toward the front door.

Now feeling as though her life was in imminent danger, she stormed through her living room before stopping dead in her tracks. Directly in front of her she could see a shadow belonging to a large man as it moved across her porch. Frozen with fear, she held her breath, and her heart stopped. The only thing that made it beat again was the knock she heard followed by the voice of her next door neighbor, Arnold Greely.

As soon as she heard him call her by name, she opened the door almost happy to see him. He was holding a few pieces of mail which were addressed to her when he said, "I meant to bring these over yesterday, but as luck would have it, the mailman struck again. Two more pieces in the wrong box. You wouldn't happen to have any of mine would you?"

"No. I don't believe so. Come on in, and I'll check, but would you mind doing me a favor?"

Arnold glanced over his shoulder before stepping inside her house. "I'm just home for lunch. So, I don't have that much time," he told her. "What is it?"

Well, someone broke in this morning, and I just discovered it in this condition. I haven't even had time to call the police yet. Could you check the place out for me while I do that?"

"Sure." She led Arnold to the kitchen showing him the damage. Picking up the receiver she dialed 911 as Arnold looked around at the mess which was left. "Was anything taken," he asked.

"I don't think so, but I can't tell for sure yet."

"It looks like maybe some kids did it." When he said that, all she could think about was the call she received from Sheriff Baker. Arnold said the first thing that entered his mind which was, "I have to admit this is terrible. Right next door during broad daylight. This could have been my house. I don't know what the world's coming to." Ilene looked at him, and he said, "I'm sorry, I didn't mean to scare you. It's not that bad. I'll wait here with you until the police arrive."

Ilene spoke to the police dispatcher giving him her name and address. "I need to report a break-in," she said as she stared at the open mail belonging to Ashley which was left on the counter next to the now empty milk carton. Suddenly, she questioned why someone would tamper with it. Hanging up the phone, she tried to dial Sheriff Baker back, but there was no answer. She wrote down the number, and waited impatiently with her next door neighbor, and that's when she asked, "would you mind keeping an eye on the place, and getting my mail for the next several days?"

Arnold agreed, and he looked at his watch. Next thing out of his mouth was, "time passes slow when you're waiting on the police." Ilene Vandershamp couldn't have agreed more. She now feared for her granddaughter's safety more than her own. She even tried calling her, but she knew she would be impossible to reach.

Chapter 41

Callahan's Mission

Captain Rollins shared the spotlight with the Chief of Police that afternoon at a press conference. The statistics he provided raised the eyebrows of the most skeptic reporters. Most all the news he delivered boded well for the police department, and those under him. The captain never bothered to give their names to reporters even though Buttweiler, and Callahan were mentioned as a special task force whose primary objective was to close a substantial number of cold cases within the next two to three months.

Pressed for details, the captain declined to comment on specifics at that point, but one persistent reporter up front demanded, "give us a number. What are we looking at captain?"

Rollins looked over at the Chief of Police receiving the head nod to proceed. Boldly he stated, "our prediction is thirty-five cold cases will be solved as a result of this effort in a shorter period of time than any of you would believe." That caused a stir.

Questions surrounding what was overlooked, and what had developed in the cases flooded the podium. The captain responded, "those are details that have too many variables to address, and although they were once cold cases, now that they are active again, you know I can't comment." It was the perfect out for the captain.

Stepping back into the limelight for a second, the Chief of Police put his hand on the captain's shoulder. That was a first. His final words to the press were, "Indianapolis is lucky to have this man. I stand by him, and our men and women in uniform. We'll keep you updated, I assure you," and with that he ended the interview. Cielinski parted company with the reporters along with the captain. "Good job back there. Always leave them wanting something, and way to go avoiding pinning us down to a delivery date."

Rollins remarked, "well, I've been watching you."

Cielinski spoke the truth when he said, "you handle the press like that on a regular basis, and you'll be filling my seat one day I imagine, after I'm done with it, of course."

On the surface, Callahan's mission seemed very ambitious, and clear to all those concerned, but the emphasis placed on him finding the killer increased some with the call he received from Sheriff Baker. Reminding Callahan he had delivered the witness he requested, he then stated, "now, I need a favor." He laid out his mandate in no uncertain terms as he told the detective, "I have a torched body in my jurisdiction, and I'm going to have to break the news to the young man's mother soon. The bastard responsible for it is, without a doubt, the one you're looking for, and I want you to promise me you'll do whatever it takes to stop him no matter what the cost."

"I'll do whatever it takes sheriff, you have my word."

Hearing those words, Sheriff Baker placed great weight in them. Somehow, it lifted a weight from his shoulders for the moment. Feeling confined within the boundaries of Jefferson County, he didn't relish sitting on the sidelines. For the time being though, that's all he could do. His duty lied in protecting those inside its borders, and he had already allowed one to fall. The sheriff couldn't permit the evil which darkened the town of Chanceville on more than one occasion, to continue its reign of terror. Needing closure himself, he made one more demand of the detective, "you call me when it's over." Confident in the palm reader's mystic abilities he added, "you can tell Sister Lee I now have my answer."

"Alright sheriff, I'll convey that to her."

Making a prediction of his own, Sheriff Baker informed him, "he's going after the girl for a second time. Wherever she is, that's where you'll find him. My guess is your witness knows the place, don't ask me how, but I'll look forward to taking that call when it comes detective." No other words were exchanged between the two men. The sheriff simply pushed the end button on his cell phone.

As much as it went against his nature, the sheriff was forced to trust in someone else's abilities to see to it the matter was handled successfully, and brought to an end. For now, he knew the wicked soul which barbequed Bruce Horvath was no longer within his reach. With any luck, he would never see any of his handiwork ever again. Saying a brief prayer for the safety of Ashley, and her grandmother, he tacked on an added request for the superior being above to see to it Callahan seized the opportunity to obliterate the son of bitch behind Bruce's death. Closing that prayer with a brief 'amen,' he pulled back on the road laying tracks for his office.

The sheriff had to make a call to a distant junkyard in order to acquire a burned out Ford Ranger, and eventually give Fred the go ahead to request a set of dental records from Doctor Avant's office. Singer, on the other hand, enjoyed taking most of the day off. It was the easiest missing person case he'd ever worked, and Ratley remained in the dark as usual. That's just how matters like this were handled in Jefferson County.

Chapter 42

Haunted By Nightmares

Mrs. Horvath phoned the sheriff's office late that afternoon hoping to hear some word from the sheriff, or Deputy Singer regarding her son's disappearance. Neither of them were in the office when Ratley took her call. She was the first to inform him her son was missing, but Ratley assured her if she had spoken to Singer about it, chances were he, and the sheriff were hard at work finding out what happened to him. "They've both been out of the office most of the day, but I'll have him call you as soon as he gets in," he added.

When the sheriff did return, Ratley made him aware Bruce's mother had called. When he inquired about what the sheriff knew concerning the case, Sheriff Baker told him grimly, "I'll take care of it. It's been a long day, why don't you go on home."

The deputy wasn't one to argue with the sheriff, but he knew something was up when he reached for his hat, and coat. Snatching his keys from his desk drawer, he walked to the door as he looked over his shoulder saying, "don't worry sheriff, Bruce is bound to turn up somewhere." All he received was a nod from the sheriff before he walked in his office, and closed the door.

Truthfully, the sheriff wasn't up for making that call just yet. He pulled the photo of Hayden Keller's burned body from the file folder he kept locked in his lower drawer. It looked much like what he discovered on Route 9. There were no do-overs in this line of work. He picked up the phone, and carefully dialed a number. It wasn't Mrs. Horvath he was trying to reach, it was Ben Goodman. The sheriff wanted to know the same thing Hayden did, which was how in the hell did he determine his name was in fact Hayden Keller.

To Sheriff Baker's surprise, the number was still good. Ben answered on the fifth ring never expecting it to be the sheriff of Jefferson County calling. He recognized him though. With little beating around the bush, Sheriff Baker told him who he was, and why he was calling. Ben's first response was, "I really don't remember sheriff." He wasn't buying that though. Nearly a year earlier he was certain the serial killer's name was Hayden Keller, now for some reason, he pretended not to know how he came by that information.

The sheriff outright said, "don't lie to me Ben. Doing that could impede an investigation. You know where you picked up that name. I just want you to tell me."

Somewhat defensive, Ben asked the question, "what's it matter at this point sheriff? He's dead, and it's over. Ashley is still alive as a result."

"I have to confirm who he really is because this thing's not over. You still keep in touch with the girl?"

"Yeah, I spoke to her a little over a month ago. She's doing pretty-good all things considered."

"Well, someone is coming after her, and the body of the gas station attendant turned up crisp. On top of that, her grandmother's home was broken into just this morning. This wreaks of payback of some sort. Maybe he had someone that took losing him personally."

"That bastard didn't have a soul that cared for him sheriff. He was a damn psychopath, and if I told you how I knew what his name was you'd never believe me."

"Why don't you try me son? You obviously know more

than you shared with me when we first met."

"He told me, okay."

The sheriff recounted Ben's statement of events he handed to him a year earlier. "You want to tell me everything that happened or do you even care what happens to that girl?" That immediately set Ben off. He cared for the girl as much as anyone. In fact, he'd face Hayden Keller down again if that's what it took to save her. Armed with only two lives, one of them was spent when he stated, "he told me right before he drove away leaving me for dead, sheriff. It happened in a dream, a damn nightmare I'll never forget. That's how I found the girl."

Hearing the truth, Sheriff Baker took a deep breath. He didn't question if Ben was being straight with him, people never made that kind of stuff up. Not fully understanding the paranormal events which led to Ashley's rescue, he knew enough to know something supernatural occurred prior to Ben's showdown with Hayden at the gas station.

"It sounds to me like you had a premonition son."

"You're saying you believe me."

"Yeah, I do. A few days ago, I probably wouldn't have, but that's not the case now. If you know where Ashley is you need to do whatever you can to see to it no harm comes to her until this guy is caught."

"Did you have a premonition of some kind sheriff?"

"I base things mostly on gut, but what I saw the other night made something clear to me. You, and the girl, are in danger. Something evil is coming for you, someone filled with vengeance. I'm not saying Hayden Keller isn't dead, but I can't say for sure that he is either."

"I don't know what to say sheriff."

"Say you'll keep her safe, and you'll be careful yourself until you hear from me that this is over."

"Alright."

"Good enough. I'll talk to you soon." Those words ended

the call between Ben, and the sheriff. Each were now tasked with their own mission, and rest would not come easy to either one of them.

Ashley was now the only one unaware of the danger that was headed straight for her. Ben made an attempt to reach her by phone, but all he could leave was a voice message. Shielding her from harm was never easy, but he even feared he might be too late after talking with the sheriff. Sister Lee entered his mind for a moment. Weird shit went on in Chanceville, and somehow, even though he wasn't there, he was being pulled back into it for a second time. Such was the experience of most that passed through the quirky little town. Strange events just seemed to follow them for the rest of their lives, and Ben was no different in that regard.

Left with little choice, he got in his car, and set a course for Des Moines. He knew where Ashley was attending school, and he planned on intervening in her life one last time based solely on the words the sheriff shared with him over the phone. It would take him all night to get there, but this wasn't the first road trip he had taken that brought him to her aid, and face to face with Hayden Keller.

All he could do was hope the sheriff was wrong, but Ben's own gut told him that wasn't the case. The closer he got to the City of Monks, the more he sensed that chill coursing through his veins. Hayden was also making that drive to Des Moines, he was just coming from the opposite direction. Being the eternal hunter he was, he knew he was getting close to his nemesis with each mile he covered. *This one won't end pretty* he thought, and he was right.

Knowing nothing, and fearing dreadful thoughts, Patricia Horvath couldn't sleep a wink that evening. Strange things occurred in Chanceville, and oftentimes they went unexplained. She just laid there staring up at the ceiling questioning what had happened to Bruce. At 2:13 a.m., she turned on the lamp next to her bed, and she looked over at a picture she kept on her dresser. For her, the next morning couldn't come quick enough. Sheriff Baker, on the other hand, wished to stretch the night out indefinitely.

Realizing he had done everything he could, the sheriff laid there in his chair questioning the future actions of others. He knew his phone would ring, eventually. He only hoped it would be good news for a change. He certainly didn't have any to hand to Bruce's mother, but a lie in this case was far better than the truth. Much weighed on the Chanceville sheriff's shoulders as he scratched old Blue's head watching a late night infomercial. Looking up at the sheriff, the dog let out a groan, and that's when Sheriff Baker admitted to him, "this is the hardest part boy, I know."

Sister Lee awoke from deep meditation. She walked quietly down the hall to Callahan's bedroom where he was sleeping. All she had to do was follow the sound of his snore. It was loud enough to wake the dead at times so, she didn't bother knocking. She just opened the creaking door far enough to lean her head into the room where she firmly spoke the first words which came to mind. "It is time to get up, he is on the move. We must go now in order to stop him."

Callahan cracked his eyelids some as he glanced over at the alarm clock. Almost unable to believe it, he yawned before informing her, "it's not even six yet. What the hell could he be doing at this hour?"

"Hunting his prey, just as you should be doing."

With that, Callahan pulled back the sheets, and placed his feet on the floor. Rubbing his face some as Sister Lee flipped on the light he looked up at her. She stood there staring at him as he sat on the edge of his bed wearing a wrinkle Colts T-shirt, and a revealing pair of boxer shorts. All he could manage to say was, "do you mind?"

Looking him in the eye, she stated, "hurry up, and put your pants on. I'll fix your breakfast," and with that she turned walking straight to the kitchen.

Callahan mumbled, "how about a shower first." Scratching his head, he questioned his new roommate situation, but he would no doubt follow her advice regardless of how far-fetched it seemed at times. In the end, he'd give anything to stop Hayden Keller, and Sister Lee had made it clear to him only he could do it. He knew where they were headed before grabbing his towel. Sister Lee had given him the itinerary before he laid down hours earlier. Stepping into the shower, he turned on the water thinking Sister Lee took preplanning to a whole other level, and what he found waiting for him on the breakfast table after getting out made him suggest a trip by Hardees on the way out of town. Oatmeal, and prune juice just didn't quite do it for him.

Chapter 43

Forever Hunted

Making up for lost time, Callahan phoned Buttweiler from his car. It was a few minutes after eight o' clock when he answered. The detective gave him strict instructions to field all his calls, and make no mention of his trip to anyone except Sergeant Gant when he calls. Buttweiler didn't have to ask how he knew where Hayden Keller was, Sister Lee was riding shotgun for heaven's sake. "You're sure you don't need me to go along?"

"No, I need you there to take care of business for me, and when we catch this guy, I want you to be the one to inform the captain."

Buttweiler looked forward to that moment. Still, he had strong concerns for his partner, but Callahan worked solo most of his career, and he had Sister Lee with him. Maybe that's why he never considered whether he would succeed in stopping their monstrous serial killer. Had he known that which Sister Lee held secret, he would have shared different words with his mentor. "I'll see you when you get back then."

Callahan shared a look with Sister Lee as they flew down the highway. She didn't say anything when the detective told his young partner, "I don't think I'll disappoint you."

Despite the early start, Des Moines was still several hours away for Callahan, and his riding companion. Little was said on the way there, except when Sister Lee gave him a description of the vehicle Hayden was driving. "It is a truck of some sort, red and very large in size, *Ford* is written on the front of it, and it's in good condition. The inside is filled with stuff." She looked over at Callahan as she opened her eyes. Left with nothing more to tell him, things seemed awkward between them. Turning her head, she looked back at the road in front of them as she apologized for making him uncomfortable when she went to wake him up.

He glanced over at her, and her face showed no sign of emotion. That's when he said, "I wasn't uncomfortable."

"Now you are lying, just like about breakfast."

"Hey the truth was I wasn't hungry at the time."

"You were not hungry for what I fixed, there is a difference. I should have known, but my energies were focused elsewhere."

"Look, it's no big deal. We ate breakfast, and everyone wears underwear."

Sister Lee gave him an odd look. "You assume much, don't you?"

"You mean to tell me you don't…"

Sister Lee cut him off saying, "what I have under my dress is none of your business."

Speaking his mind, Callahan replied, "well in all fairness you got a pretty good look at me this morning."

"Like you said, it was no big deal. I just never saw a pair with balls all over them."

Callahan shot her a curious glance as she clarified, "the shorts you were wearing."

For the first time, Callahan saw the emergence of a smile make its way to her face, and that's when he said, "of course you were." Suppressing his laughter, he turned his attention back to the road, and the awkward feeling between them no longer existed.

Hayden Keller was already there watching, and waiting as he combed the college campus in search of his precious prey. Ashley Pennington would surface sooner or later, and he would be ready. Parked outside the freshman hall, he knew he would find her, eventually. He couldn't wait to see the look on his face when she saw his. Few were given a second shot at meeting Hayden. This would be interesting to say the least, and there wasn't much in Hayden Keller's world that fell into that category.

Nearly an hour had elapsed, a long one indeed for Hayden to endure, but he could sense what he was searching for was getting closer with each slow passing minute. Ben Goodman was nearing Des Moines, dialing Ashley as he drove. Sheriff Baker's words rang in his ears, and Ben never stopped to think if it was his eternal destiny to save the girl. He wasn't one to ponder the possibility of past lives though. Reality was he had already spent one of his. He had faced his demons once, and the results were life changing for both he, and Hayden Keller. Sister Lee knew their next encounter would not end well.

She could now sense Ben's presence, and although his intentions were good, Sister Lee could not allow him to intervene in this matter. Closing her eyes, she concentrated on his exact location. Callahan noticed, but he said nothing. Whatever she was doing it appeared important. Knowing Sister Lee as he did, he never disturbed her concentration with small talk. He wasn't much for it anyway.

Not wishing to harm Ben, only to halt him, Sister Lee orchestrated a chain of events that would prevent him from reaching Grandview College in time. Her face appeared concentrated, and strained as she did her best to place obstacles in from of the man with two lives. The closer Ben came to Des Moines, the more shit he had to contend with. Suddenly, everything stood in his way from never changing red lights to slow moving drivers, but the debris in the road, and the traffic jam that ensued from an overturned rig which blocked most of the highway, would see to it he wouldn't meet Hayden a second time.

Sitting there locked behind miles of cars, he could feel the connection to Sister Lee again. It was mentally distracting like someone else was occupying the same space in his head. After the encounter between them in her parlor, she had the ability to see things though his eyes at will. The only drawback was Ben was able to recognize when that link was re-established. The growing chill he felt warning him of danger waned as he sat idle on the highway.

He felt his window of opportunity closing fast, and Ashley's well-being was his primary concern. Struggling to fight his way over to the shoulder, he clipped the bumper of another vehicle as he sped over into the safety lane. Ben didn't stop to trade insurance information. That eerie feeling he had where his blood almost ran cold grew once again intensifying as he gunned the gas pedal. It was then he knew for certain the sheriff was right. The girl was in danger, and he doubted for the first time if Hayden Keller was dead, regardless of what he had seen with his own eyes. Something evil was coming for her.

Stopped by police before he could reach the next turnoff, Ben grabbed his phone as he was ordered to get out of his car. His first words to the officer were, "listen, there's a girl in trouble. Someone is going to kill her if I don't reach her in time."

"What do you think you are some kind of cop? No, wait a minute. I bet you're one of the FBI guys, right."

Ben could tell he wasn't buying it based on his smart-ass response, but how many guys made that kind of claim given the circumstances. He informed the officer, "I am a software designer. Look, if you don't believe me talk to the sheriff, and ask him yourself." Holding his cell phone in his right hand he pressed three buttons calling the number Sheriff Baker had dialed him from. Hearing the ring, he handed the phone to Officer Penn as he approached.

"Let me see your ID, and keep your hands where I can see them."

As he held the phone to his left ear, Ben did just as he was instructed, telling him to ask for Sheriff Baker. Before he could say a word in response, Ratley answered, "sheriff's office."

Officer Penn looked at Ben. Glancing down at his license, he cleared his throat before saying, "let me speak to the sheriff. I've got a man here by the name of Ben Goodman that claims a girl is in danger, or being murdered. I need to know if he knows anything about it."

Ratley recognized the name instantly. He hastily stood jamming his knee into the corner of his desk nearly tipping over his chair in the process as he said, "hold just a damn minute." He hollered for the sheriff since he had his door closed, and when he opened it, the deputy held up the receiver telling him, "you need to take this one, Ben Goodman's involved."

Taking the phone from Ratley, the sheriff confirmed the name of the girl in question. "If he says the girl is in danger, I'd trust him. He's already saved her once before." Officer Penn listened as the sheriff gave him some background on what had taken place previously, and he mentioned the recent break-in at her grandmother's house which he believed was actually an attempt on her life.

Penn's only response was, "I'll call it in then. We'll let the local police in Des Moines handle it. You have a description of this guy, what he driving?"

Ratley recognized the description right off the bat as the sheriff hesitantly said, "tall, probably in excess of six feet, short dark hair, a notable scar on his left cheek, driving a flashy late model red Ford pickup crew cab, I believe. I don't have a plate number for you."

Ratley volunteered, "that truck had an Alabama plate sheriff. I don't remember the number, but it started with a two. I'm sure of that." The sheriff passed that along to Officer Penn, and he asked to speak with Ben. His final words to him were quick, and clear before handing the phone back to Ratley.

The deputy had a number of questions for the sheriff, but few he felt like answering. When asked about the guy with the scar, he informed the sheriff he never noticed it. "It was easy to miss, you only spoke to the guy for a minute," he replied. The sheriff turned heading back to the office when Ratley questioned if the eye-catching truck he saw was stolen. "Yes, I believe it was, but it's out of our jurisdiction now. None of that's important." Even Ratley drew the connection between the scared man driving the truck, and the disappearance of Bruce Horvath. When he went to mention it, the sheriff informed him, "that's just a coincidence nothing more. Bruce was killed in an auto collision several nights ago. I've been waiting for the dental records to confirm that before I contact his mother. Now do you have any more questions?" Ratley said nothing, he just shook his head no.

With Ben Goodman, and Ashley Pennington involved, he felt certain the sheriff knew a great deal more than he was sharing. Ratley's loyalty to him went just as deep as Singer's did though, and Sheriff Baker relied heavily on that as he picked up the phone to speak with Fred. It was now someone else's job to hunt down evil, and stop it before it could strike. Sheriff Baker's money was on the detective from Indianapolis, and Sister Lee.

Chapter 44

With No Mercy

Callahan and Sister Lee were a little over an hour away when Hayden spotted Ashley Pennington exiting the Student Center. From a distance, he compared her to the picture he stole off of the refrigerator. The glimpse he gained of her left little doubt he had finally found her, and she could clearly sense that something wasn't right. She looked over her shoulder as she walked toward the library feeling as though someone was watching her with every step she took. Her mind drifted from finding a quiet place to do research to self-preservation. Last time she experienced that feeling, she was in his clutches. Just the mere reminder of that traumatic point in her life caused her to walk faster. Hayden certainly noticed, but he didn't care. She would be in his clutches once again soon enough, he could feel it as he climbed out of the truck leaving it double parked.

Stewart Nettle drove a security golf cart around campus. His life's work consisted of seeing to it everyone adhered to school policy regarding parking. Armed with a radio, handcuffs, a flashlight, and taser, he was ill-equipped to take on Hayden Keller to say the least. Fortunately for him, the killing machine was nowhere near the vehicle when he discovered it. Hayden had just entered the library in high hopes of seeing Ashley again, this time close up, and personal. He constrained his urge to kill the kid working behind the counter who asked if he could help him with something. Hayden turned to him placing his finger over his lips without uttering a sound, and his scar was in full view of the young man serving as the library assistant.

Figuring he was one of the contractors working upstairs, Myron went back to his duties of placing books on a cart, but the scar on Hayden's cheek was something that would remain forever etched in his mind. Myron mumbled the word, "freak," under his breath once Hayden was a fair distance from him.

As for Stewart Nettle, it had been over a month since he was able to tow a vehicle, but Hayden made it easy for him. Double parked without a sticker plastered to the rear window, it was everything a guy like Stewart could ask for. That sporty oversized pickup was going down, and the owner of it was going to have to pay dearly to get it back. Following routine protocol, he pulled out his ticket pad, and jotted down the tag number. Calling it in, he waited several minutes to hear back that the vehicle he was looking at was believed to be stolen. Police were dispatched to the scene immediately. This one was out of Stew Nettle's hands. His job was to see to it no one moved the vehicle. Cops were on the scene in a matter of minutes. The description given to Officer Penn by Sheriff Baker added a great deal of urgency to their response time. Those were factors Stewart was totally unaware of, and little did he know he was about to be featured on the evening news as a result.

Hayden perused the reference section in search of the girl. The library was fairly empty when he saw her pass by a large set of bookshelves on the other side of the room. He stood perfectly still just watching her, only his eyes moved as he traced her footsteps. Stalking was his second favorite thing to do. Waiting for the perfect moment was as much of an art as the kill itself, but Hayden knew things wouldn't end quick for her. He peered at her from a distance through the bookshelf as she walked up the stairs. Following her path, he took in the smell of her hair. His palms began to sweat, and his mouth became wet with great anticipation of what lied ahead. Hayden still had plenty of bodies to harvest before the Sabbath, and he desperately wanted to add Myron's to the list. Hayden planned on permanently embedding his head in the copier before leaving. The librarian wannabe would have to wait his turn though. Hayden knew proper etiquette, even if he didn't follow it. Ladies first, he said in his twisted mind while he watched Ashley take a seat at a table in a secluded part of the library on the second floor. Glancing out the window, he spotted the security guy parked in his patrol cart next to his truck. Hayden had held onto it way too long. He knew it too. Up until then, he just couldn't bring himself to part with the thing. Feeling the need to make a quick change, that's when he noticed the paint van pull up. It was close to the building, just feet away from the service entrance, and it certainly beat the hell out of a bread truck.

Needing to act swiftly, Hayden turned his attention back to Ashley. Carefully inching his way toward her with each step he took, he remained hidden behind the bookshelves closest to her. Ashley could sense danger was near at that moment, and she didn't need to hear it from her voicemail. Her blood ran cold as she paused from reading. She felt a hand hit the table next to her, and another one landed on the back of her chair. Almost paralyzed with fear, she raised her head some, not sure of what she would find staring down at her. Tears started to fill her eyes before she even cast them on his retched face. Just for full effect, Hayden leaned down so she could get a good look at him. His breath smelled like rotten potatoes, and the scar on his cheek took her breath away, instantly preventing her from making a sound. The first thing he said as he looked right through her was, "long time no see, I bet you missed me."

Hayden's sinister glare was unmistakable. He smelled as if he hadn't bathed in over a week, and although she saw him die with her own eyes, his face was now different with the same gruesome cut running down the length of his cheek. She couldn't explain it. She barely had time to think, but she wanted to put as much distance between herself, and him as possible. Trying her best to make a quick escape, she bolted from her chair as he reached for her hair. Clinching it tightly in his fist, he confidently informed her, "you ought to know you'll never get rid of me." Ashley let out a life or death scream which filled the building. Grabbing hold of one of the chairs, she hurled it at the window. Hayden jerked her to the floor as it shattered the double pane glass sending fragments flying outside the building. He hastily threatened her with her life if she didn't tell him where to find the guy that saved her at the gas station.

The noise from the busted glass caught the attention of Stewart, and the three policemen now on the scene investigating the inappropriately parked stolen F350, and the current whereabouts of Ashley Pennington. Two of the officers rushed straight for the library, and the other one radioed in the call for more back-up. Stewart Nettle stood by almost helpless, but seeing the officers swing into action he quickly followed even though he was fifty feet behind them once they entered the library.

Hayden wasn't playing any longer, "live or die, what will it be Ashley?" He was enraged knowing his timeline just became a great deal shorter than he had planned. Extracting the information from her wouldn't be as enjoyable as he once thought. She wasn't talking even when he struck her hard with his fist until Hayden said, "I know where your grandmother lives. How about I pay her a little visit." It was his last ditch effort to gain that which he sought. Ashley was going to die either way, but Hayden never expected Gus Grossman to step in, armed with a painter's tool, that old son of bitch meant business.

Ashley's eyes widened as the shadow of the old guy covered both she, and Hayden. He looked nothing like Ben, but she was glad to see him even though he was almost as ugly a Hayden. Reaching down with one arm he rapidly took the sharp end of the metal scrapper, and plowed it into Hayden's lower back embedding it deep into one of his kidneys. The pain spiked through his central nervous system, and he released his grip on Ashley to face a more imminent threat. Surprised by the attack much the same way he surprised Ashley, Hayden Keller turned to face his opponent. Gus smelled like a blend of cheap beer, turpentine, and cigarettes. Gritting his yellowed teeth, he held firmly to the handle of the tool he carried in his hand. Ready to take another stab at Hayden, he groaned, "take this you son of a bitch." The old painter nailed him once in the gut slicing him open some as Hayden reached for his throat realizing the first wound inflicted was most likely fatal. Not sure what to do as he did his best to choke the life right out of Gus, Hayden stared into his eyes.

Gus's face quickly turned red as Ashley rose to her feet. She went to reach for another chair planning to club Hayden with it, but what she saw take place caused her to stare in pure disbelief. Hayden's body twitched, and he loosened his death-grip on the painter's throat. Gus fell into the wall behind him, and his body convulsed in much the same way. Ashley stared at him as he shook his head gaining his bearings. The man that had hunted her laid lifeless on the floor, but that didn't stop her from striking him with the chair for good measure. Looking up at the old man, she asked if he was alright. That's when he took the painter's tool, and scored the side of his face with it. The same venomous stare overtook his eyes as blood dripped steadily from his cheek. Snarling just the way Hayden Keller did, he growled, "I told you, you'd never get rid of me."

Ashley's screams rang out as she fled for the stairs. She dashed in the direction of the policeman's voice yelling hysterically. Hayden, of course, followed until he met the officers near the bottom of the stairs with guns drawn. His story at that point was, "I was trying to save her." He said little other than that. He could only afford to take three more souls before the Sabbath, and he had three times that many staring at him. Based on the situation, his options were limited. Holding the bloody tool in his hand, the police weren't convinced based on Ashley's panicked statement.

The officer closest to Hayden ordered him, "drop what you have in your hand sir." Ashley clung to the other officer as Stewart Nettle stood there listening to her frantic claim. "His name is Hayden Keller, and he killed my family a year ago. Now, he's going to kill me, and my grandmother." Her eyes were filled with tears as she spoke. Pointing his taser right at Hayden's heart, Stew Nettle let loose as he pulled the trigger delivering four million volts right to his chest. He didn't let go either for almost twelve seconds. That's when Officer Britt stepped in. "What the hell are you doing trying to kill him?"

Myron stuck his head around the corner snapping a picture of the whole thing with his iphone as Ashley requested he shoot him again. Stew was willing to do so, but Officer Britt instructed him to put it away. "Better yet give it to me," he said as he pulled it out of his hands. Myron was a journalism major, and he had no doubt the picture would make the newspaper.

By the time they carted the dead body down the steps, and out the doors of the library, Channel 3 News was there on the scene filming the whole thing. Stew Nettle was the one willing to say the most, and that's why he was chosen to be featured on the evening news. The fact of the matter was, local security guard thwarts killing spree at major university, made for a great headline. The story he told while the cameras were rolling could easily lead one to believe he was an integral piece in stopping mayhem from taking place on the college campus. "I was the one that made the call," he said. Once my back-up arrived we stormed the library cutting off all possible exits knowing this guy was somewhere inside." A passing shot of the body bag was taken along with some footage of Gus Grossman's body being loaded into a nearby ambulance. Hayden was still unconscious at that point, but he had a pulse, and Officer Aldridge's handcuffs securing him to the gurney. Stew Nettle continued spewing information when asked by the reporter, "so you're the one that actually took the suspect down?" A serious look formed on his face as he confessed, "the scene inside the library was intense. There was a standoff, and the suspect was armed. It left little time to think, really. I just acted on instincts I guess, knowing someone had to pull the trigger."

The camera panned down at Stew's empty nylon covered holster. When asked about the gun he used to take down the subject, he cleared his throat informing them, "well, it was actually my taser. It's in the hands of police at this time, an internal part of the investigation you understand. I'm sure I'll have it back in no time."

Closing out the interview, the reporter turned looking at the camera saying, "well, there you have it. The scene at Grand View could have been much different were it not for this security guard, and police." With his name left unmentioned, Stewart Nettle was compelled to ask, "is there any chance this is going to be on CNN?" The camera stopped rolling at that point.

Chapter 45

A Startling Discovery

Sergeant Gant had no idea what he was in for that afternoon when they hauled the man believed to be Hayden Keller into questioning. His eyes were wide open as they placed him in the chair inside interrogation room three. He was still handcuffed, but he hadn't spoken a word to anyone since being revived inside the ambulance. The ID he had on him pointed to him being Gus Grossman, but the girl on the other side of the glass swore up and down his name was Hayden Keller.

Ashley appeared unstable, and traumatized. She was fearful of anyone that came near her. Police knew one thing - whatever took place in that library was more than she could bear emotionally. The name she kept saying sounded extremely familiar though. It didn't take long for Gant to put two and two together. One of the officers suggested they question her at the hospital where she could receive proper medical care, but the lieutenant in charge ordered them to take her into another room. "I want her statement before she leaves. I don't care how incoherent it is, just record it." He was almost certain Ashley was on something. He never voiced that thought though.

Observing the suspect through the window, Lieutenant Landers directed his question to Gant, "what do you make of it?"

Honestly, Gant didn't know what to think. Based on what Ashley had already told police, it was clear she was completely delusional, and the guy they were viewing through the glass seemed out of it as well. He had a thousand yard stare sewn into his eyes just like Manson, and he either remained perfectly still, or he twitched uncontrollably. "Keep them right here," he said. "I'll be right back." He left the lieutenant alone in the viewing room while he went to his desk, and immediately started searching for Detective Callahan's number. Unable to find it, he barked at one of the other officers, "have you seen anyone screwing with my papers?"

"Someone's always laying crap on your desk. What's the big deal?"

"The big deal is I might have a serial killer sitting in that room, and I can't find the number to the guy that brought him to my attention." Nearly at his wits end, looking up, he yelled at one of the junior officers, "Osprey, get me the Indianapolis Metro P. D. Ask for the number to a Detective Callahan."

The corporal grinned as he said, "Dirty Harry, sure thing."

Gant qualified his order shouting, "do I look like I'm kidding? Someone show him how to use the damn phone, would you."

Osprey changed his tune instantly informing him he was right on it. "Indianapolis, Detective Callahan…"

Less than two minutes later, Buttweiler received the long awaited call from Gant. He knew it was coming, but still, it amazed him how spot on their unconfirmed source was about everything. Sister Lee's abilities would forever be a mystery to him. Gant tossed out his name prior to requesting to speak with his partner. That's when Buttweiler informed him, "he's on his way there now." Glancing up at the clock on the wall, he added, "he should be there shortly."

Gant was at a loss for words when Buttweiler offered to give him Callahan's cell number. "Who the hell are you again?"

"The name is Buttweiler, and congratulations by the way on apprehending Hayden Keller."

Gant immediately questioned him as to what he knew about the suspect, and Buttweiler had to mention the jagged cut on his left cheek. He also told him not to let anyone near him until his partner arrived. When Gant questioned why, Buttweiler said, "that was all I was told to tell you."

"And you guys believe this guy could be tied to multiple murders here in this area?"

"Quite a few Sergeant, all across the country. Callahan will explain when he gets there. He has a list for you, some cases you might want to look into." Gant ended the call with more questions than he had to start with, but he looked forward to talking to Callahan in person.

When the sergeant returned to the observation room, he found Lieutenant Landers in the midst of interviewing Officer Aldridge. "You mean to tell me he didn't say anything on the ride over here?"

"No sir, he was unconscious most of the way until the paramedic gave him the atropine. That's when he about scared the hell out of me."

"What do you mean?"

"Well, at first he didn't move, a couple of seconds later his eyes just popped open, and he started jerking. It was like he was having a seizure. Maybe it was a bad reaction to the shot, I don't know, but that's when he grabbed the EMT. The next thing I know he's inches away from the guy's face."

The lieutenant took another look at the cuffed man sitting motionless in the chair as Aldridge added, "that old guy shook him like a rag doll even wearing the cuffs, and after what I've seen - I wouldn't underestimate him."

Gant cut in asking, "did you have to intervene?"

Officer Aldridge responded, "I was going to, but before you know it our guy let him go. After that, he just laid there staring up at nothing with that crazed look on his face."

The lieutenant turned to Gant and said, "well, let's get this over with. You want the honor, or would you prefer Pippin handle it?"

The sergeant replied, "I have a detective on his way here from Indianapolis. He claims this guy could be connected to numerous cold cases. I say we speak to him first before we try to question this guy."

"Indianapolis is a long way, and I don't plan on missing dinner."

"Shouldn't have to, I just got off the phone with him, and he should be here in thirty minutes."

Lieutenant Landers took one more look at their murder suspect before he turned toward the door saying, "fine. Maybe he can shed some light on this for us, but he's not taking our suspect. We've got an active case, and a ripe dead body to prove it."

Gant quickly said, "I couldn't agree more."

The lieutenant nodded his head spouting, "I don't guess it'll hurt to let him sweat it out in there a little longer." On that note, Gant and Aldridge just shared a look with one another. Gus Grossman wasn't sweating anything. He was catatonic. Landers was now more concerned with reviewing the security footage from the library, and the surrounding buildings to compare what it showed to Ashley's outlandish statements.

Key members of the Des Moines Police Department mulled over the recorded camera feeds provided to them as Officer Britt gave his account of things. He pointed out the chair came crashing through the upper level window shortly after the man they had in custody entered the building.

261

Another camera captured Hayden following Ashley through the library for a short distance. The timestamp on that piece of footage put it prior to police arriving on the scene.

At the time of the attack, Ashley Pennington was sitting in a blind spot as far as the security system was concerned. So, they couldn't see any part of the altercation which occurred between the girl, and the two men. A latter piece of footage caught Ashley fleeing from the man they were holding in interrogation room three, and the entire scene on the stairs was captured right down to the second where Stew Nettle went Rambo on him.

The recording was grainy in some places, but able to make out entirely. Since it lacked audio, that of course, required the two officers who were present on the scene to fill in some blanks for the lieutenant. He could see Gus's mouth move slightly as he stood at the top of the stairs holding the sharp bloody cutting tool in his hand. Landers pointed at the screen asking the officers, "what did he say right here?"

Britt stated, "the only thing he said initially was he was trying to save the girl."

Referring back to the piece of footage where Ashley was running for her life, and their suspect persistently followed, the lieutenant spoke his mind asking, "does this look like he was trying to save her to you?"

Aldridge was quick to point out, "I told him to drop what he had in his hand, but he wasn't complying, obviously." Landers looked at him before turning his attention back to the security footage just in time to see the show of force administered via taser. He felt like saying thank God for this guy, but he refrained after seeing his subject hit the stairs hard.

Pippin had to chime in with, "damn that's gotta hurt. Run that back, and play it again, would you."

The lieutenant quickly questioned him, "why, what did you see?"

Gant just shook his head, he knew what was coming when Pippin opened his mouth to say, "I just saw a guy get his clock cleaned. Now, that was entertaining. That guy would still be holding the trigger had Britt not stepped in." Several of them tried to hold back from laughing. The situation was serious, but Pippin always managed to lighten the mood in a room.

Noticing several smirks on the faces of his officers, Lieutenant Landers sternly made them aware, "we're not watching America's Funniest Home Videos." That dose of reality set the tone for the rest of the investigation. The lieutenant stated in no uncertain terms, "I want motive, I want those print results, I want the connection between this guy, and that girl. In short, I want answers - how about working on getting me some."

Chapter 46

Need For Deception

As the D.M.P.D. attempted to sort things out, Sheriff Baker broke down, and made the call he'd been dreading. He didn't pick up the phone to do it either. This one he made all by himself personally. As soon as he pressed the doorbell, Patricia Horvath pulled back the drape. Seeing the sheriff's car in her driveway with no sign of her son present meant one thing. Tears were already forming in her eyes as she opened the door. Pressing her lips together, she attempted to remain composed praying she wouldn't hear two words, but as a mother she knew.

Sheriff Baker proceeded to tell her, "there's no easy way to say it, but we found Bruce's body." She drew her shaking hand to her mouth as the sheriff explained, "it was a bad car accident, and your son was the one behind the wheel. No one else was involved, but the whole truck caught on fire, and he didn't stand a chance. I'm sorry."

"Why," she cried.

Sheriff Baker stood there with his hat in his hands. All he could offer in response was, "I don't know. These things just happen sometimes. It was a sharp curve with slippery road conditions. This could've happened to anyone. Maybe, he swerved to avoid hitting an animal. I'm just sorry I have to deliver this kind of news to you." Helping her over to the couch, he asked if she had anyone she could call. Patricia Horvath reminded the sheriff how important her son was in her life, and he assured her with time, she'd get through it with the full support of the community.

Nearly seven hundred miles away, Ilene Vandershamp hoped for better news. She had made the trip to Des Moines after being unable to contact her granddaughter. Just about the time Callahan, and Sister Lee reached the police station, she arrived at the university to find the place still buzzing about what had taken place earlier that morning. The police, and reporters were no longer on the scene, but crime scene tape spanned the doors leading into the locked-down library. Naturally, she feared the worst when she could find no sign of Ashley in her dormitory. As soon as she spoke to the resident assistant, she was promptly directed to the admin office.

Informing the old woman of the events which led to the capture of an armed man, and the death of another, the assistant to the dean assured her Ashley Pennington was still in one piece. The woman explained, "I don't have all the details, but I'm certain your granddaughter is just fine. Police just took her down to the station as a precaution to get her statement, and probably pick someone out of a line-up." She passed it off as if it was just a routine event of some sort, but Ashley's grandmother knew better than that. She asked for the phone book in order to find the number to the nearest police station, and still concerned about her granddaughter's well-being, she spoke her thoughts openly. All the woman said in response to that was, "I hope this doesn't mean she won't be back next semester."

Callahan escorted Sister Lee inside the precinct virtually unannounced. The detective was in his element of course, but the gifted palm reader from Chanceville collected a few curious onlookers. When he spoke to Gant for the first time face-to-face, he introduced her as a special witness, and the sergeant fired back, "we've got one ourselves."
Sister Lee looked at Callahan informing him, "the girl is

265

still here. We must see him now."

The sergeant observed the two of them as he asked, "how does she know about the girl?"

Callahan responded, "it's all over the news," as he handed Gant a list of unsolved murders still on his books in hopes of sidetracking him. "The reason I came here was to deliver these to you in person."

Gant made the comment, "on the very same day we find this guy. What are the chances of that?"

Callahan explained, "we've been tracing his path for some time. When I spoke to you on the phone, I told you I believed he'd strike again soon, but maybe we shouldn't jump the gun until we allow her to take a look at him."

The detective turned gesturing to Sister Lee, and Gant nodded his head saying, "follow me."

The truth was Callahan couldn't wait to lay his eyes on him. Sister Lee didn't appear to be nearly as optimistic, but she cautiously followed him into the observation room, and Gant closed the door shut behind them leaving the light off. They had a perfect view of Gus Grossman, and it wasn't pretty, a painter by trade just dodging sixty. He continued sitting there in the same position they left him in a half hour ago. The distant dismal look he carried in his eyes, and the bandage he was wearing on his left cheek appeared promising. Callahan had no doubt what lied beneath the tape and gauze. In one word, he looked hideous just the way a serial killer would appear in the minds of most people.

Hardly casting her eyes on him, Sister Lee walked up close to the glass placing her left hand on it. Her fingers instantly spread apart as soon as she touched it. Closing her eyes, she focused her senses on the energies within the room. Not even giving Gant a chance to ask what she was doing, five seconds later she opened her eyes informing

Callahan, "he is not here, but the girl will be useful." Ashley Pennington was her primary focus. She looked over at Sergeant Gant saying, "now you should take us to her."

The sergeant had to ask, "what kind of witness is she? She barely looked at the guy. The girl swears up, and down he's Hayden Keller."

Callahan started to explain she was also a police consultant, but Sister Lee's response was quick, and cutting. "That is not all she claims, and I tell you anything is possible." With the sergeant fully aware of Ashley's statements, Sister Lee's words appeared right on target. How the hell she appeared to know things no one else did left him alarmed, and mystified. Callahan put an extreme amount of faith in her abilities, but he was looking at the suspect with his eyes. Taking in what he saw, he found it hard to believe the man sitting in that chair wasn't their guy. Against his better judgment, the detective questioned her. "You're sure that's not him. I mean he looks like he could fit the description."

Sister Lee stared at him only a moment before saying, "trust not what I say, and he will get away, but ask him any question you wish to satisfy your concerns." Speaking sternly she added, "I would start with the most important one, but he will not answer you no matter what you say to him."

Callahan turned to Sergeant Gant asking, "do you mind if I question him?"

Gant informed him, "I'll have to go in there with you."

Callahan replied, "not a problem." That's when the sergeant looked over at Sister Lee not knowing what the hell to do with her. She stared straight ahead through the glass as she stood motionless. Her eyes appeared locked with Gus Grossman's for the time being.

As he opened the door, Gant told the detective,

"someone's going to have to stay with her."

Callahan started to say he wouldn't have it any other way, but Sister Lee informed the sergeant, "Lieutenant Landers will do quite nicely." She never looked in his direction as she said it. Ironically, he was headed straight down the hall to the interrogation room. Gant stepped out telling him he was just in time to oversee the questioning of the suspect.

A brief introduction between Landers and Callahan led to the lieutenant informing him, "that guy in there is all ours till we're done with him. I've got one dead man that appears to be responsible for a car theft, and possible murders, and the guy you're about to interview definitely took him out according to the preliminary evidence. To make things more confusing, our witness claims he's your serial killer." He paused for second before adding, "she also claims the dead guy was too."

Callahan nodded telling him, "I happen to have a witness of my own in the observation room." He, nor Gant, had to ask the lieutenant to babysit her. Landers was eager to talk to her, and he figured that witness would have to be more grounded than Ashley Pennington ever was.

Within seconds of entering the room along with Officer Aldridge, the lieutenant told her who he was, and Sister Lee replied, "I know."

"Callahan tells me you're a key witness when it comes to this Hayden Keller character."

"I have seen much of the blood he has shed." Staring straight ahead through the glass, she informed the lieutenant, and Officer Aldridge, "you are no longer looking at him." Her statement came across as odd to say the least.

Sister Lee was calm, and concise with her words. She and Ashley Pennington were definitely at opposite ends of the spectrum, but their statements were confusing to law enforcement officials. Wishing to ask her to clarify her remark, Landers started to speak, but he paused just as Gant, and Callahan entered room three to talk to the man in question. Nothing gave a rise out of Gus Grossman though. He sat there staring into the reflective glass on the wall in front of him, not recognizing himself or anyone else for that matter.

Gant was first to address him telling him the detective he was with had a question or two for him. That invoked no response from Gus, and he didn't flinch when the sergeant informed him, "you know you could be facing murder charges." In hopes of grabbing the old guy's attention, Gant firmly slammed his hand on the table as he walked up beside him. Raising his voice some, he felt compelled to ask, "what the hell made you come after that girl?" Silence was all that was present in the room after that.

Callahan just observed realizing Gus's reaction wasn't normal. Taking Sister Lee's advice, he chose the question he felt Hayden would have to respond to. The first words out of the detective's mouth were, "you never kill on the Sabbath, why is that?" Gus Grossman didn't have an answer for him. He couldn't even speak his name, or form understandable words. The interview was over in a matter of minutes, and when they went to leave, Gus lunged grabbing Gant's arm. Clinching it tightly, he tried to plead for help, but the word never fully made itself heard. Other than that faint outburst, he showed no ability to communicate.

Callahan was convinced Sister Lee was right. Hayden Keller had found a new host, and it was his job to find him while there was still time. As they left the room, Callahan told Gant, "I need a list of everyone that had contact with him." Put on the spot, Gant gave the names of Officer Britt and Aldridge. Callahan then asked, "they both seemed okay to you?"

"Yeah, they're good officers. What's the deal? Is this your guy or not."

Lying to buy time, Callahan replied, "without speaking to the girl, I can't be sure yet."

In the brief amount of time Sister Lee spent bonding with Lieutenant Landers, and Officer Aldridge she managed to convince them it was imperative they get the girl to the nearest hospital immediately. She knew that move would draw Hayden out from wherever he was hiding. She also knew he wouldn't wait forever for her to be released from protective custody, and as much as she preferred not to use the girl as bait, there was no better way to find him.

Chapter 47

The Unexplainable

The consensus was Ashley Pennington was suffering from shock. The events which took place one year ago had now been brought to the lieutenant's attention. Clearly, the psychological impact from that event directly affected this event, there was no getting around it. Agreeing to let the detective speak with Ashley prior to her being transported to Mercy Medical Center was rather odd. Gant knew something was going on that Callahan wasn't sharing with him.

Sister Lee never entered the room with Gant and Callahan to speak with Ashley Pennington. She simply observed through the glass just as she had done with the tasered painter held in handcuffs. Eager to listen to every word that was said, hoping to make sense of it all, the sergeant allowed Callahan to do most of the talking, and first thing the detective did was turn off the microphone, and video recorder. As far as he was concerned, the official interview was over.

Proceeding with caution, he attempted not to intimidate. For once in his life, he spoke gently with compassion, and given the circumstances, he didn't find it difficult to do. He even asked if she would mind if he took a seat. Choosing the one on the other side of the table from her, he made himself at home for all five minutes he was given to speak with her. After stating his name, he informed her, "I promised Sheriff Baker I would return a favor, and part of that involves seeing to it no harm comes to you."

Ashley paid close attention to what he said after that. She felt no one could shield her from Hayden Keller, not given what she had seen. Callahan appeared physically capable, and willing, but she thought she knew something he didn't. Wishing her words were not true, she confessed, "no one can stop him. I know that."

Callahan gave her a nod as he mouthed the words, "I believe you." Gant appeared not to notice since Callahan's back was turned to him. The detective admitted, "I know you've seen things most could never imagine." Speaking just as softly as he did upon entering the room, the detective posed a question to her. "What if I told you I was the one chosen to see to it this ends?" Ashley looked skeptical until Callahan added, "I know about Ben Goodman. I also know what led him to find you. Do you trust me?" Ashley was having difficulty processing everything. Callahan said, "I know it's hard to do that after what you've been through, but now, I'm making a promise to you - good will win over evil in the end." The crucifix she wore around her neck caught his attention. He stared at it a second before saying, "everyone needs to have faith in something. That's a nice necklace by the way."

Ashley thought back to what Ben had said to her the night he pulled her from the black SUV. Now, Hayden wanted to know his identity just so he could hunt him down and kill him, probably out of revenge. She didn't know his full intentions, yet she never gave him Ben's name. There were many details Ben hadn't shared with her about his encounter with the palm reader in the dream which led him to find her. Ashley knew enough though. She looked up at the detective saying, "he knows where my grandmother lives. If you don't stop him, he'll find me again, but I won't give him what he wants."

She reached for her necklace, and she held it between her

fingers as Callahan responded, "I know. I'm asking you to put your faith in me to do what's necessary to stop it once and for all." Ashley nodded her head.

The detective turned to Gant requesting a minute of privacy. The sergeant didn't wish to leave the room, but he looked at the girl saying, "well, that's up to her."

Ashley said, "sure," without much pause.

Gant replied, "okay, then. I'll be right outside the door, but after you're done talking to her, I have a question for you."

"Fair enough," Callahan replied, and hearing the door close he said, "tell me exactly what you saw take place between the two men in the library." In less than sixty seconds she gave him an accurate picture of what happened, and their discussion was over. The detective informed her, "they plan to transport you to the hospital, and contact your grandmother. I plan to see to it you get there safe, and I won't leave until this is over."

Stepping out of the room, Callahan met Gant in the corridor.

The sergeant seemed antsy when he bluntly put forth the question, "what the hell is really going on?"

Callahan looked at him knowing he couldn't handle the truth. Sincerely, he said, "if I told you, you wouldn't believe me."

"Well, why don't you try giving it a shot because at this point I'd believe about anything."

"Okay, my partner, and I have been researching old murders, some of them going back decades. I hate to say it, but certain consistencies showed up. Timelines coincided, and the death count continued to grow beyond anything I can ask you to fathom, but the period of time we're talking about goes too far back for one man to be our killer, yet one name keeps appearing ever so often connected to them in some way. You care to take a stab at what it is?"

"Hayden Keller, I'm guessing."

"Correct, and either the guy in the morgue is just a random stalker choosing to come after a girl he's never met who lost her family to a man known only as Hayden Keller, and the guy that stepped in to stop the attack felt the need to pick up where the other guy left off, or we're dealing with something else here."

Gant considered the facts presented to him. Supernatural forces didn't seem plausible, and the scenario Callahan painted didn't satisfy him either. Callahan stated, "the guy that came after her approximately a year ago is the one that committed the murders still filling your books. Everything tying him to them is right in the folder I handed you."

Gant had a nose for the truth. He could sense the detective was being straight with him, but he refused to accept it. "How do you plan on stopping something like that," he asked purely out of curiosity.

"Through a power greater than myself," Callahan answered. He carried a look of self-assurance in his eyes when he openly said, "you don't believe me."

"You knew I wouldn't before you told me." They walked toward the door of the viewing room as they talked.

"Well, maybe that proves some can tell the future."

"Like your friend Sister Lee, I presume." Desperately in denial, Gant warned him, "don't buy into it Callahan, you're too good a cop for that. Psychics rarely provide any help. You ask me - it's a bunch of bologna."

The sergeants final words caused Callahan to inform him, "make no mistake, she's not my friend, but the woman in that room can tell you what you ate any given day of the week last month, and she can tell you where you'll be ten years from now. Don't underestimate her, she will help me find who I'm after."

"I guess you don't need our guy is what you're saying."

Callahan spoke fast as he did his best to enlighten the

sergeant. "The one that doesn't talk, no you can keep him. You're holding what's left of someone after Hayden Keller's through with them."

Gant never bothered to thank him for the folder or wish him a safe trip back to Indianapolis. He had a feeling where Callahan was headed, and he purposely never asked.

As Sister Lee left the observation room, Callahan started to lead her in the direction of the doors to the precinct. Finally, they were leaving, but not before the gifted palm reader addressed the sergeant one last time. She turned facing Gant saying, "Carbonara, and lettuce with tomato. Once you taste it, you will have a call to make." Befuddled by her words, Gant just stood there waiting on Aldridge to show up to transport Ashley to the hospital. The look of bewilderment faded from his face though as he shook his head hardly able to believe he allowed the fortune teller to get inside it temporarily. He watched as she, and the detective, proceeded toward the exit thinking they formed the ultimate odd couple.

Leaving the station, Callahan asked, "what was all that about?"

Sister Lee replied, "a meal suggestion, that is all. How many friends would you say you have?" Callahan looked at her not knowing what to say. She earnestly confessed, "I have none."

A doubtful smirk crested Callahan's lips when he suggested, "maybe you have one you're unaware of."

"Perhaps," Sister Lee said in response. The tone in her voice expressed a mild sense of question.

"I could always use one more, I'm just saying."

With little sign of emotion present on her face, Sister Lee informed him, "I shall consider it," and that ended the personal talk between them.

Chapter 48

Hunting The Hunter

Callahan opened the door to his car, and Sister Lee took her place in the passenger seat. The detective questioned her, "are we too late?"

"He will try once more for the girl. When he does, you will face him, I guarantee it." The conviction in her voice put him on point. Closing her door, he stood there for a second just thinking. Looking at vehicles, and foot traffic outside the police station, the detective grew concerned. Hayden Keller could be anywhere in the body of anyone, and that made his job a hell of a lot more difficult. His only option was to maintain a safe distance to lead the bastard to believe Ashley was unprotected, but at the same time stay close enough to her to keep him from laying his hands on her. Callahan wasn't exactly the type to blend in, and he knew it. The fact was he had been a cop so long it was written all over him.

Walking around to the other side of the Crown Vic, Callahan pulled his phone from his pocket. His eyes remained busy searching for any sign of Hayden present in the faces of passing people. He dialed Buttweiler to inform him, "the hunt is still on," as he climbed inside his car.

Buttweiler replied, "I thought Gant had him in custody."

"I did to, turns out otherwise." Callahan wasn't about to inform him Hayden Keller had the ability to takeover someone's body simply by coming in contact with it long enough. That secret was held between him, the girl, and Sister Lee. Gant would eventually come around to join them though.

Callahan's focus was on Aldridge, and Ashley as they exited the precinct through the side door. That's when his partner informed him, "Captain Rollins wants to know where you are."

The detective cranked the car with little time to talk instructing him, "tell him I'm in Des Moines on business. We've got a strong lead on our serial killer." That news certainly sounded good to Buttweiler. He couldn't wait to inform the captain, Henley too, for that matter.

Enthusiasm was present in his voice as he pried for more details saying, "you must be really close then."

The detective looked over at their unconfirmed source. She heard Buttweiler's comment through the phone, and Sister Lee nodded her head only once saying nothing. Her face appeared solemn, and her eyes peered straight through the windshield in front of her. That's when Callahan said, "we're so close it's scary, but I gotta go." Ending the call, he put away his phone keeping his eyes peeled for any possible danger.

Trailing Aldridge to the hospital, Callahan allowed no more than two cars to come between him, and Ashley. She seemed calm in the backseat of the police car, but that was where she felt safe. Looking over her shoulder, she spotted the detective, and his sidekick. Instantly, Sister Lee made an impression on her. The palm reader worked to establish a mental connection with her. Soon, it would become very valuable in the effort to stop Hayden Keller from living. Ashley was visually drawn to Sister Lee once the psychic link was made between them. Callahan wasn't sure what she was doing, but he didn't question her as she invaded the mind of Ashley Pennington gaining the ability to see through the girl's eyes. When they arrived at Mercy Medical, Callahan pulled into the parking garage closest to the west entrance. Finding a space facing the hospital, he sat there patiently allowing Aldridge, and Ashley time to make it inside the building. His eyes were trained on them using his side view mirror, but Sister Lee's focus was elsewhere. She stared at a place on the sidewalk near the entrance to the building. Her head moved suddenly, and she started to turn her eyes away from it. Callahan was forced to ask her, "what is it? Did you see something?"

She looked back at the place that had her attention saying, "it is there where you shall face him and..."

"And what?"

"It shall end."

Another ambulance pulled into the parking lot across the street closest to the building, and a chill coursed through Sister Lee's body as she sat up straight, her spine perfectly erect. Her neck quickly stiffened. Looking over at Callahan, she questioned him, "do you feel that?"

His senses were already on high alert, but when she reached over touching her hand to his cheek, he felt what she did. Surprised by the eerie chill of death which he could feel emanate through her hand, he blurted out, "what the hell? He's here, isn't he?"

"His mark will not give him away, but you will sense when he is close, and you must act swiftly." She knew he would take action at the appropriate time. If there had been another way to stop Hayden Keller from acquiring that which he sought, Sister Lee would have surely seized it. She knew balance had to be restored though, and with it would come her chance to separate herself from the evil one forever. The cost she would pay would be a high one.

Callahan watched as the officer, and Ashley breached the main doors of the hospital. Remaining at a distance, he could see them clearly through the tinted glass as he stepped out of his vehicle. He wasn't the only one watching though.

Hayden Keller often enjoyed the hunt before the kill, but he never cared for enduring the wait. Still occupying the passenger seat, Sister Lee told Callahan, "I shall wait here," but the detective insisted she accompany him inside the building.

"You know how many crimes occur in parking garages?"

For once, Sister Lee was handed a question she didn't have the answer to. "You'll be safer inside, I promise." Suddenly, Callahan was the one making predictions. Sister Lee had never seen the inside of a hospital with her own eyes, not even at the time of her birth, but she saw no need to inform Callahan of that. She just did as he requested knowing it would all end soon. Not wishing to encounter Hayden up close while he still breathed a breath of life, she immediately picked out a seat far away from the window in the corner of the lobby. From that vantage point, she had an unobstructed view of the place she saw in her vision, but she refrained from casting her eyes on it for the time being.

Outside the hospital, Hayden Keller took in the sight of the cross adorning Mercy Medical Center. In his mind, there was no more fitting place for Ashley to meet her maker. Sitting idle behind the wheel of the ambulance, grinding his teeth some, he pondered what he'd like to do to the girl before killing her. Watching her from a distance, he plotted his next morbid move figuring he had only two left he could kill in the process. Not particularly caring for the restriction, he grumbled under his breath, "fucking rules." The upside for him was after assessing the situation, he was convinced he had the perfect getaway vehicle. That's when he took his eyes off the target long enough to check his appearance in the mirror.

Feeling the need to enter the hospital without revealing the jagged cut he now carried on his face, he stepped to the back of the vehicle. The body of the real ambulance driver was stretched out on a gurney. One leg hanging off the edge of it, Joel Dyson had seen better days. Stationed there permanently with his eyes frozen wide open, he appeared as though he was staring at the set of shock paddles dangling from the defibrillator. That wasn't weighing heavy on his mind though. Joel Dyson was dead, his neck was broken, and no amount of medical care was apt to bring his ass back breathing. Hayden managed to crush his windpipe during the struggle to take-over the driver's seat. The paddles were hanging because that's where Hayden left them after applying them to each side of Joel's head. He shocked the shit out of Joel multiple times just for pure amusement. Hayden watched his arms and legs flop around in odd directions each time he hollered, "clear!" That game continued until the battery ran low, but he had to pass the time somehow until he could gain another shot at the girl.

The detective was already aware of Sister Lee's quirks, and he knew she wouldn't ride the elevators. Her concerns about getting on them paralleled her sentiments about planes for some reason. Whatever they were rooted in, he didn't have to psychoanalyze them. The irony was she would do next to anything to help him catch a demonic serial killer which defied death, but she wouldn't step foot on something that left the ground.

Ashley caught a glimpse of the detective, and Sister Lee while waiting to be admitted. From the other side of the room, he gave her a wink for reassurance. Officer Aldridge stood right beside her until the transporter arrived pushing a wheelchair. His only words to Ashley were, "it looks like you're in good hands here." He never admitted seeing the detective. Truthfully, he hoped the girl received the care she desperately needed. Ashley felt silly taking a seat in the chair. She told the guy pushing it, "I can walk, alright."

Not knowing why she was being admitted, he just responded, "it's hospital procedure. What are you trying to do put me out of a job?"

Officer Aldridge said, "you better listen to him. I think he's serious." In an effort to put her more at ease he said, "don't worry. I'm sure your grandmother will be here before you know it." Once she was taken to her room, Aldridge went to get himself a cup of coffee.

Even though she could no longer see him, the girl seemed more at ease knowing Callahan was in the building, but the truth was she couldn't wait for her grandmother to get there. When they placed Ashley in a room by herself, the nurse's assistant flipped on the television for her. The news showed Stewart Nettle being interviewed, and Ashley grabbed the remote to cut it off as she tried her best to block out certain images while Callahan panned over the lobby looking for one person. The detective read the room noting entry, and exit points. A security officer was seated at his post on the far end of the admissions desk closest to the door. He was busy chatting with the girls behind the counter whenever they were in between accepting patients. The place appeared safe enough. Callahan asked, "will you be alright here?"

"I will be fine. You must watch over the girl. He is coming, I can sense it."

Callahan took her at her word then instructed her to stay put. Removing his jacket, he placed it over the back of the chair next to her. In a quick attempt to camouflage himself, he planned on donning a white coat instead, something that would hide his gun, and help him blend in with others working there inside the hospital. "Don't go anywhere," he reminded her as he opened a door which read *HOSPITAL PERSONNEL ONLY.*

Chapter 49

No Longer A Skeptic

Callahan stood at the end of the hallway near the elevator holding a clipboard. It was merely a prop to make him appear he belonged there, but apparently it worked for him. Despite the fact he didn't have a visible ID badge, and he never attended medical school, he certainly looked the part. Presenting the image one would expect of a doctor was a hell of a lot easier than being one though. He soon found that out when one of the nurses asked him a question regarding a medication dosage. Dodging her question long enough to point her in the direction of a real physician, Callahan hardly made eye contact with her. He constantly observed people approaching Ashley's room. It was located on the other side of the nurses' station, and between the sound of the phones, chatter, televisions, rolling carts, and beeping monitors, it was hard to hear anything, especially, that close to the elevators. Ducking into an empty room, he stood near the door keeping watch while pretending to read over something that had his interest.

Back at the precinct, Sergeant Gant read over some of the cases in the folder which Callahan had pointed him to. More details had emerged about the man Gus Grossman killed in the library with the painter's tool. Weighing the facts, it was damn near impossible to connect all the dots without leaning in the direction of something paranormal taking place. Still refusing to admit it to himself, he grumbled, "it's about time," when Pippin placed a styrofoam box filled with food on the edge of his desk.

Engrossed in what he was reading, he opened up the box paying little attention to what was inside. Forking a bite of salad, he crunched on the lettuce and tomato. As soon as he took a bite of his sandwich, he noticed it tasted different. Calling Pippin's attention to it, he asked, "hey, does this look like Sodona Turkey to you?"

"No, that's Chicken Carbonara. They were out of turkey. What are you bitching about? It comes with a side salad."

Gant sat motionless as Osprey looked at him saying, "Sarge doesn't like it, I can tell."

Pippin's response was, "fine, if he doesn't want it I'll eat it. Someone has to feed the vending machines."

The sergeant stood telling Osprey, "you get a hold of Aldridge, and tell him if he's already left to get his ass back over to that hospital, and stay with that girl until I get there, and don't let anyone come near her. I mean it!"

Gant left his food where it set, and he was gone in a flash leaving Pippin to ask, "what's his problem?"

Hayden entered the hospital through the emergency entrance carrying a bag he acquired from the ambulance. One of the girls at the check-in desk recognized him as Darin Banner. She even said hello to him addressing him by his first name before noticing the bandage on his face, but Hayden paid her little attention. Cutting him off as he started to pass by her workstation, she almost blocked his path when she questioned, "what happened to your cheek?" Hayden just looked at her. He knew better than to say a single word. He desperately wanted to thumb Crystal's beautiful blue eyes out, but there wasn't time for that. He continued walking just as if he had never met her, and she turned in disbelief, her mouth still partially agape. Confiding in one of her co-workers, she spoke her thoughts, "I can't believe that."

"What? Guys are assholes."

"Yeah, but there was something completely different about him."

"Just be glad you didn't sleep with him."

Hayden's search for Ashley took time even though it was done efficiently. Callahan began wondering if he was going to show, but soon he would have his answer. Armed with a .40 caliber semi-automatic pistol, and advice he received from Father Tomas before making the trip, Callahan clearly felt prepared for the task. He believed, based solely on Sister Lee's vision, he would spot Hayden somewhere inside the hospital, and the actual showdown would take place outside, but there was much more to it than the palm reader revealed to him.

The harvester of souls checked with each floor nurse tossing out the name of the special patient he wished to pay a visit. Finally, he pinned down her exact location. As soon as he stepped foot off the elevator, Callahan knew he was close. Experiencing the chill of extreme present danger, the detective turned seeing the face of evil heading straight for Ashley's door.

The detective's actions were quick, and seamless. Peeling off the white coat, it hit the hospital floor as he drew his gun. He immediately yelled across the room ordering Ashley to run. "Everyone get down!" Hayden was the only one willing to defy him. As Callahan drew down on him, he only picked up speed planning to take Ashley hostage, just as he had done with her father. Callahan fired two rounds to prevent that from happening as Ashley took off toward the stairwell as fast as she could move with a slightly injured ankle, and bruised clavicle. The bullets did little but buy her a few seconds. He wasn't able to pin Hayden down though due to the obstructions behind the nurse's station.

Losing sight of his target, the detective dodged panicked people in the hallway outside the patients' rooms. Some that were less fortunate tried to crawl to safety as he raced to gain a bead on Hayden Keller. Callahan knew he had to see to it Hayden made contact with no one. Otherwise, he could walk out of there, and no one would be the wiser.

The detective's adrenaline was pumping as he stumbled over shit on the floor. He couldn't look down, he was busy scanning for any sign of the demonic bastard dressed in an EMT's uniform. His mind raced pulling the trigger yet again. With no sign of Hayden's head, or torso exposed to his line of fire, he took the next best thing. Two more rounds fired toward his leg. Shockingly enough, even through the maze of swivel chairs, a bullet actually managed to find its target piercing the lower part of Hayden's thigh. He never gave Callahan the satisfaction of knowing he hit him though.

Pulling a pistol from the bag he was carrying, Hayden returned fire shooting wildly over the heads of hospital employees hoping to hit the detective some place vital. Even though he missed, laying down the cover-fire allowed him to make it to the stairwell. Desperate to stop him, Callahan expended two more rounds before the door closed shut leaving Ashley trapped inside the stairwell with a fiendish man she knew all too well.

Hollering to the nurse as, he himself, raced to the door leading to the stairs, Callahan ordered her, "call security! Tell them to seal off all exits to the stairwell on each floor on the west side of the building. Do it now!" Chancing it, he didn't even hesitate entering. He dove through the door pointing his weapon knowing full well Hayden had the upper hand at that point. Dodging two bullets, he took the third one in his right arm as Ashley scrambled up the stairs headed for the roof.

Utilizing what little cover he had between the steel handrail, and the concrete steps, Callahan returned fire. Hayden was done screwing with him. He figured his unfinished encounter with Ashley Pennington was long overdue. Chasing her to the roof, Callahan followed fast. Hearing Ashley scream, he knew Hayden Keller was close just when he saw the light enter the upper part of the stairwell. One shadow blocked it only for a split-second, and Callahan pointed his gun using his left hand, full well knowing Hayden, and he, were the only ones left on the stairs.

Both of them injured, they continued their climb upward, Callahan aiming his weapon at each turn, and seeing the second shadow pass overhead he fired once again. All he had left were three bullets. Hayden fully expected him to come busting through the door just as he had done before, and he turned to face him as Ashley tried to put distance between her, and her assailant from hell.

Hayden had the high ground, and the one thing Callahan swore to protect at all costs. The detective knew Hayden would unload on him as he kicked open the door, yet he did it anyway, but all Hayden Keller hit was air, the wall inside the stairwell, and the door itself. Callahan was lying on his back at the top of the stairs when he kicked it open, and once Hayden expended most of his clip, the detective raised his gun taking advantage of the situation.

Using both hands to steady his weapon, Callahan placed one .40 caliber slug in Hayden's shoulder, and two in his chest. With no more than one or two bullets left, Hayden refrained from returning the favor. His plans had changed. Ashley stood near the edge of the building trapped in a corner with no means of escape as Hayden steadily continued making his way toward her. He found the body he was in no longer suitable. Callahan had managed to Swiss cheese him somehow, but he knew the detective's limits. Hayden growled, "you might kill me, but you won't kill her."

Callahan could see from the look in his eye, Hayden Keller didn't plan to kill Ashley at that point, he planned to inhabit her. He thought about nothing, but making good on his promise to Ashley, and Sheriff Baker. He didn't flinch acting swiftly just as Sister Lee knew he would. Charging Hayden at full force to prevent the soul exchange from taking place, they locked horns. Hayden looked him square in the eyes, and both of them started to violently shake as if they were suffering an electric shock, but Ashley had seen this transformation before. Terror filled her heart. She couldn't breathe.

Sharing a death-grip on one another's throats, Callahan could feel his blood start to run cold. He knew what was happening, and he had only a split-second to act. Dragging Hayden to the edge of the building, he did what was necessary to end it. Sister Lee, and Father Tomas' words showed their full impact. "A breath of life is given to man in an instant, yet it can be taken away just as fast." Both men left the roof staring into the other's eyes. When they hit the concrete sixty-five feet down, screams were heard near the entrance to the hospital.

Callahan, and the body that once belonged to Darin Banner lied facing one another feet apart. Sister Lee saw them leave the roof through Ashley's eyes. Forcing herself, she looked out the window as she stood retrieving Callahan's jacket. It was confirmed, her vision was right. The death of a great man sealed the fate of another that was a plague on mankind, and for that she shed one tear. More would've been a waste, though she deemed her only true friend worth it.

Falling to her knees near the edge of the roof, Ashley Pennington cried many tears, enough for them both. She questioned in her mind if it was really over as Sister Lee severed her mental connection to her. The palm reader stood motionless staring out the window waiting on a call. Looking at the symbol she carried on her hand, and the one on her wrist she had worn for centuries - she knew balance had been restored, but this time it came at a very high price. Sister Lee told herself there could be no more loss, and seconds later she heard Callahan's cell phone ring.

Sister Lee retrieved the phone from the detective's coat pocket only to hear Buttweiler's voice on the other end of the line. She knew it was him, and when he would call. Instead of a normal hello, he heard, "you need to come here. It is over, but your partner is no longer with us. I am at the hospital known as Mercy Medical. Hurry, I shall be waiting at the west entrance." She hung up the phone giving Buttweiler no more information than that. There would be plenty of time to talk on the long ride back, and then all of his questions would be answered. Eventually, he would be tasked with making the call to Sheriff Baker to inform him his partner had made good on his promise.

Aldridge arrived just in time to see the crowd forming near the entrance of the hospital. The security guard had things partly under control when he exited his car. People were pointing up at the roof, and Aldridge could see part of the girl's silhouette against the setting sun. He went into reactionary mode. Speaking to the security guard, and an off duty deputy in uniform, he instructed them, "keep everyone back, don't let anyone touch these two men until more police arrive. Is that understood?" His fear was Ashley would jump herself. "I need to get to the roof. Where's the access point?" The security guard pointed to the interior part of the west wing, and Aldridge took off in that direction thinking *this is like something right out of Flashpoint.*

Gant was on the scene by the time Aldridge made it to the roof to retrieve the girl. After the drama was over, he had questions for Sister Lee. The first one was, should he leave an officer stationed outside her door. Sister Lee didn't answer him though. Gant stated, "things being what they are, I'll just go ahead and do it to be on the safe side." When he asked her what happened, Sister Lee honestly said she saw nothing with her own eyes other than bodies lying dead on the concrete outside the lobby where she was sitting. He had to accept her statement whether he liked it or not. The palm reader never traveled beyond the ground floor. Just for his own edification, he had to ask, "did you have a sense it would end this way?"

"It does not matter now. What's done is done."

"Why didn't you tell him?" Gant waited for an answer which never came until he stood to leave. Walking away, he heard Sister Lee speak her peace, "he never asked."

Gant just nodded, never looking back at her before exiting through the doors in which he entered. He was fully aware Callahan's partner was coming for her.

Just minutes after Gant left, Ashley's grandmother arrived to find blood, and chalk on the sidewalk near the entrance to the hospital. Crime scene tape had already been stretched, and it seemed to follow her granddaughter wherever she went. Ilene Vandershamp was left with no answers other than Ashley was now under sedation, and resting comfortably after being pulled from the roof by police. Nothing was said to her about the incident that occurred on the fourth floor. Everyone thought that was best for her sake. The real facts of what had happened would never be revealed to her, and they'd never make it into Gant's report either simply cause the lieutenant would never buy it.

For Callahan's partner the drive back to Indianapolis was a difficult one. Buttweiler placed eyes on both of the bodies before leaving Des Moines, and Sister Lee road shotgun doing her best to explain what happened based on what she had seen through Ashley's eyes. Certain details she left out though. The only words she handed him which bordered on reassuring were, "it is finally over. You will see one another again I assure you." In a way Sister Lee's words filled a hole somewhere deep inside his chest. Buttweiler didn't completely understand the keeper of secrets seated next to him, but he trusted her in much the same way as Callahan once did.

Chapter 50

Honoring A Hero

Father Tomas observed the rank, and file members making up the various branches of law enforcement as they walked past his casket. Almost every one of them carried a look of loss mixed with a hint of stern resolution. One thing was clear, Callahan's years of work on the force had cultivated many relationships. It brought with it honor, and respect from his peers, and he'd even gained the admiration of his superiors. He had to question if his fellow priests would take the time to send him off in such a way when the day arrived. It didn't matter much to him though. Point of departure never compared to one's final destination in his mind. The question which plagued him at that moment was - where was his former parishioner, and friend. He believed he had the answer, yet, he couldn't be certain. Thoughts came into his mind, and left being replaced by others as he earnestly searched for the right words to share with those that had come to pay their final respects to the fallen police detective.

This was not a run of the mill ceremony. Few of them were, it seemed. Father Tomas knew him personally, even though he seldom saw him in church. Callahan was much like a stray member of his flock that surfaced on occasion only to gain a word or two to chew on. Cops were inherently riddled with doubt, and full of questions, some of them ran deep too. Processing that for a moment, Father Tomas reasoned, whatever Callahan believed was between him and God, but the priest was certain he would've never consciously made the decision to become catholic - he was born into it like so many others. The priest could certainly identify with that. It was one thing he, and Callahan had in common.

As Sister Lee boarded the Greyhound bus, Father Tomas felt a connection to Callahan he had never experienced. He knew, without question, what the detective would wish to have shared with the men, and women gathered there that day. The eulogy was one many would remember. The twenty-one gun salute was warranted in the minds of all those attending the graveside burial, and there were few flowers just as Callahan would have preferred, but the releasing of the doves symbolized a new beginning. Many found hope in it, but those closest to Callahan would forever miss him dearly.

As people straggled away from the service, Henley just stood there looking down at the hole where they intended to place him permanently. He was frozen there, unable to move to save his own soul, and Buttweiler turned looking back at him. He gave Henley a moment to himself. He knew the admiration he felt for Callahan. Knowing the detective would've wanted he, and Henley to carry on, Buttweiler walked over to him, and just stood beside him without saying a word. Henley confessed, "he's gone."
Buttweiler just threw his arm over Henley's shoulder saying, "come on partner, we should be going too."

As they lowered Callahan's casket, and covered his grave, Sister Lee's Greyhound pulled into the station. Sheriff Baker was the one who came to meet her when she stepped off the bus. That's when they really got to know one another. A total of twenty words were shared between the two of them during the twenty minute ride to her small white house which sat close to the Jefferson County line.

Now that she was back, and Hayden Keller no longer breathed, all was right in Chanceville again, but elsewhere things would never be the same. What the stars held for Ben and Ashley's future, only Sister Lee could tell.

The months ahead were peaceful, almost pleasant, despite poor weather conditions at certain points. Looking to a brighter future for all who breathe the breath of life, Sister Lee followed the stars as she did since being handed the task as a child. Nearly six months had passed since she left Indianapolis, but what she saw in the celestial bodies above reminded her of what was buried there.

There was a blood moon coming soon, and it foretold of great unrest, a disturbance in the balance that existed beyond what she had ever seen before. There was no question blood would run deep, and evil would find her. She was certain there would be no escape. Time, and space had culminated once again forming pathways through lower realms. The misalignment of the watchtowers of time themselves signified something ominous to come. It marked the point evil reentered this world. There was no mistaking it, Sister Lee had seen it many times before. She drew her breath dreading what she knew lay ahead. Restless and worn, virtually depleted of all her energy, she looked up from her star chart saying, "not again."